The Great Expectation by [...]
Marissa plays upright ba[...] [...]es their
schedule. She loves trav[...] [...] always
worries about the care of her prized Afghan. When she hears
that the kennel she uses is under new management, she immediately investigates the new owner and realizes her worst fears.
Can she move past her first impressions of Jason Easton? Can
they help each other find renewed faith?

Harmonized Hearts by Lynn A. Coleman
Tyrone has a dream of putting the psalms written for string
instruments to music. He works tirelessly while at home only to
disturb his new neighbor with the noise. When Cassy sees him
again playing his cello at a wedding, she must admit her attraction. Will Tyrone admit his inability and open his heart and
soul to Cassy, allowing himself to create harmony with her for
the rest of their lives? Or will they both be as mournful as the
psalms he's been trying to put to music?

Syncopation by Bev Huston
Cynthia left Miami six years ago to pursue a singing career, and
Tristan has often thought about the love he let slip away. When
she returns for a visit, he is disappointed to see her faith faded
behind the push for stardom. Still Tristan pursues his rekindled
love even though his friends caution him. Cynthia shows signs
of renewed love and faith—until a shadow from her life in LA
threatens to steal her away. Can Tristan let her go again?

Name That Tune by Yvonne Lehman
Music is Eva's life. She wants to make music for the Lord
always, longs to have the quartet respected as the professionals
they are, and dreams of creating a violin that a famous violinist
would play in concert. Her hopes and dreams seem to be coming together. She has a romantic interest who is, of all things, a
handsome, famous violinist. But why does he not stir her heart
like plain and fun-loving Jack?

STRINGS
of the
HEART

Members of a String Quartet
Find Love Under a Miami Moon
in Four Novellas

GINNY AIKEN
LYNN A. COLEMAN
BEV HUSTON
YVONNE LEHMAN

BARBOUR
PUBLISHING

STRINGS
of the
HEART

The Great Expectation

by Ginny Aiken

Dedication

To the best support system:
Elizabeth, Karl, and Natalie, critiquers extraordinaire;
Ivan and Shiloh, Greg, Geoff, and Grant,
the best kids in the universe;
Goldie and Buffy, my creative canine contributors;
and as always, to George, who didn't realize
that first computer was a Pandora's box in disguise.

*They sing to the music of tambourine and
harp; they make merry to the
sound of the flute.*
JOB 21:12

Chapter 1

Present-day—Miami, Florida

"Honestly, Rissa," Ty said with a grunt. "Are you packing rocks in Bertha the Beast?"

Marissa Ortíz glanced at her fellow musician. "Quit griping, Tyrone Carver. We're a *string* quartet, and I play a bass. Bertha's no heavier today than she was yesterday."

"Easy for you to say," Ty countered, as his six-foot frame handily maneuvered the unwieldy instrument. "You have me to haul the Beast around."

Rissa gave her best friend—well, one of her three best friends—a knowing look. "Want to trade jobs? I can give you the schedule roster anytime, anywhere."

Fear widened Ty's hazel eyes. "Don't you dare. You know how much time it's taking me to compose—"

"Don't try to pull that one on me. I know what your secret project means to you and how much time you've committed to it, but the truth is, you just can't be bothered with schedules, keeping track of dates, times, or locations. As long as you lock info in your head, you're fine, but where would that leave the rest of us?"

Clattering footsteps prevented Ty's response. "In the dark," chirped Eva Alono, hugging her violin case. "We'd never know where or when we were expected to perform."

The lights in the dim Sunday school classroom suddenly went on. "The Lord did say, 'Let there be light.'" Viola player Tristan Reuben acknowledged the others' groans with a profound bow, then turned to Rissa. "Is this lug complaining about dear Bertha again?"

Rissa arched a brow.

As the others laughed, she winked and grinned. "I still love him—even though he's a nut bar."

Eva chuckled. "You should know. Me? I just want to know where you pack your candy calories—you're wispier than fog."

With another wink, Rissa tossed her hair over her shoulder and struck a dramatic pose. "I'm blessed."

As she said the words, she wondered if she would ever feel that blessing deep inside her heart. She recognized the gifts the Lord had given her, and she'd developed them so she could use them to His glory, but was she truly blessed?

She thought of her family, her world-renowned harpist mother and late grandmother, her Nobel Prize nominee physicist father. A father who hid in his office at East Central University of Florida and a mother whose physical disabilities and uncertain mental state kept her, if not hidden, then certainly unavailable.

Pushing back the imminent self-pity as she always did, Rissa reminded herself that God loved her, that she and her fellow quartet members made up a loving family since they'd met in college, and that she'd recently found herself the perfect companion.

Soraya.

What joy the lovely Afghan hound brought her each and every day, how loyal she was, how unconditional her love. The dog's innate goodness made Rissa's decision about pet care during the quartet's upcoming twenty-one-day South American tour even tougher.

"Earth to Rissa," Ty called. "Is there intelligent life under those beautiful curls?"

She ducked away from his approaching hand and strove for a scrap of dignity. "Enough, already. The Altamonte wedding's this Saturday, and today's my only chance to rehearse—I'm giving ten hours of back-to-back lessons over the next three days. Let's get to work."

Eva's perusal intensified. "What's wrong?"

A rueful smile curved Rissa's lips. "I can't hide anything from you, can I?"

Hurt flickered in and out of Eva's eyes. "Do you really want to?"

"No, Silly," Rissa said, patting her friend's shoulder. "It's just that—well, it's kind of dumb for me to worry, but. . ."

"Okay, Kid," Ty ordered, "tell Big Brother what's wrong. And don't give us any more of that 'it's dumb' stuff. I've been wondering what put the flagpole in your spine and the tight smile on your mouth."

Rissa gusted a sigh, then grabbed her nearly waist-length hair, twisted it, and drew it into a knot at the base of her neck. "I can't believe you guys. The FBI could use you—"

"Quit stalling," Tristan said, concern on his face.

"That's right, Ris," Eva concurred. "You don't have to carry the world on your shoulders. We're here—you know, 'A friend loves at all times, and a brother'—or a sister—'is born for adversity,' " she quoted from Proverbs 17:17.

"Okay, okay." Taking a deep breath, Rissa forced her shoulders to relax. "You guys are right. I am stressing about this next tour. Mom. . .well, she's not doing well these days. Her pain meds are failing her, and you guys know what that does to her state of mind. And Dad. . ."

A murmur of sympathy rippled through the friends. Rissa held up her hand to ward off further pity. "That's just part of it. You guys remember Soraya's breeder, right?"

All three nodded. "Mrs. Gooden decided to retire a few months ago and sold her entire operation. That wouldn't have been half bad, but you guys won't believe who she sold to."

Expectant silence followed.

"Well?" Ty asked. "Who has enough cash to buy all that property and those luxe kennels?"

Rissa worried her lower lip, shook her head, and finally shrugged. "None other than the infamous, unethical, and slimy Jason Easton, Attorney-at-Law."

Eva frowned. "The shark? The one from that millionaires' firm? What's he doing with pampered pooches?"

"You know as much as I do," Rissa said, "but not as much as I intend to learn."

"Uh-oh," said Tristan. "The guy doesn't stand a chance. The hypermeticulous Marissa Ortíz is on the case. She'll sniff out even the most minute vestige of slime, clean it up, and have the place running by the book in less time than it takes to sneeze."

"Hey!" Rissa jabbed her pal on his solid shoulder. "If I weren't careful, we'd never make any of our bookings. You guys don't pay much attention to details."

"Yep," he countered, "none of us is particularly neurotic about minutes, dates, and stuff like that. That's why we love you so much."

"That's beside the point," Ty said. "I want to know what Rissa's planning in that overzealous little mind of hers."

"I'm just checking it out," she said with a nonchalance she didn't feel. "I know how Mrs. Gooden ran the place, and if anything's not as it should be, I'll make sure the ASPCA and the police learn all about it. Less than one minute after I do."

"How'll you know if he's really running a decent show or not?" Tristan asked.

"That's why I'm going there," she said. "I bet he's the kind of absentee owner who buys an operation as a tax write-off, hires out the dirty work for peanuts, and then rakes in as much as clients will shell out. After all, he's the one who got that. . .that Elliott-what's-his-face—the SEC crook—off a year ago."

She thought back to the splashy trial of the man who'd cooked the books at a snooty investment firm. "Southwycke!" she exclaimed. "Elliott Southwycke, who's now living in a mansion in the Bahamas. Jason Easton's the one who got him off on some shady loophole or technicality or some other slimy lawyer-thing."

Ty gave her a narrow-eyed stare. "So you're going out there loaded for bear."

"Yes, and that's why we have to finish the gabfest. The Altamontes are paying us a nice chunk of change to waft their daughter up to the altar and then triumphantly march her down the aisle a high-society matron." She rummaged through her black leather portfolio and withdrew a well-thumbed Vivaldi score. "Thankfully, they chose 'Spring' for the processional,

13

Pachelbel's 'Canon' as background, 'Amazing Grace' for communion and the lighting of the unity candle, and finally, 'Lohengrin' for the recessional. We know all that and only need a run-through. Once we do the sound check in the sanctuary, we're done."

They then plied their craft, the art that soothed and brought them joy and comfort in times of turmoil. Rissa reveled in the sparkling notes of "Spring," put her whole heart into praising the Father with her music, and thanked Him for this, the one blessing she had no trouble identifying.

If only she could as easily identify anything questionable in the kennel at the mercy of the shady man now at its helm. . .

Two hours later, Rissa turned her geriatric yet still strong European station wagon into the palm-lined drive of Silk-Wood Kennels. The place looked no different than it had four months ago when she'd retrieved Soraya after the quartet's last trip. Then again, looks could be and often were deceiving.

As she pulled up to the yellow-stucco office building, however, dismay swam in her stomach. She counted three teens—one walking a gorgeous brindle Affie on a leash, while another danced to the rhythm in his earphones as he hosed the chain-link-fenced run closest to the parking lot. The last one stood not ten feet from the faded gold hood of her car, a quizzical look on his face.

"D'you bring it?" he asked as Rissa opened her door. "I thought it'd been sent overnight."

She stood. "Bring what?"

"You know. The. . ." He blushed under his deep Florida tan. "The. . .*stuff.*"

Oh, no. Matters were worse than she had imagined. Drug dealing was the order of the day. Well. Not only had SilkWood lost a regular customer, but they'd also gained themselves an imminent visit from the authorities—as soon as she called them.

Hoping to extract more incriminating info from the shaggy-haired kid, she played along. "No. Was I supposed to?"

Overlong wiry arms swung upward. "I don't know. All's I know is that Jase's all bent out of shape about the delay, and you don't even have—" Again, his flushed golden-olive skin highlighted his chiseled features. "You don't have the *stuff* with you."

In the interest of gaining the unsuspecting canary's confidence and subsequently getting him to sing, she went for the basics. "So. What's your name?"

He narrowed dark, lushly lashed eyes. "Why?"

She strove for nonchalance. "Just being polite."

Evidently she hid her ulterior motives well. "I'm Paul," he said. "Who're you?"

In the further interest of her budding investigation, she opted for veracity and held out her hand. "Pleased to meet you, Paul. I'm Marissa. Are you new around here?"

"Yeah. Jase needs help, and I would do just about anything for him."

No doubt. Most addicts were under their dealers' total control. Poor child. She wondered how she might help him leave his destructive lifestyle. "You must know and love dogs a great deal."

Paul gave her a wry grin. "Nope. Never had one, but I sure am learning fast."

Inexperienced and ignorant, to boot. Poor dogs. "Afghans are wonderful, aren't they?"

"At least they're not rat-sized yapping dust-bunnies."

Rissa laughed at his patent disgust. Loud rumbling on the gravel drive then caught their attention. A parcel delivery truck stopped behind her station wagon and a sandy-haired man leaped out, holding a package embellished with FRAGILE stickers.

Paul grinned. "Finally."

"Are you the new owner?" the driver asked Rissa, staring at her as though she'd oozed out from some disgusting mire.

She read his name tag. "No, Sean. I've been a kennel customer for some years now, and I came today to meet the shys— Mr. Easton."

Sean studied her, then reached into the truck's cab for a clipboard. "If you're not the owner, then who's signing for this?"

Paul stepped forward. "They gave you the. . .stuff? Freeze-dried and all?"

Sean shrugged. Then the teen's words seemed to register. "Freeze-dried?"

Paul blushed even more. "They'd have to, otherwise it wouldn't be any good by the time it got here."

Marissa frowned. What kind of drug were they dealing? She'd never heard of any that required freeze-drying. Before she thought of a clever way to ask, Sean glared at the box.

"If I'd known what it was," he grumbled, "I might have. . . oh, dropped it—accidentally, of course."

Huh?

Paul reached for the unprepossessing box. "Gimme that. If Jase heard what you just said, he'd call and report you."

"Some of us have principles."

Paul rolled his eyes. "Shoulda known you're one of *them.*"

"And proud of it. What you guys do here is unethical."

"You're nuts."

Rissa's gaze ping-ponged between the two. What was going on?

"Really?" asked Sean. "I bet this is twenty- maybe thirty-year-old sperm—"

Her eyes popped wide open.

"And I bet the donor was the bitch's late great-great-granddaddy," Sean added. "Inbreeding leads to nasty mutations. Besides, aren't there enough dogs around already? Why do you guys have to make more?"

Relief left Rissa lightheaded. "You mean. . .that's just a specimen for breeding?"

Both turned and glared.

"What'd you think it was, Lady?" Paul asked in disgust. "I sure haven't spent the last three hours out here to work on my tan. Jase runs a breeding kennel, you know."

She waved a hand before her face, needing every drop of humid Florida air she could dredge up. She shrugged. And waved some more.

Finally, when she found the starch to firm her voice, she said, "If it's so important, then sign and take it to Mr. Easton. I'll go with you, since I did come all the way out here to meet him."

Paul graced her with a head-to-toe-and-back-again scrutiny. "Jase's going to be busy for awhile yet. Why don't you come back day after tomorrow—better yet, Saturday afternoon."

His attempt at a brush-off wasn't about to dislodge her. "I'm busy from now until Sunday after church. As I said, I'll follow you."

Forehead furrowed, Paul signed the paper on Sean's clipboard and held out his hand. The delivery truck driver glared at the controversial box yet again, then relinquished it. Without another word, he hopped into the truck and sped away, tires spewing gravel. Marissa winced as a couple of pieces dinged her car.

"Shall we?" she said to Paul, marveling at Sean's intensity. Animal rights' activists were, if nothing else, committed to their cause. She supported many of their efforts, but extremism didn't appeal to her. Besides, SilkWood Kennels' breeding program had produced Soraya. There couldn't be too much wrong with that.

As Paul led Rissa into the long building of runs, she took the opportunity to check out their condition. She didn't see food spilled on the cement floors or nastier stuff, either, and the water pails were full. Most of the dogs had come inside to enjoy an air-conditioned reprieve from the fiery Florida sun, and they looked well if excited by the stranger in their home away from home.

Way at the back, however, in a dim run to the right, Rissa finally found what she'd expected. A wadded pile of rags, damp-looking at that, surrounded a man in a ratty T-shirt and jeans that had seen better days. A pair of bowls had rolled into the central aisle and lay overturned, soggy kibble scattered all around.

The silver Affie in the run let out a pain-filled wail. Rissa's hackles went straight up, and she marched right to the abuser's side.

"That's it," he murmured as she reached him. "Good girl!"

The Affie moaned, relaxed somewhat, and then dropped shoulders and head onto her portion of the rags.

"Just what do you think you're doing to that poor, suffering animal?" she demanded.

The man turned.

Rissa gasped. "Jason Easton?"

Those clean-cut good looks had stared out from the *Miami Herald*'s front page too many times for her not to recognize him. What shocked her was the unadulterated emotion on his features. . .and the tears in his deep blue eyes.

"Helping God with a miracle, Ma'am," he said, his voice rough.

Then she noticed his outstretched hands. A tiny creature snuffled and wriggled in the well of his big palms, seeking its mama where only a scrap of towel could be found. Pale wet fuzz on its body suggested a future coat to match that of its mother.

A lump filled Rissa's throat. She dropped to her knees at Jason Easton's side and reached a careful finger to the newborn. It rubbed against her, full of promise.

Her eyes welled. "The miracle of life."

Their gazes met, and, to Rissa's astonishment, his reflected the reverence and awe she felt for the Master's power. This couldn't be the real Jason Easton. Not the one who'd let crooks get away with ill-gotten gains.

Yet it was. As she cupped her hand over the pup in his, she found herself unable to look away. A shimmer ran through her, the acknowledgment of a precious, shared moment.

She drew in a ragged breath. Somehow her life had just changed.

Irrevocably.

But had it changed for good?

Or had it changed for ill?

Only the Lord knew.

Chapter 2

Rissa shook free of the spell around them. She felt disoriented, as though one of Florida's hurricanes had tossed and turned and dropped her upside down. Nothing was as it should have been, as she'd imagined.

Well, that wasn't true either. Since arriving at SilkWood, she'd seen only kids—just what she'd expected. To find Jason Easton wearing ragged clothes, kneeling in a run on a pile of wet, bloody towels, and moved to tears by the miracle of birth. . .she hadn't expected that.

Oh, sure, he was a hunk. That build, chiseled features, and blue eyes impressed whether he wore his usual three-piece suit or these garment industry relics. His almost palpable genuine emotion, however, moved her. It didn't match her expectations. It was too real, too similar to her reaction, too easy to share.

She didn't know how to handle it. Or her response to it. . . to him.

That frightened her.

"Sorry you had to see this mess," he said, breaking into her thoughts.

Rissa blinked, then looked where he indicated. Ah, yes, the

rags, the littered kibble, his disheveled appearance. She brought her gaze back to his face and took note of the self-deprecating smile. Before she could say she understood, he spoke again.

"Mahadi and her puppies come first, then the mess." He ran a gentle finger over the chubby newborn. "Now that this last one is out, Mama and brood can become acquainted while I clean up."

He rose, wiping his hands on a relatively clean towel, then held a hand to Rissa.

She took it and stood at his side. "I would have done the same."

His sincere grin made something tickle from her throat to her middle. Whoa! This guy's smile was potent. As was that down-home honesty he presented. Was any of it real?

It looked real. But he was a killer-shark lawyer, too.

He hung up the towel on a hook in the metal support beam and faced her again. "I'm Jason Easton, the new owner, and you're. . . ?"

Still off guard, she said, "Oh, yes. . .ah. . .Marissa—*Rissa* Ortíz."

"I won't shake your hand again until I've washed mine," he added, smiling yet another time. "What brings you out here?"

Yes, Marissa, why did *you come out here?* "Well, you see. . . I. . ." *Get a grip, Woman!* Firming her posture, she went on. "Mrs. Gooden sold me one of her pups, and I've kenneled Soraya here every time I've traveled. I'm preparing for another trip, and I wanted to see you—meet the new owner. . . ."

She fought to gather her scattered thoughts. "I wanted to make arrangements for her stay while I'm gone."

I can always cancel if things go sour out here.

21

"In that case," Easton answered, "let's go to the office and take care of business."

Rissa nodded and followed him from the kennel to the yellow-stucco offices. Would she come to regret this? She was too shaken to make a sound decision, and she knew she'd second-guess herself until she dropped off Soraya, then every day of the tour and right up to the minute she returned to SilkWood to pick up her pet.

Father, help me do the right thing. I can't tell what's up or down anymore, but I know You know what's best.

Sign for the reservation and get out of Dodge seemed like the best course right then.

❧

As Jase opened the door for the breathtaking woodland nymph who'd floated into his kennel, he shook his head. *Lord, couldn't You have kept her away a few minutes longer? Just until I had time to wash up and put on something besides rags?*

Nothing like making a rotten impression on the most beautiful redhead he'd ever seen. Marissa Ortíz looked like something out of an illustrated fairy tale, tall, whisper slender, fair skinned, and blessed with the greenest eyes this side of heaven. She had to be a model or maybe an actress, one of those who'd bought land around Miami since a prominent Cuban band had helped popularize Key Biscayne, SoBe, and the mansions dotting the waterfront.

He'd never seen her at any event, and he'd suffered enough of the artificial parties and benefits to know who was who in Miami. Then he realized she stood expectantly at the counter. He grinned again, amazed by his unusual lapse of attention. "When do you leave?"

Rissa pulled a black-leather planner from her caramel-colored bag and flipped through scribbled-on pages. Slender fingers with short, well-kept nails danced over the writing to stop almost at the bottom edge.

"Our flight leaves at 6:51 P.M. on Tuesday, the seventeenth of June," she answered, "so I'll drop off Soraya at. . .hmm. . . I'll have to leave her at 3:25 P.M. if I'm to have any hope of clearing the security at the airport on time."

"Okay," Jase drawled, amused by her extreme precision, "and you'll be back for her. . . ?"

More page-flipping and finger-dancing. "Our flight gets in at 11:23 A.M. Sunday, July thirteenth. By the time I clear the baggage claim. . .and you're seventeen and one-quarter miles west of the airport. . ."

As Rissa microcalculated times and distances, Jase watched a length of wavy strawberry-blond hair slip from behind her ear and slide across her cheek. Gold strands and red strands blended in the same exotic richness found only in old-fashioned rose-colored gold.

"I'll factor in three minutes for what little traffic I might find on a Sunday morning. . . . I should be here between 11:53 and 11:58."

What a tortured way to say she'd arrive around noon. "Okeydokey," he said with humor, marveling at her eccentric ultraprecision. "Noon on the thirteenth it is."

The hint of a frown brought her light auburn brows close, but she didn't comment on his rounded-up estimate. Thankfully.

"We're all set then," he added when she made no move to leave.

She nodded. She zipped her hobo-style handbag open, and

the maw swallowed her planner as she ran her free hand through miles of red-gold waves. Still, she stood at the counter.

"Is there something else I can do for you?" he asked, feeling somewhat stupid.

Rissa looked right through him—more accurately, past his left ear to the wall at the back of the office. She squared her shoulders and took a deep breath. "Yes," she then said. "You can tell me who will care for Soraya while she's here."

Now that was a new one for him. "Uh. . .I will, and my kids. . ." He paused and gestured toward the front window through which he could see Paul, Alida, Jamal, Dale, Matt, and Tiffany. "We'll do some of everything here."

Her dainty nose tipped up. "I was afraid of that."

Great. "Why?"

The green eyes narrowed. "You expect me to trust my baby to an inexperienced kennel owner who's at home with the crème de la crème of white-collar criminals and a bunch of goofy kids."

Jase steamed. His instincts told him to kick her snooty attitude, preconceived expectations, and pretty self off his property and back to Miami, but he knew she wasn't the only one who saw him that way. And he wouldn't alienate a customer with the kind of behavior expected of a shark.

Help me, Lord. "I don't intend to defend myself to you. You have two choices. You can leave Soraya here and assess her care after your trip, or you can take your business elsewhere. I'd rather you didn't, since I know what I'm doing and I love dogs—"

"I'm not questioning your feelings. I saw your response to the pup's birth and I know how much it moved you. My concern stems from your inexperience running a kennel—not to mention the lack of experience of the juveniles out there."

He could have told her they were actually repentant juvenile delinquents in the process of rehabilitation, but that wouldn't help.

"Again," he said, "it's your choice. Look, you have time to think about it. I hope you choose to leave Soraya with us, but I won't beg for your business. As far as my kids go, I'd trust them with my life. I don't say it as a cliché—I know them and know what they can and will do."

Rissa turned to leave, then stopped and stared out the window. Jase groaned. Paul and Jamal were on the ground locked in an esoteric wrestling move while the other four cut up the figurative rug in a wild salsa. They sure knew how to choose their moments.

"What do you want from them?" he asked, taking in the tight white edge of her lips. "Everyone needs a break, especially those who work as hard as they do."

Glancing over her sundress-bared shoulder, Rissa's eyebrow arched up above her right eye. "Do you know where your specimen is?"

"Huh?"

"Do check with your hard-working Paul. Who knows where the prized sperm you received awhile ago wound up."

She left in a swirl of green-and-white foliage-print crinkle cotton and the hint of jasmine he'd failed to notice before.

❦

As Rissa opened the car's door, Handel's "Hallelujah Chorus" tinned out from her handbag. "Hello," she said into her cell phone.

"*Buenas tardes,* Marissa," her mother responded in her most polite and fear-inducing querulous tone.

Alarm stole her breath. First Jason Easton, now her mother. *Oh, Lord Jesus, help me. I'm not prepared to deal with her, not now!*

"*Buenas, Mamá.*"

"How are you?" Then, as usual and without waiting for an answer, Adela Ortíz went on. "I am terrible. I'm sure the end is near. A person cannot bear such pain—*if* she wants to keep living. *If* she has something for to live. . ."

Rissa sat down hard in the driver's seat. With her free hand, she clutched the steering wheel as she would a lifeline. *Please, Lord, please.*

"Did you take your medicine?" she asked.

"What you say, *niña?* That I'm addict? Or that I'm crazy and need drugs?"

Rissa took another deep breath. "No, *Mamá.* Nothing of the sort. I just know how hard it is to tolerate the pain, and the doctors have urged you to make sure you take the prescriptions round the clock."

Adela huffed. "Of course, I have take all the pills. *Y nada.*"

This wasn't the first time her mother's painkillers stopped helping. "Have you called the doctor?"

"Hah! *¿Para qué?* For what?" Then, again without waiting for Rissa's answer, she went on. "I'm think all those doctors is the problem. They too happy taking your *papá's* money. Maybe they giving me drugs to make me hurt more for to keep the dollars coming."

"*Mamá,* that's outrageous, and you know it. The doctors wouldn't do such a thing. They're experts on spinal injuries." A thought occurred to her. "Have you said that to them?"

Dreadful silence confirmed her worst fears. "You should be ashamed of yourself, Adela Ortíz. You owe them an apology."

"I do *not!* They owe me a new body for all we pay these years."

They'd reached today's impasse. "Look," Rissa said, "I'm on the way to my condo. What if I call Dr. Kaszekian from there? I'm sure he can find something to help you."

A high-pitched wail came from the other end of the call. "You just want be rid of me. See? I have nothing for to live. I cannot play my beloved harp, your father. . .bah! He's always play with numbers, and you? My flesh and blood? You don't take time for to talk to me. I have nothing for to live. . . ."

A knot twisted Rissa's innards and searing tears welled up in her eyes. "I love you, Mother, but I'm ninety minutes away from you and can only do so much. I'll call Dr. Kaszekian when I get home, then I'll check on you after he's had time to prescribe something new. I do need to go now."

She cut off yet another stream of misery. She wondered where Mrs. Janssen was. Her mother's nurse-companion rarely left her unattended. Then again, the poor woman did occasionally need to use the bathroom or prepare Adela's meals.

Rissa turned the key in the ignition, then left SilkWood.

"Why, Lord? Why is she like that?" she asked in the silence of the car. "And why me? I don't know what to do with her. . .for her." She swallowed hard and blinked even harder, to no avail. The lump in her throat didn't budge, and the tears spilled down her cheeks, followed by many, many others.

Doubting she'd sleep that night, she slipped in a CD and forced herself to focus on the lyrics. Rissa knew that if she took her mind off God's glory and power and might, even for a scant moment, she'd never make it home in one piece. The tears would return, and who knew what she'd fail to see in the road ahead. Joining her voice to the singer's, she sang the Lord's praises, wondering how the day could have gone so wrong.

In His Word, God promised to be with her during the bad as well as the good days. Today was one of the bad. Yet He remained the Best of the best. King of all kings. Jehovah, Messiah, Almighty God. In Him she would place her trust. . . relinquish her fears. . .confide her heartache. In Him she would find peace. Only in Him.

❧

The Altamonte wedding went off without a hitch. The quartet's music, even if Rissa did say so herself, was the perfect accompaniment to the exchange of vows at the altar. The bride, with her olive skin, exotic brown eyes, and masses of black hair piled under coronet and veil, looked lovely, excited but solemn. Her voice trembled when she pledged herself to her groom before God and man.

Even though Rissa was in no hurry to marry, she hoped she would someday reflect the same emotions and commitment she'd witnessed.

Now, at the reception, the quartet would play until the multicourse dinner. At that time, a pianist and harpist would take over, and the foursome would eat with the other guests.

As Ty huffed and griped about Bertha's imaginary ever-increasing weight problem, Rissa scanned the vast ballroom in one of Miami's most venerable hotels. She recognized many of the guests from their appearances in the *Herald*'s society pages. A smattering of politicians, local and state level, was also in attendance.

Then she spotted a familiar snow-white mane. Dread filled her. It couldn't be.

The crowd shifted, and Rissa caught a glimpse of what she'd feared she'd see. *Papá*, elegant in his dinner jacket, wore the vague expression that indicated the presence of convoluted computations. At his side, Adela's wheelchair reflected the sparkle of the crystal chandeliers overhead. Not a single hair strayed from Mother's dyed-to-perfection auburn French twist.

Rissa wished she'd realized ahead of time that her parents knew the Altamontes, even though she shouldn't be surprised they did. Her father had been prominent in certain pre-Castro Havana circles, and now, as a result of his Nobel Prize nomination, he was highly sought after as a guest at numerous society gatherings.

Praying for strength, she tuned her bass as the others joined in. Then she saw Ty glance up.

He turned to her, frowning. "Isn't that. . . ?"

Rissa swallowed hard. "The one and only. I had no idea she—*they'd* be here."

"Would you've backed out if you'd known?"

She worried her bottom lip. Would she have run out on her friends? "I'd never do that, no matter how difficult my parents are."

Ty reached out and squeezed her shoulder. "Even if you had, you're not alone, you know."

Rissa felt her friend's love as a special gift, the Father's warm blessing. "Thanks. I know you guys are here for me, and I know the Lord will see me through tonight."

"Amen," he said.

As she rosined her bow, she heard a hiss to her left.

"Pssst!" her mother called again. *"Marisita,* over here."

When she turned and made herself smile, her mother pressed one of the wheelchair controls and propelled herself near. Rissa saw Eva's eyes narrow and Tristan's jaw jut forth. Ty took a protective step forward.

Love bubbled up for her three friends. "It's okay, guys," she murmured. Then, turning to Adela, she said, *"Hola, Mamá.* I had no idea you'd be here tonight."

"Of course we're here. We know Rodrigo and Estersita Altamonte since university in Havana. We couldn't miss Sarita's wedding."

Adela seemed calmer than she had earlier in the week. Perhaps her new prescription was helping. Rissa hoped so. She knew the toll the unrelenting pain had taken on her mother—and the family—over the years.

She smiled tentatively. "I hope you enjoy the pieces we've chosen. We're doing some of the mellow old *danzones* you like so much."

"Ah, *sí.* The music your father and I loved so much when we were *novios,* before we married." A dreamy expression softened Adela's features. Rissa breathed a prayer of thanksgiving and felt her friends' tension ease.

Then *Papá* approached. "Come, Adela, we must take our place at the table. It takes some doing to arrange your wheelchair so that no one jostles you."

Mamá's features hardened. *"Sí,* Francisco. *Vamos ya.* Marissa, I wish you'd open your eyes. Why you must to play that great masculine thing, I no understand. The harp, *niña,* the harp you should play. You're my daughter and the great Brigitte Cardoza's granddaughter."

Rissa winced. She hadn't escaped this encounter unscathed. She lowered her head to keep her feelings to herself and watched her father propel the wheelchair to the opposite side of the room. As she blinked to keep the tears from melting her mascara, she saw Eva put her treasured violin on the floor.

"I'm so sorry," her friend whispered, wrapping her arm around Rissa's shoulders. "I'm sorry for her suffering and for the misery she spreads as a result. The Lord knows your heart, Ris. He knows you want to praise Him with your music, and you do. A quartet—*we*—couldn't perform without a bass. Besides, you can always play your marimba instead. Not that I want you to abandon us for some percussion ensemble or anything, but you do have that, too."

A cross between a sob and a giggle escaped Rissa's lips. "Don't even mention the marimba in the same room where *Mamá* might overhear. You should hear what she says about 'cacophonous percussion *things*.'"

Eva came around and gripped Rissa's forearms. "Just answer one question: Are you doing God's will?"

The two friends had hashed out this point frequently since college-roommate days. Rissa shrugged. "I believe with all my heart that I am, but it's just. . .well, she's my mother."

"And He's your Father in heaven. With God beside you, no one can stand against you, remember?"

She nodded and donned a weak little smile. "I'm okay." At Eva's roll of the eyes and Tristan's snort, she added, "No, really, I am. Let's do what the Altamontes hired us to do. Let's play."

As Eva retrieved her violin, Rissa squared her shoulders and settled Bertha in the curve of her shoulder. She drew her bow, poised to glide it over the thick strings that enriched the sound of the other instruments, and looked at the glad-handers in the receiving line.

She gasped. "Great, just what I needed."

"What's that?" Ty asked.

"Look who just arrived."

"Uh-oh."

"Mm-hmm. The slimy shark-*cum*-kennel-owner himself."

And dressed to the nines. This was the Jason Easton she pictured as she drove to SilkWood the other day. Polished, impeccably groomed, his evening whites in gleaming contrast to his tanned face, his blue eyes shining with intelligence and shrewdness. This was the man who worked for the wealthiest and most unsavory present here tonight.

The man to whom she'd contracted to entrust Soraya for three weeks—in a moment of utter discombobulation, of course. The man who, just by his mere presence, made her heart beat a little faster, her cheeks burn a little warmer, and her senses perk a little livelier.

The man she expected would prove himself unequal to caring for a kennel full of dogs, but thanks to his legal knowledge, would get away unscathed by his incompetence.

Chapter 3

Upon entering the ballroom for the Altamonte–Echeverría wedding reception, Jase spied the gleam of rose gold in an unforgettable waterfall of hair. He'd never expected to see Rissa Ortíz at this Miami society wedding, but after one glimpse of those almost waist-long waves, no one could mistake her for anyone else.

Then he noticed the massive instrument in her embrace. Hmm. . .so she wasn't a model or an actress after all. He'd heard of the Classical Strings Quartet, and he'd attended events where they'd performed, but he'd never taken note of the musicians. Now he wished he had. He might have met her when he could have made a better impression on the ethereally beautiful woman.

Rissa displayed a mixture of dramatic contrasts. Her exquisite delicacy belied her strength—it took an abundance to handle a full-size upright bass. And while she looked as though she belonged in an illustration of woodland beings with her willowy frame and old-master coloring, she grounded herself in precision, as her exacting focus on time and schedules testified.

She'd caught him off guard at the kennels, and after she left, his senses reeled hours later with her jasmine scent and feminine loveliness. Now, witnessing yet another of her facets, he found himself flat-out intrigued.

And attracted.

To his dismay, the kind of woman who'd make him a logical partner never appealed to him, yet the much-prejudiced Rissa Ortíz drew at him more than any of the earlier inappropriate candidates.

Lord, help. Show me a suitable woman so that I can set aside this attraction to one who hates me because of my former job.

Jase donned a smile and congratulated the Altamontes and the Echeverrías, both families longtime clients of his father and friends of his parents. Then he spotted his law-school mentor, the frail and gray Dr. Pierpont, holding court near a floor-to-ceiling window, and joined the debate on the more esoteric points of habeas corpus. He snagged scrumptious seafood and Cuban delicacies the wait service offered on silver trays. He drank geranium-scented iced tea seemingly by the bucketful. He smiled, nodded, shook hands, and chatted.

But he couldn't evict the musician from his thoughts.

Conceding the futility of his efforts, Jase leaned on a fluted column and watched Rissa and her fellow performers. He noted the camaraderie between the foursome, their obvious love and respect.

He envied them. He had nothing similar in his life.

Then Rissa's posture changed. The fluidity of her movements and the poise she displayed, even while kneeling at Mahadi's birthing, vanished. With jerky spurts of motion, she tuned her instrument, head lowered close to the bass's bridge.

When she looked back up at the gathered guests, a chill grimace replaced her smile.

He followed her gaze. "So that's who you are, lovely Rissa."

The still-famous former harpist, Adela Ortíz, whirred her motorized wheelchair to Rissa's side. Mother and daughter shared a resemblance, but Rissa looked most like her legendary grandmother, Brigitte Cardoza, the height by which all harpists were measured since the 1940s. Even Adela never reached Brigitte's level of mastery, and many said that failure still fueled her burning bitterness. Her career, cut short by a fall down the marble steps of a European opera house, never fulfilled its promise.

Whatever mother and daughter, now joined by Nobel Prize nominee Dr. Francisco Ortíz, were discussing couldn't be pleasant—at least not for Rissa. She grew pale, drew in sharp breaths, winced, and then finally, when the professor wheeled his wife away, lowered her head again, letting the spectacular cascade of curls hide her face.

Jase had the distinct impression she wept.

Something impelled him toward her, the urgency significant. Despite the three concerned musicians converging upon her, he kept on. As he approached, she smiled weakly at her friends, squared her shoulders, leaned her head back, and shook the wealth of hair away from the bass. She then drew her bow, poised to perform.

Admiration filled him.

The music began. Rissa's rigidity disappeared, and she shuttered her eyes, the softest, most reverent expression illuminating her features. As the lush notes of Corelli's "Sarabande" underscored the murmur of the gathering, she gave in to her art.

The attraction deepened. His need to know her better grew, and Jase knew that, regardless of how she felt about him at the moment, he was going to try to change her opinion.

He wanted her to look at him with the emotion and trust she showed her friends. And, if God so willed it, he would become a part of the circle Rissa showered with love.

After cajoling the bewildered Estér Altamonte into squeezing his place card between Rissa's and that of some other guest relegated to the musicians' table, Jase soaked in the quartet's music.

When the maître d' announced dinner, he took his new seat and watched the quartet store the instruments. All displayed a profound respect for the magnificent tools of their trade, even Rissa, despite her struggle with the unwieldy bass. As Jase pushed his chair back to go help her, the African-American cellist assumed the onerous task. The familiarity between the two sent a foreign pang through Jase, and, to his amazement, he recognized. . .jealousy?

Moments later, his tablemates approached.

"I'm telling you, Ris, you overfeed the Beast," her good-looking and overly helpful friend said. "My poor back suffers more each day."

Rissa tossed her glorious hair over her left shoulder. "And I keep telling you, Ty, you're just a big baby."

The other two musicians pulled out their chairs and sat, chuckling. Ty struck a pose, one hand on Rissa's chair back and the back of the other at his forehead. "You wound me, oh, Carrottop!"

Rissa narrowed her gaze. "Them's fighting words, brother mine."

"Nah, nah, nah," Ty chided and slipped into his chair. "We're too mature for sibling rivalry."

Then Rissa noticed Jase. *"You're* sitting *here?"*

Her dismay rubbed him the wrong way, but he controlled his response. "That's what the card says," he answered. "I must congratulate you—all of you. You've extraordinary talent."

The praise pleased Rissa's partners, but it brought a skeptical gleam to her eyes. Thank-yous rang out, hers the most muted. Turning to the other woman in the group, she made it plain she would not be furthering their acquaintance. Jase bided his time.

Moments later, a starched and ironed waiter delivered a lobster first course. As Jase lowered his head to pray, he noticed subtle movement among the others and glanced sideways. He caught his breath. Rissa and her partners, holding hands, were about to ask a blessing over their food.

He said, "May I join you in prayer?"

Shocked green eyes met his. While Rissa seemed unable to speak, the viola player raised a brow. "You're a Christian?"

"Nearly twelve years now."

"Then welcome, Brother. I'm Tristan Reuben. And you're. . . ?"

"He's Jason Easton, Tris," Rissa said, rousing herself from her stupor. "The new owner of SilkWood Kennels."

"Aren't you a lawyer?" Ty asked.

"Passed the bar many years ago."

The other woman's eyes darted from Rissa to Jase and back again. "I'm Eva Alono," she said, "and Tyrone Carver's the last of our group. Let's pray, shall we?"

The lobster chunks in lime butter were delicious, as the

hotel's reputation led one to expect, and the conversation remained polite. Then the last guest at the table arrived.

Resplendent in gray swallowtails, pink shirt with white collar, sunset-orange tie, top hat in hand, and spats over shiny black shoes, the diminutive elderly dandy took the seat to Jase's left, cresting a wave of liniment and aftershave over the lobster and lime.

He plopped his chapeau in the center of the table in front of his plate. To Eva, he said, "Evenin', Chickadoodledee. My name's Horatio Davenport Jones, but all my friends moniker me Wem—don't ask me why, 'cause after eighty-three years, I still haven't clairivisioned the whyfore to that. Still, I'd be mighty honorized if you'd call me Wem." He glanced at the others. "All of you, too."

Jase suppressed a chuckle and held out a hand. "Pleased to meet you, Wem. I'm Jason Easton."

Bushy white brows beetled together. "The advocate, eh?"

Jase nodded.

"Well, rattle my rafters, sonny-boyo! I've got me a question for a legal beagle like yourself." Plunking both elbows on the table in a sidesaddle sort of way, Wem fixed Jase with his beaming brown eyes. "D'ja think I got me a case against the ambulance chaser that refused to sue city hall for me when I stubbed my toe and tripped on one of them too-tall nuisance curbs over on Hialeah Boulevard? At night, and under one of those dim-bulbed streetlights?"

To Jase's relief, the well-pressed waiter arrived right then and slid before him a fragrant, golden-skinned Rock Cornish hen accompanied by asparagus soufflé and three-peppered baby corn. Wem received his lobster as well as his hen and, from his glee, would not soon return to his imagined matter of jurisprudence.

Jase suspected that, despite the sartorial excess and advanced age, a laser dwelt in Wem's mind. But Jase no longer practiced law.

For the rest of the meal, Wem entertained his neighbors with tales of a long career as a jockey and greyhound breeder. Nowadays he ran a race-dog retirement home and dabbled in the market—he took a bath in the dot-com crash. Racing ran in his blood, he said, and Jase saw the man's need to replenish his caloric output in the speed with which he inhaled vast quantities of food.

"Now," Wem said, "after all those years, I've got PETA nuts marching at my front gate, accusing me of treating my dogs like dogs. I take good care of my old-folk-dogs. Where'd they get the imprescription that canines are people, too? I've never hurt a soul—not even a dog's—yet."

The lights went out with those words. A line of waiters marched flaming Baked Alaskas through the ballroom, eliciting the guests' appreciative oohs and aahs.

Wem raised an interesting issue, but a wedding reception wasn't the place to debate the topic. Jase decided to hunt down the free-spirited philosopher some other time and continue the discussion.

As he forked up a bite of ice cream and cake dessert, Rissa asked, "Why can't one hate animal cruelty and support good breeding practices?"

Jase, noting that Wem, busy with his Alaska, seemed impervious to Rissa's question, answered. "I don't think the two are mutually exclusive, but there are those who believe breeding interferes with the flow of nature and produces too many unwanted animals."

"Hmm. . . ," she said, "sounds like what the delivery guy told Paul."

"Paul? The delivery guy?"

Rissa nodded. "The day I visited SilkWood, Paul was waiting for your breeding specimen. It arrived via a parcel service, and the driver made a negative comment when he realized what he'd delivered."

The pianist and harpist who took the quartet's place during the meal packed up their instruments as a small orchestra set up. Throughout the ballroom, chairs scraped against the polished terrazzo, indicating the end of the banquet.

Jase stood and held a hand to Rissa. "May I?"

To his surprise, she accepted. The warmth of those talented fingers imprinted his palm with evidence to her vibrancy.

"Thank you," she said with a smile.

They turned from the table and, through the room's enormous windows, Jase caught sight of the blazing sunset. Shards of light shone the same shade as her hair.

"It's beautiful," he said, tilting his head toward the west. "I'd like to enjoy it from the balcony. Care to join me?"

Rissa hesitated. Jase tugged on her hand. After a shrug and a glance at her scattering friends, she nodded. "Miami's sunsets are gorgeous."

No more than you are. The words nearly slipped from Jase's mouth, but he managed to exert his considerable control over his tongue. This wasn't the right moment.

When he opened the glass door, humid evening warmth met them.

She shivered. "I didn't realize how chilly they keep the ballroom until right now."

"It is cool inside," he commented, then grinned. "Well, as long as Horatio 'Wem' Davenport Jones isn't in the vicinity, the room feels cool. He certainly spices things up."

An indulgent smile lit her face. "He's an original, isn't he?"

"I don't think God's in the copy business."

She turned, stared at the setting sun. "You surprised me," she said. "I wouldn't have thought you knew the Lord."

"Why?" he asked, not sure he wanted to hear her answer.

With a deep breath and that squaring of the shoulders he recognized as a bracing, courage-giving gesture, she leaned sideways on the stucco banister and met his gaze square on.

"Your legal triumphs don't strike me as particularly Christian."

He *hadn't* wanted to hear her answer. "You mean my defense of clients to the best of my ability, as required by law?"

Green eyes blazed. "How can you defend criminals? You know they're guilty, and you set them free to rob and steal again."

"I couldn't choose between defending them or not—it was my *job.*"

"It may be your job, but is it what God expects from His own? Does it rise to the level of integrity Jesus exemplified?"

Jase clenched his jaw. He'd argued that point with himself—and his late father—many times, but he now chose to reiterate reality. "The law requires equal representation and due process for all."

"Then that law should be changed."

"How would you change it? And how would you decide who deserves legal representation? Only the innocent? Then perhaps you should remember Jesus' admonition about casting stones."

She bit her lower lip. "I can't judge," she answered, a troubled expression on her face. "But you, as a Christian, can choose another career or to practice another branch of the law. You don't have to help criminals escape the consequences of their crimes—their sins. You don't need to betray the cause of Christ."

The memory of heated arguments with his father, of endless nights on his knees in prayer, of interminable wrangling with himself flooded Jase and brought the anguish back. "You're right," he said. "I betrayed the cause of Christ. But then I walked away."

He walked away again, difficult though it was.

❧

You're right.

Two simple words, yet they bore an impact Rissa didn't expect. They followed her through the remainder of the reception as she sought but failed to find Jason Easton.

Evidently, her questions chased him from the event.

She avoided thinking about it as long as she could. But by the time she stood in her bathroom removing the remnants of mascara from her lashes, she could no longer dodge the queasy feeling that started when he left her.

Water dripping from her chin, she met her gaze in the mirror. Jase mentioned casting stones. Was she without flaw? Without sin?

No.

Her conscience forced her to avert her gaze. She wasn't sinless, especially in view of her judgmental attitude toward Jase. The Father alone had the right to judge His children.

She'd put herself in His place.

If that wasn't the height of pride, she didn't know what was. Pride was sin, the log in her eye. No wonder her stomach lurched all evening long. Faith in Christ honed one's conscience to a fine point.

She sopped up the mess on the vanity top, finished her ablutions with a light coat of moisturizer, then turned off the light and picked up her Bible on the way to her prize piece of furniture.

The soft sage green chaise by the window was her one and only brand-new purchase. Its chenille upholstery felt like pure indulgence against her skin, and the down filling molded itself to her body in a comforting embrace. Although new, it didn't look out of place in a shabby chic room full of antiques and flea market treasures.

She prayed for guidance from tonight's passage and opened God's Word. She found she couldn't concentrate at all.

She had to confess her sin, not just acknowledge it to herself. She also had to ask forgiveness, of God, and of Jase. Sliding to her knees by the chaise, she figuratively crawled into her Father's lap and let her troubles flow from within. She confessed, sought absolution, praised, and worshipped her Master and King.

And, eventually, acknowledged she had to swallow her pride and seek Jase. The sooner, the better.

Feeling more at peace, she devoured the Bible passage and spent time meditating on its teaching. Then she went to bed.

Taking her cue from her mistress, Soraya approached the padded dog bed Rissa kept next to the nightstand, spun tonight's requisite turns, nosed the rim in various spots, and finally plopped down with a heartfelt sigh.

Turning off her bedside lamp, Rissa knew how she would approach Jase. Soraya and the newborn pups gave her the reasons she needed—and another chance to see him again. Despite their argument, he appealed to her. Honesty made her admit she wanted to know him better, even though she'd rather deny the fact.

With a clearer conscience, she dropped off to sleep, her dreams filled with beautiful sleek baby Affies, rolling and tumbling under their mama's watchful eye.

Chapter 4

After church the next day, Rissa retrieved her pet from her condo. Butterflies churned her stomach as she drove to SilkWood, while Soraya, as usual, simply enjoyed the drive.

"You lucky dog," Rissa said to the Affie strapped in the front passenger seat of the car with a canine safety harness. "You don't have a bellyful of trepidation about this visit."

Soraya turned loving eyes toward her. At a red light, Rissa reached out and rubbed the silky head. The dog closed her eyes and leaned into her owner's caress.

"Yep," she said, "you're innocent, Soraya, but I'm not. I have to apologize. Apologies never come easy, but this one promises to be harder than most."

The need for honesty made Rissa acknowledge that today's difficulty came from the height of the fall for which her pride had set her up. "Oh, yes, the bigger we are, the harder we fall."

Soraya then yipped her response—she would remain noncommittal.

Rissa added, "Funny how when one's at the receiving end of a cliché, it becomes an unfunny truism."

The Affie tipped her head, shot her a quizzical look, and added a soft yap.

"Hey, that's why you're lucky. You don't have to worry about sticking your foot in your mouth. For you, that's fun. Me? I made a very dumb move."

Then Rissa faced the moment of truth. She'd reached SilkWood. As she turned onto the long gravel drive, her pulse raced and the butterflies became dive-bombing buzzards. She stopped at the parking area in front of the office building and opened her door.

The heavy throb of hip-hop's bass line buffeted her ears. Soraya's excited if outraged yowls at her restrained condition set Rissa's already rattled nerves on edge. She hurried to the passenger-side door and released her hound. With the ease of familiarity, Soraya ran to the kennel run closest to the car. She sniffed up and down its length, stuck her long, slender muzzle in and out of various links in the fence, and barked in exuberant joy.

The hip-hop beat mercifully stopped at the end of the song.

Rissa approached the office, a prayer for courage and humility on her lips. She pushed the door inward, shivered at the blast of arctic-conditioned air, and called, "Anyone here?"

"I am," Jase answered, "but why are you?"

Oh, great. He wasn't going to make this easy. "Umm. . .I—well, I felt. . ." She cut short her stammered efforts when she failed to see him. Rissa needed a face by which to gauge the effect of her apology. "Where exactly are you?"

He sighed. Something scraped across the floor. Then, with obvious reluctance, he rose on the opposite side of the laminate-covered divide. His chiseled jaw jutted and a muscle in one lean cheek twitched. "So you're the kind who likes to lob attacks eye-to-eye."

Rissa winced. "That's a fair jab, considering my actions last night, but it's not why I came."

He stared, arms crossed over his ratty T-shirt.

She didn't blink. "I came because I had to." A deep breath and another quick prayer gave her courage. "After you left—at least, I assume you did, since I didn't see you again—I couldn't forget what I'd said, and believe me, I tried."

He arched a brow.

"By bedtime, my conscience burned hotter than the sun"— Rissa gestured toward the window—"and the Holy Spirit's convicting worked."

The jaw eased by a hint—*just* a hint.

She leaned on the counter. "I owe you an apology. I was wrong. I had no right to set myself up as your judge and jury, never mind convicting you. I know only God can do that, but I let pride take over. I put myself in the Father's place, and. . .well, we both know that's sin, plain and simple."

His shoulders relaxed a fraction.

She'd hoped for more, the uncrossing of those arms or a gentler light in his blue eyes. He offered nothing more.

"Last night I asked the Lord's forgiveness," she continued, "and now I ask yours. I know I don't deserve it, but I hope you can forgive me at some point. I'm sorry for what I said and for hanging onto an opinion without even hearing your side."

Then his demeanor changed. He exploded out of his internal constraints. He flung his arms to his sides. He looked away. He ran a hand through his dark blond hair. He turned and walked to the desk at the right rear corner of the office. He didn't say a word.

Still, Rissa sensed that she'd reached him. "What's worse," she added, her voice soft, "I did to you what my family has done to me for years. I boxed you in by my preconceived notion. I expected you to be a sleazy lawyer out to make a buck, and then you sent me and my expectations on a roller-coaster ride when you said you were a—"

"Christians can't be lawyers?" he asked, spinning to face her again. "Or are they only supposed to follow the law when it's convenient? God called us to respect the earthly rule under which we live, and last time I looked, in America we live by the rule of law."

Rissa bowed her head. "Yes, He did, and if I'd listened to what you tried to say instead of only my judgmental thoughts, I would have heard you. I didn't want to hear it, just as my family doesn't want to hear what I have to say about my life and my choices. As wrong as it is for them, it's equally wrong for me."

A shudder racked her. "You said you walked away from the law—"

"I *did* walk away. That's why I'm—"

"Give me a chance, please." She dropped her purse on the counter and reached out as though to touch him, but he was too far on the other side of the chasm. "If only I'd given some thought to your actions—which I only did later on—I probably would have seen the truth. You haven't represented anyone in nearly a year, have you?"

"No, I've—"

"Wait! Let me finish. You spent a fortune buying out Mrs. Gooden, right?"

At his nod, she continued. "You can't litigate while mucking out runs, and I've never heard of a lawyer who wears torn jeans and T-shirts to court."

He glanced down at himself, groaned, and to her amazement, blushed. "I suppose I could wear my three-piece suit to feed and walk the dogs, but that wouldn't make much sense. I changed when I got home from church."

Rissa gave a tentative chuckle. "I'd judge you a raving lunatic if you hadn't."

He smiled back. "You'd have every reason to."

As he rounded the counter and came to her side, Rissa allowed herself a measure of relief. Then she noticed the unusual sparkle in his blue eyes.

"You weren't exactly dressed for labor and delivery the other day," he said. "You reminded me of illustrations of fairylike beauties in old, Victorian storybooks."

His words stole her ability to respond. She stared at him, stunned by what he'd said. He'd called her a beauty.

Her silence seemed to make him bolder. "You look like that again today. This lacy dress you're wearing looks very old-timey, and your hair. . ."

His words died as he reached, paused, then caught the lock of hair resting on her arm. Twirling it around a finger, he reeled himself right up to her, a look of wonder on his face. Rissa's breath caught in her throat, and his intense eyes snagged her gaze.

"Beautiful. . . ."

Somewhere in the back of her mind, the thought of panicking wafted in and out—mostly out, since right then she felt more than thought. The frigid air in the office suddenly turned sultry, weighty. Time paused. Seconds drifted rather than passed. All the while, Jase continued to stare, his face approaching.

She suspected he hovered just a breath away from kissing her, and she didn't know how she felt about it. She merely felt the warmth of his nearness, the excitement of his interest, the pull of their attraction, the beginnings of—

"Hey, Jase—Oops!" Paul careened to a stop in the open doorway.

Jase and Rissa turned, virtually cheek to cheek.

"Bummer," the blushing teen said. "I'm sorry. I just—umm, well, I'll be seein' ya! Later, *much* later."

As Paul turned, Jase tore himself from Rissa's side. "Hold it. What's up?"

The teen stopped, but kept his face averted. "Nothing much. We were just with Mahadi and the babies, and her pooch"—he pointed at Rissa—"flipped for the pups. She's crazy for them. You should see it. But it's not important, you know." He sidled along the door he still clutched in one hand. "I'll be getting back now. You're cool. Just go back. . . . *Never mind.*"

He ran out as though the Hound of the Baskervilles had set its sights upon him and licked its chops.

Rissa smiled. Then she chuckled.

Jase turned and sent her a questioning look.

She laughed. "It's—*he's* just too funny!"

A lopsided grin widened Jase's lips. He ran his hand through his hair, then shook his head. "Kinda killed the mood, didn't he?"

Rissa only laughed harder.

He joined in.

Moments later, when they both caught their breath, Jase opened the door and gestured for Rissa to precede him outside. "We may as well join them, don't you think?"

Stepping into the late afternoon heat, she said, "I'm a dog lover and Affie crazy in particular. I'd love to take a look at that cutie I met the other day."

They went to the building of runs, hurried down the center aisle, and met up with four teens, a curious Soraya horning in on the action, an anxious, defensive Mahadi, and her litter of sweet pups.

"Oh!" Rissa exclaimed, looking at the wriggling infants. "They're beautiful." She turned to Jase. "Do you think she'd let me come close? Pick one up?"

Jase tipped his head, studied the canine family. "I don't think she'll mind if you come into her kennel and go right up to them, but you may have trouble touching. She's a fantastic mother, and she might take a snap since she doesn't know you."

"I was afraid of that," Rissa said. "It's disappointing, but I should know better. Soraya's mother went crazy when I came to visit her and her litter."

"Affies are very protective of their pups," Paul stated with surprising certainty.

Stepping around him, Rissa placed a hand on his shoulder. "Looks like you've learned a thing or two about dogs."

The shoulder rose in a shrug as she dropped down to his side. "They're pretty cool," he said. "Just watch them play. They roll all over each other, and they don't even have their eyes open. Yeah, they're cool."

Rissa turned her attention to the "cool" dogs. A soft rumble rolled from the new mother's throat, warning Rissa away from the infants. Remembering her experience with Soraya's mother, she sat quietly, not moving, letting the dam get used to her scent. In the meantime, she watched the puppies romp.

The plump little wigglers wore soft fuzz quite unlike the long, silky hair they would later grow. Mahadi's litter promised a variety of traditional Affie colors. One sported silvery fuzz, very much like its mother's. Two were dark, and their coats would probably grow in glossy black or rich brown. Another looked like it would be red, and two had blond fuzz, similar to Soraya's coloring.

Rissa heard a sniffle behind her. She glanced over her shoulder and saw tears on the stocky brown-haired girl's face. Jase placed a hand on the teen's shoulder.

"You okay, Tiff?" he asked.

Tiffany drew a shuddery breath. "Yeah. It's just that. . .well, it's kind of hard. I can't forget, you know?"

Jase placed an arm across her shoulders, and with the ease of familiarity, Tiff turned into his chest. He held the girl as she sobbed, patting her back with a fatherly tenderness that brought a lump to Rissa's throat. There was just something about Jase. . . .

When Tiff's anguish lessened, he said, "You were so sure you were doing the right thing. Do you regret it now?"

"Yes—no. . . ." She met his gaze. "No, I don't regret giving my son away. The O'Malleys really wanted a baby, and they have what mine needs. I don't, not now."

Rissa's throat burned and tears filled her eyes.

"But you will someday," Jase stated.

"You bet. The next baby I have will have a mother *and* a father who want it and are ready to really take care of it." She lifted a shoulder and rubbed her wet cheek. "It's just that a baby is a baby, dog or human, and a mother *feels*. I'm really glad you helped me find the O'Malleys. I don't know if I could have done the right thing if I'd just had to hand him to just any old couple."

So Jase *had* done more than represent crooked rich guys. She was glad she'd apologized—God didn't convict without reason.

The slam of the kennel door put an end to the emotional moment. "Well, howdy-dowdy-do there, Counselor," crowed a familiar voice.

Rissa stood. Wem? Here? She glanced at Jase.

He said, "I'm surprised to see you, Wem. I meant to call, since I hope to debate some points you made last night, but I never expected to see you so soon."

"Ah-ha ha *ha!*" Wem said. "Even the pretty, red-topped chickadoodledee is here, too."

Rissa voiced a weak "Hi."

Wem removed his snappy tartan golf tam, grabbed her hand, enveloped her in the aroma of liniment and aftershave, then kissed her fingers. "You're a better sight and scent and sound than even my dear, sainted great-aunt Gertie's lively Sunday chicken dinners."

Rissa didn't know whether to run for her life or laugh. She glanced at Jase and recognized the error in *that*. The mirth in his eyes made chuckles bubble up from her middle. She clamped her lips tight.

Wem noticed nothing. "I reconfiggered that, having nothing better to do today, I could come and pick your jurisprudicious brain, sonny-boyo."

Jase groaned.

Tiffany giggled.

The boy named Matt snorted.

Paul sidled behind Rissa, making for the great outdoors.

The movement caught Wem's attention. He looked at Paul, narrowed his gaze, and lost his amiable expression. "You!"

Paul stepped lively.

Wem snagged Paul's arm in the curve of his carved ebony cane. "Hold it there. I thought you were locked up tight."

Paul's eyes flashed. "I did my time."

Rissa gasped.

"Not nearly enough," bellowed Wem.

"I didn't take it," argued Paul.

"You and your pals did."

"So what?" Paul shot back. "That junky old Studebaker wasn't worth my two years. It only had scraps of metal around the rust."

"You hoodlum, you—"

Jase stepped between them as Wem's free hand shot out for the boy's neck. "Now listen here, you two. Paul was in the wrong place at the wrong time, and he paid for his poor choices. Last night you looked familiar, Wem, but I'd forgotten the case."

Wem sputtered, as though Jase had spouted heresy.

Jase added, "I believe insurance paid for your loss."

Wem dithered. He hemmed and hawed. Finally, he glared at Jase. "It's the memories, Counselor. You can't go putting dollar signs on a man's recollections, and this. . .this hooligan stole a passel-load of mine. From the best years of my life, I might add."

Jase narrowed his gaze. "I thought you'd recently bought the car."

Wem blushed so bright that even the dim light in the kennel couldn't hide the red. "It's the memories it joggered loose in my mind that he stole from me."

With an indignant "Harrumph!" Wem marched down the kennel hall, opened the door, then slammed it in his wake.

A pregnant teen. An auto thief.

A tinge of suspicion colored Rissa's thoughts. "Mr. Easton?"

Jase blinked, shook himself. "Huh?"

"Might I ask you a question?"

He nodded.

"In private," she added.

The jaw clenched and the muscle leapt in his cheek. "Follow me."

As soon as they left the building, she turned. "How many of your employees have juvenile records?"

He fisted his hands, and the expression on his face hardened further. "They all do."

Lead landed in Rissa's stomach. "You expect me to trust my valuable pet to a class of junior thugs?"

He took a step closer, and Rissa gulped.

"As I told you before," he said, "the choice is yours. Tell you what. Leave your animal with us, as a test of sorts, overnight if not for a couple of days—free, of course—and judge us then."

With great obvious effort, he opened his hands and stepped toward the office building. "Just keep in mind that God will forgive your sins as you forgive those of others."

Chapter 5

The next day, Rissa puttered around the condo as she usually did on her rare free days. She saved Sundays for the Lord and Mondays for herself, and today she'd finished the boring necessities before noon. But nothing felt normal. She missed Soraya and couldn't relax. She wouldn't until she picked up her pet later that evening.

She regretted accepting Jase's challenge, but he'd left her little choice.

She turned to her favorite hobby, despite the lousy outdoor light, and set up her easel in front of the patio doors. The lofty palm visible through the slider's frame looked disheartened and reflected her mood—not to mention that of the day.

As she squeezed generous blobs of black, phthalo blue and green, alizarin crimson, and a dab of titanium white onto her palette, she mentally composed the painting. But as her thoughts ran images of an intriguing lawyer and a mental recording of their parting words, she found she couldn't concentrate. She hated admitting—even to herself—how much Jase appealed to her. They shared a common faith, a love of dogs, and she couldn't deny the sizzle between them. Still, that wasn't enough—he thought her as judgmental as her parents, and she had serious doubts about his connection to former criminals.

The doorbell rang, and Rissa responded, glad for the reprieve from her thoughts.

"Surprise!" chorused Eva, Tristan, and Ty.

"Huh?"

Ty reached around and tugged the long braid running down Rissa's back. "What is *wrong* with you? You never forget the year, the month, date, day of the week, hour, minute, or even the millisecond. You really forgot your birthday?"

Rissa frowned, then realized she hadn't checked her planner. "You're right. This is unusual for me. And it is my birthday."

Tristan pushed past Ty. "Phew! I balanced this frosting extravaganza for three whole blocks while Eva drove. I'd hate to think it was for nothing."

"Hey!" Eva closed the door behind her bouquet of helium balloons. "I'm an excellent driver. You're just doing a guy thing because you hate to have someone else behind the wheel."

"Maybe," Tristan said with a grin, "but you have to admit a car ride is scary with this sugar-and-butter football field on your lap."

Ty feinted a jab to Tristan's shoulder. "Get over it."

"Watch it, funny guy," the cake-bearer warned as he dodged and landed the dessert on the kitchen counter. "I bet you'd rather eat it than have the birthday girl's pooch slurp it from the floor."

Rissa gulped. "Soraya's not here."

Three shocked faces turned her way.

"Jase challenged me to trust her to him for one night to see how she does before I leave her there during our tour."

Her friends changed the subject, and Rissa appreciated the ongoing good-natured banter. It let her mask her dismay. She prided herself on her attention to detail, and forgetting the date—her birthday, no less—was not at all like her.

Last night's heated argument still troubled her. Missing her dog didn't help.

"Earth to Rissa," called Ty.

"I'm here, I'm here," she answered. "You guys are too sweet. You didn't have to do this. No one celebrates birthdays once they turn twenty-one. At least, no woman does."

"Those are the ones who fork over fortunes for so-called miracle wrinkle cures," Eva countered. "They prefer to eliminate the beauty God created for every age."

Ty howled. "How old are you, Miss Wise *Old* Sage? The same twenty-eight as Rissa, only five months sooner, last time I checked."

Tristan waved Rissa's message pad and pen. "I'm recording Eva's statement for posterity. I'll reread it on her fiftieth b-day."

"I'm so glad you guys came," Rissa said, laughing. "It's gross and gray, and I can sure use your nuttiness."

The impromptu party went off with great success. Gag gifts balanced true tokens of affection, and the hot dogs, chips, veggies and dip, and cake soon vanished. They played excellent recordings throughout the afternoon, enjoying the new Aaron Copeland CD Tristan gave Rissa. She loved the twentieth-century American composer's music, and as his adaptation of the Shaker hymn, "Simple Gifts," soared around her, Rissa finally began to feel more like her normal self.

Then her mother called, ostensibly to wish her well on her

birthday, but in truth to relate her latest tiff with Mrs. Janssen, her nurse/companion.

"Are you okay?" Eva asked as Rissa hung up the phone.

She nodded. "Mom seems better. I hope it lasts."

"We all do," Tristan added. "She's not a happy woman. We know how trying she can be, but her situation would be tough for anyone."

Rissa's eyes welled. "Thanks for understanding. Even though she has no feeling from the hips down, she suffers a lot. Her middle back and neck are in bad shape, too. I pray—"

Another phone call let her escape without voicing a specific prayer. She offered many for her mother. "Hello?"

"Rissa?" Jase said.

Oh, no. She wasn't ready for him. "Yes."

"I regret bothering, but you must come to SilkWood right away."

His formal tone disturbed her even more. "Why?"

"I wouldn't ask if it weren't important." He fell silent for a moment, then went on. "Mahadi's only girl pup is missing. No one's seen her since yesterday afternoon in the kennel."

"That's awful," Rissa said, "her eyes aren't even open. She couldn't have gone far. Have *you* looked for her or did you have the kids do the searching?"

His silence grew ominous. Then, "No, I didn't dump the search for a valuable, already-sold dog on the kids. They helped. We all looked for her, even the police."

That put matters in a different light. "I don't understand. If everyone's already looked for her, why do you need me?"

"Because *they* need to question everyone who's been here since noon yesterday. You were, remember?"

The memory of everything—their near kiss; Wem's kennel invasion; the revelations about Tiffany, Paul, the other kids; Jase's parting words—hadn't left her, no matter how hard she tried to shake them. She didn't want to think through the implications, but she didn't seem to have a choice.

"Have the police questioned Paul?" she asked.

"Just get out here," Jase said, his voice curt. "It's theft—she's valuable—and the cops want to talk to you."

He hung up.

Rissa stood, staring at the palm she'd wanted to paint, holding the phone partway between its cradle and her ear. Why was Jase so insistent on her presence? He couldn't possibly think she had anything to do with the pup's disappearance. Not with that crew of criminals running his place.

What a pity. She'd grown to like Paul. But he was a thief, tried and convicted. What could you expect?

And Jase? That moment, the shared intimacy that led to the near kiss. . .she'd foolishly thought it might lead to something. He was a poor judge of character, however, putting any chance in doubt.

Ty took the phone, and Tristan took her by the shoulders. "What's going on?" he asked.

She shuddered. "One of Mahadi's babies is missing."

Eva erupted from the rose velvet settee. "Who's Mahadi? Is she divorced? Could it be drug related? Did they call in the FBI?"

Rissa patted Tristan's hands, then removed them from her shoulders. She went to Eva as though slogging through the heavy steam that replaced the earlier rain and pulled the two of them down onto the settee.

"Mahadi's one of Jase's Afghans," she said. Eva rolled her eyes. Rissa continued. "He'd sold the pups before she gave birth last Wednesday, and one's missing. He thinks someone took her for the money. The police are there, and he says they want to question me—I don't know why. I know he knows I had nothing to do with the theft."

Ty joined the women in the seating area. "Didn't you say you left Soraya there yesterday? It's police procedure to talk to anyone who has contact with a crime scene."

"But I haven't even touched the babies. Besides. . ."

"Besides what?" Tristan asked. "You can't just leave us hanging. What else do you know?"

Rissa glared. "You don't have to grill me like some TV cop. I'm going to face the real ones soon enough."

He stared on, unrepentant.

She stood. "It turns out the teens that work for Jase have juvenile records. One of them stole Wem's Studebaker."

Ty frowned, also rising and heading for the door. "The old jockey from the wedding? One of Easton's employees stole his antique car? Anyway, wouldn't the kids know the pup's too young to survive without the mother?"

Rissa sighed. "The junior car thief knows nothing about dogs."

"If he's no longer in custody," Eva said thoughtfully, "then he must have paid his debt and been rehabilitated."

"Who knows how rehabilitated he really is," Rissa said.

Ty led Eva and Tristan outside. "God knows, Ris. Please pray before you say anything. Only the Lord knows the kid's heart."

Rissa closed the door and headed for her room. She'd need sturdy shoes, as the rain must have made a mess of SilkWood's grounds. She glanced at her computer and realized she hadn't checked her E-mail yet. Mondays usually brought potential business for the quartet.

Moments later, she was glad she'd paused to check. The sponsor for their upcoming tour had written to request an earlier departure and the Ramos gallery about performing at an exhibition.

Rissa didn't like the tour change. She had to retrieve Soraya. SilkWood was no longer safe; she needed safer accommodations, the sooner the better.

Mulling over the pros and cons of various other kennels, she logged off, donned socks and running shoes, slung her bag over her shoulder, and left for SilkWood, dreading the upcoming ordeal.

❦

Rissa stormed from the police interview, hot tears scalding her face, rage burning her stomach, pounding her temples. No wonder Jase had been nowhere in sight when she arrived.

"There you are." She ran toward him. "How dare you not tell me Soraya's missing? She's mine, and someone took her from *your* property. I demand you find her—"

"I'm doing all I can to do just that," he said, his voice revealing exhaustion. Worry plowed furrows on his brow. His blue eyes looked irritated, and the circles under them were deep and dark. "I wanted you to drive safely. If you'd known, who knows?"

"You assured me I could trust you." Another sob ripped through her. "But you let someone take her."

The crunch of gravel muffled his response. Rissa turned and saw the parcel delivery truck followed by a well-preserved, copper-colored Pacer, circa 1978. As the truck stopped in the parking area, the car darted around it and pulled up mere inches from where Rissa and Jase stood near the office door.

Wem, in blazing white pants, neon green-and-purple plaid shirt, and Stewart tartan tam-o'-shanter extricated himself from the car. "Hey, there, Chickadoodledee," he said, bowing over Rissa's hand in a cloud of liniment and aftershave. "Fancy seeing you here again. Of course, it's a pure-dee-pleasurement, you know."

"They took my dog, too," she said bitterly, "and I just spoke with the police—not much pleasure there."

Wem's shaggy brows shot up. "Surely they don't suspect you."

She scoffed. "I didn't steal my dog. They questioned me as her owner and because I was here yesterday afternoon—just as you were."

The aged man spun his walnut cane in the air. "And just like you, *I* know nothing of the missing pups." He pointed at Jase with the prop. "I bet your thieving pup of the human variation does, though."

"I'll vouch for Paul any day," he said, sparks in his eyes. "And I'm sure you want your interview over as soon as possible. The police are waiting in my office."

Hearing Wem voice her fears, Rissa's anger flared again. Jase hadn't represented many innocents. "I don't know how you can trust delinquents," she said. "Especially Paul. He stole Wem's Studebaker."

Jase stepped forward, standing toe-to-toe with her. "Paul was with his brother and two friends when the older boys stole the car. And yes, he did share in the profits from the sale of the parts. At the time, he had a drug habit."

Rissa reared back and pointed at the boy, now cleaning a fenced run. "There you are. He probably wanted another hit."

Jase took her accusing hand, using it to reel her in. "There, Rissa," he said once she faced him, "is a repentant sinner. Like Saul, our Paul had an epiphany. He kicked his habit and accepted Christ during one of my Bible studies at his halfway house. He loves the Lord and wouldn't betray Him."

"But—"

"Do you question that Bible conversion?"

"No, but—"

"Then consider this one real, too. If God can turn a man like Saul into an apostle, then He can change a drug-addicted boy. I trust Jesus' redeeming power. Do you?"

As though he'd landed a physical blow, Rissa couldn't catch her breath. As Jase's words whirled in her head, she noticed Sean, the delivery truck driver, hold out a stack of parcels. She gestured to Jase.

He took it, forcing a smile despite his obvious anger. "Thanks."

Sean grunted, then stomped back to the truck. He peeled away, scattering gravel, just as he had the other time.

"That's one strange guy," Jase said.

Wem strolled from the office, a grin spanning ear to ear. Despite their serious situation, Rissa couldn't stop a smile. "There's another one," she murmured.

Jase's steely stare softened enough to acknowledge her effort at levity. "No argument there."

Cane hooked on his right arm, Wem approached, his left hand picking imaginary lint from his fluorescent shirt. "Cleared of any imprevarication, sonny-boyo! I knew I would be. Not like some others I won't mention."

He didn't need to mention anyone. His gaze flew straight

to Paul. Rissa shared the gent's certainty, but couldn't discount Jase's words. If Paul had sincerely accepted Christ, then he now lived by different standards than before. Had he really chosen God? Or had he just chosen the easy way to con a powerful champion?

From what she knew about addicts, recidivism was nearly a given. Had Paul fooled Jase? Was he using again? Had he ever stopped?

A purebred Affie sold for a good bit of change—times two, in this case. And Paul might not know that separating the pup from her mother would lead to death without sophisticated supplementation.

"I'll be moseydrifting along, now," Wem said, hastening to his car. Something in the way he admired the kennel buildings set off Rissa's mental alarms. He'd mentioned investment losses at the wedding reception, and although his sense of style was. . .oh, one could call it unique, the outdated garments looked expensive. The compact car wasn't, but it dovetailed with recently reduced financial means.

"Jase," she said, her gaze following the copper-colored ovoid car down the drive, "could Wem have taken the dogs?"

"Why would you think that?"

She drew a bracing breath. "Well, he said he lost a bundle in the dot-com crash, and he takes in old greyhounds. I expect it's expensive to care for them, and his coffers are probably pretty empty by now, since he retired from racing years ago. Besides, he'd know how to keep a newborn alive."

"It's possible. Anything is. But you know? Something else troubles me even more."

"Really?" she asked, desperate for any nugget of information.

"Yes, really." His eyes narrowed, not in suspicion or anger. He looked puzzled, yes, questioning, bewildered. "I'm concerned about your expectations of everyone you meet. They're pretty negative."

She gasped.

"If people don't fit your assumption, then you try to shoehorn them into that mental mold. You said you're the victim of your family's expectations. I think you're twice a victim."

Anger filled her. "What do you mean, twice a victim?"

"Yes, twice."

As she went to speak, he placed a finger on her lips. "Hear me out," he urged. "Yes, you're a victim of their expectations, but it strikes me that you're also a victim of the expectations you put on others. I don't think you can see those around you for who they really are. You seem to see only what you expect to see."

His indictment left her speechless.

He went on. "I fought to break free from my father's expectations, and because of my clumsiness, we parted on bad terms. He died before I had a chance to mend our relationship. I have no intention of letting anyone else's opinion cage me again. I decided at my father's funeral that I would concern myself only with God's greater expectations and trust Him to deal with what others expect of me. You should examine your heart. Maybe you're letting your expectations bind you in ways far worse than the family ones you say you've fought to break."

Rissa severed the connection between them. She ran to her car and drove home through a blinding flood of tears.

How could Jase say such hurtful, untrue things? She of all people knew how expectations hurt. She didn't put expectations on anyone. People were people, temptations were tough, and change harder, even with God's help. She certainly wasn't bound by any bizarre backlash of the expectations he thought she imposed. She didn't force expectations on others, she simply saw people as God's flawed, sin-prone children—just like her.

Didn't she?

Chapter 6

It was the worst week of Jase's life—other than the one after his father's death. Then, the failure to bridge the breach he carved when he told his father he could no longer in good conscience practice law as he had deepened his sense of loss. The elder Easton saw Jase's departure from the firm as a personal insult, a betrayal. Jase saw it as part of his commitment to Christ. Father hadn't understood. He'd never recognized his own need for the Savior.

This time, in addition to the loss of two lovely, valuable animals, Jase also felt the loss of what might have been. He'd sensed something special growing between him and Rissa. Now, in her view, he'd been negligent with her dog.

He also had to deal with the buyer who'd paid for the pup in advance. Jase had used that money and his savings as down payment for the future King's Kids Downtown Ministries building—his secret dream. He couldn't return the money. He couldn't replace Soraya.

Both weighed heavily on him, each important in its unique way.

His heart said Rissa was special, that if somehow they

overcame this crisis, they might have a future together. But he couldn't see how, not unless he found the missing Affies. The police had no leads.

As he turned off the lamp on his nightstand, he couldn't stop a grimace. What a way to spend a Saturday night. The cops had grilled him for hours again, then he'd seen to all the dogs' needs, locked the kennel building, and finally returned to his lonely home.

In spite of the day's busyness, Rissa hadn't been far from his thoughts. "Lord," he whispered as he drew the cotton sheet over his shoulders, "will she ever be?"

❦

"There's no question," Rissa said into the phone, "this was the worst week of my life."

Eva didn't answer right away. Then, "Worse than the time after your mother's accident?"

"Maybe not worse, but pretty close. I was little when *Mamá* fell. Grown-ups took care of things then. Now—"

"Yes," Eva said, chuckling, "now you have to fix what you goof up as well as deal with the problem."

"Oh, spare me. I apologized to you guys about a zillion times."

"And we forgave you. You're just lucky we didn't have anything else scheduled for tonight besides playing at my parents' restaurant. They understood when I told them we'd had a glitch in our schedule."

Rissa sighed. "I'll say we had a glitch—me. I can't believe I didn't write down the info when Robert Ramos called on Tuesday."

"I think you had a few things on your mind. Like your missing dog and a very intriguing kennel owner."

"Intriguing nothing," she countered. "He's negligent. A lawyer should know better."

Again, silence reigned. As Rissa went to ask Eva to share her thoughts, her friend said, "I think you protest a bit much."

"*What?* The guy challenged me to leave Soraya at SilkWood so he could show me I could trust him with her during the tour. Less than twenty-four hours later, he let someone steal her."

"As I said, you're protesting too much. You know that little deters a determined thief. I think you're just a teeny-tiny wee bit scared of the *guy* in question."

Rissa's cheeks began to burn. "I'm not scared of Jason Easton."

"Sure, you might not be scared of *him*, but I think you're scared of the sparks between you."

Thankfully, Eva couldn't see her blazing skin—and hadn't witnessed the near kiss. "You're crazy, you know?"

"Mmm. . .maybe," her friend said. "Time will tell."

"Umm. . .well, yes. Speaking of time, it's late and I do teach third-grade Sunday school. I'd better turn in, otherwise wildman Tommy Young will run circles around me in the morning."

Eva laughed. "You think Tommy's pretty special, and you know it. But it is late, and performing tonight with only a mini run-through wasn't easy on the old nerves."

"Okay, okay," Rissa conceded. "I'm sorry, *so* sorry I forgot to tell you guys about the gig at the Ramos Gallery. Thankfully, Robert called this morning to request some Mozart. Otherwise"—she shuddered—"we would have been a no-show. And then—"

"And then you'd spend even longer beating yourself up for not keeping track of every last second that goes by. You're forgiven. Now go to sleep."

After a quick good-bye, Rissa perched on the edge of the bed and faced facts. She'd changed since meeting Jase. First, she forgot her birthday. Then she forgot to write down the gallery engagement for the quartet—not to mention forgetting to tell the other members their services were needed. What else did she forget?

Jase scared her. Not personally, but the way he made her feel. Especially since, despite her anger over Soraya's loss, she still wanted to see him.

He wasn't responsible for the dogs' theft.

Somewhere in the back of her mind, she wondered. . .what if that kiss *had* happened? What would it have meant? To her.

To Jase.

To them.

Tommy Young behaved like an angel, as did all the third-graders. The sermon inspired Rissa to listen more closely for God's voice, and, after lunching on a Cuban sandwich bought on the way home, she curled up on her chaise and mulled over the pastor's words.

Honesty was a virtue, one she valued, and as an honest woman, she had things to confess. For one, she cared about Jase. The worry she'd seen etched on his face, the lines on his forehead, the circles under his eyes, all testified to his concern for the missing animals. It moved her.

For another, since Jase remained adamant about Paul's faith, she couldn't blind herself to the possibility of the boy's innocence.

And last, she did put rigid expectations on others—expectations that colored her response to them. She expected unconditional love and nurturing from her parents, and since their personal frailties kept them from giving it, she stayed at arm's length and withheld forgiveness. She'd expected Jase to be a pricey if rank ambulance chaser, but his love for Mahadi had surprised her. She hadn't known how to respond, even though his true nature proved him admirable.

She could love Jason Easton.

And Paul. . .dare she trust Jase's opinion of the boy? Or would her expectations of a former drug addict and thief color her actions?

She thought about what Jase had said, and in view of the morning's sermon, she admitted he was right. She'd tried to take God's place. What's worse, she'd failed to trust in Him. He had the situation in control. He knew everyone's heart. She had to trust and obey, since He remained sovereign regardless of what she did, said, or, for that matter, expected.

She had to ask Jase's forgiveness. Not the easiest thing to do, but the honest one, and so she soon left for SilkWood, feeling lighter than she had in ages, despite her pain over Soraya's loss.

"I'm surprised to see you," he said, rising from his chair as she walked into the frigid kennel office.

Although flustered, Rissa refused to let nerves keep her from doing what she had to do. "You shouldn't be. You were right—about the cage I've built for myself with the expectations I place on others."

Jase rounded the counter. "I was right because I used to do it, too. I desperately wanted—expected—my father to see the error of his ways. I expected him to face his need for Christ, and instead of emulating the Savior, I hung on to my judgmental attitude."

The crease on his forehead deepened. "I never had the chance to ask forgiveness for trying to be his Holy Spirit, for judging and convicting him instead of loving him as God called me to do."

"Oh, Jase, I'm sorry for your loss and for being so blind. I did that to you, and you were still kind when you pointed out where I'd gone wrong." She gave him a crooked smile. "I don't think I'd have been as kind. I'd have put on my pride and self-righteousness, and demanded—expected—you to see the error of your ways."

She touched his arm. "Will you forgive me? For being blind? Self-righteous? Prideful? Obnoxious?"

He covered her fingers with his, smiling back. "I wouldn't go so far as to call you obnoxious. In fact, I. . ." Blue eyes sought hers, asking the question that hovered between them.

Rissa took a step closer, laced her fingers through his.

He cupped her chin in his free hand. "As I was saying, I. . . I've come to. . .care for you. A lot."

She placed her other hand on his cheek. "Me, too." She chuckled and blushed. "I mean, I care for you, too—*you* know."

"Yes," he said, "I think I do." He brought his lips to hers, and she closed her eyes, relishing his tender, warm caress. Her senses sang, joy filled her, and she soared in a crescendo of hope, happiness, and the promise of more. Love.

When the kiss ended, she whispered, "Please forgive me. I know you had nothing to do with Soraya's disappearance, not even through negligence. I was angry and scared, and I dumped my anger on you."

"What were you scared of?" he asked.

She squirmed. "You're not going to let me off easy, are you?"

"What do you mean?"

She lowered her gaze. "Ever since we met, you had a strong effect on me, and I'd never felt that before. I'd always controlled my emotions, so I didn't know how to react. That scared me."

"More than your fear for Soraya's well-being?"

She shot him a hard look. "Just as much, I'll have you know."

"Then, Rissa," he answered, a smile on his lips, in his eyes, "there's only one thing to do. We need to pray."

Holding hands, they asked the Lord to bless their budding feelings, to forgive them for their occasional trespasses on His authority, to bless them with courage and strength as they grew closer and in their search for the missing dogs.

After hushed amens, they went outside, Jase's arm around Rissa's shoulders. She marveled at the thrilling newness of the contact, the unaccustomed intimacy, and smiled, knowing something wonderful was happening between them. For a moment, she let herself forget about Soraya and basked in the glow of romance.

Movement in the saw grass to the left rear of the SilkWood property caught her attention. "Look! There's Paul, sneaking away. I bet he knows where the dogs are. I'm going after him."

"Rissa!" Jase yelled as she ran across the parking area, past the kennel building, into the overgrown area where Paul had gone.

As she waded through the grasses and wove around the malaleuca trees, she prayed, asking the Lord for guidance, for wisdom in dealing with the teen, whatever she uncovered.

She came to a halt when she found him. In the shade of a huge malaleuca, he knelt, eyes closed, hands fisted at his hips.

"Father, please," he prayed, his urgency stunning Rissa.

"Help us find the dogs. I can't go back to court, especially since this time I wasn't even there when someone else did the stealing."

Rissa heard a whimper in the distance, a familiar sound. Evidently, Paul recognized it, too. He stood, rustling the grass.

"Shh!" Rissa hissed.

He spun. "Where'd you come from?"

"I followed you, but that doesn't matter right now. Let's go find them, and quietly, so that we don't scare away the thief."

She took the lead, her ears keen on the faint cries of the newborn. Was she all right?

"If anything's happened to that baby," Paul muttered, his expression grim, "I'm gonna kill whoever took her."

"No," Rissa whispered, "you won't. You're going to trust the Lord to deal with those responsible."

"*You're* a Christian?"

Her cheeks flamed. "Yes, even though I haven't acted like one toward you. I'm sorry, Paul. I judged you by your past, a very unfair thing to do. Please forgive me."

He shrugged, never looking up from the ground. " 'S okay. Everybody does it. Except Jase, but he's different."

"Yes, he is. I promise to be more Christlike, too."

They fell silent as they approached an abandoned cement-block building that might once have been a garage.

"Do you think they're here?" Paul asked.

"I don't know," Rissa answered, her heart beating like tympani at the hand of a demented drummer. "Let's listen. We can't just barge in without knowing what we're getting into."

He bristled. "I'm not scared. The Lord knows what I'm doing. He'll protect me and see us through this."

"You know what?" Rissa said. "I've got a lot to learn from you."

He measured her mettle. "You just might be cool, you know?"

She grinned. "I hope so."

Just then, Jase ran up. "What do you two think you're doing?"

"Looking for the dogs," Paul answered. "We heard the puppy."

Jase looked at the decrepit building. "You think they're here?"

Before Rissa or Paul could answer, the puppy whimpered again. Then Soraya sailed into sight from behind a half-wild red-blooming bougainvillea at the far corner of the garage, baby in her mouth. She trotted to an old wooden door on that side of the structure, and Rissa noted the splintered bottom panel. The canines vanished.

"There you girls are," a man said. "Look what I brought."

Jase's jaw squared. "You two stay here. I'm going after him."

"Not alone, you're not," Paul countered.

The older male frowned at the younger, who glowered right back. Rissa slipped past them. Let them posture. She was going after her pet—and the tiny infant who should still be with her mother.

She walked in through the gaping hole left by another, long-gone door. When her eyes adjusted to the dark, she watched a familiar figure in a corner pour a white liquid into a baby bottle. On the floor beside him, she noted a sack of Soraya's favorite kibble, two metal bowls, a can of specialized dry puppy formula, and a clean but torn flowered bedspread.

"Glad I spotted you the other day," he told Soraya, who lay curled on the blanket, the puppy suckling at her belly. "I'd never thought you'd take off with a baby, but you did, and I'm glad. Now they won't turn either one of you into puppy-incubating machines."

"It's called grand theft, Sean," Rissa said.

The deliveryman dropped the bottle. He paled, shot a glance at the door as if to make a run for freedom, but Jase walked in. "And I intend to press charges," he said.

Soraya gently pushed the baby aside, trotted to Rissa, rubbed up against her thigh, and licked her mistress's hand. She yipped, then ran back to the pup.

Sean faced his accusers. "I didn't steal the dogs. When I brought last Monday's delivery, I saw her running through the saw grass. I drove around your property, parked by this old place, and found her nursing the puppy in here. Even though she can produce milk, that amount's limited, and I was afraid the little one might starve, so I brought formula from the ASPCA hospital where I volunteer. I've taken good care of them."

"You're telling us *her dog* stole the puppy?" Paul asked, eyes big as saucers.

"That's what happened. I just didn't return them." Sean stared at Jase. "What breeders like you do to dams is abusive and cruel. All you want is litter after litter to sell pups for all you can get. The world doesn't need more dogs. We have too many at the shelter."

Whereas Rissa's anger simmered and threatened to boil over, Jase's steely expression showed signs of softening. "You didn't take the dogs?"

"No," Sean answered. "I found them and took care of them. I made sure they had water, food, and even comfortable bedding." He pointed to the blanket. "It's not my fault the older one insists on carting the little one around. She thinks she's the puppy's mother."

"Oh, Soraya," Rissa chided. Hearing her name, the gorgeous

golden Affie gave a happy bark, nudged the pup into a mound of blanket, and pranced to Rissa. She danced before her mistress, barked again, then returned to the pup and studied the gathered humans.

When the Affie barked again, Rissa glanced at Jase, shrugged, then joined her. "You goofy dog, this baby's not yours." Wrapping her arms around the lovely animal's neck, she pressed her face against the warm silky fur. "You needed more than just my love, didn't you?"

Jase knelt behind her, reached around Soraya, and cupped the baby in his hand. "God is love," he murmured, "and love is essential. Even though dogs don't have the capacity to know Him, they know how to love—unconditionally, generously, and without expectations."

Rissa nodded. "But she needs to return the pup she stole."

"Do you think she might enjoy the company of my dogs? On a regular basis?"

"What do you mean?"

"Well, I can't deny that I'd like to have you here, with me all the time, but it's too soon to ask you something like that."

Rissa's breath caught in her throat. Was he saying. . . ?

He continued. "We can start by kenneling her here during your trip. That way she can visit her little pal and maybe make other friends or find a mate. Dogs are pack animals, and they can do weird things because of their need for company, for a partner with whom to share their lives."

"Like people," she whispered.

"Yes," he answered, hugging her back against him with his free arm. "Like us."

GINNY AIKEN

Ginny Aiken was born in Havana, Cuba, and grew up in Valencia and Caracas, Venezuela. The former newspaper reporter discovered books early on and wrote her first novel at age fifteen, burning it when she turned a "mature" sixteen. That effort was followed years later by award-winning and best-selling titles in the secular and Christian markets. Ginny holds certificates in French literature and culture from the University of Nancy, France, as well as a B.A. from Allegheny College in Pennsylvania. She lives in South-Central Pennsylvania with her husband, four sons, daughter-in-law, two dogs, and a steady stream of her sons' musician-friends. When she's not busy with the duties of a soccer mom or band mom, Ginny enjoys reading, writing, classical music, and assorted needle arts.

Harmonized Hearts

by Lynn A. Coleman

Dedication

This story is dedicated to my granddaughter,
Serenity Paige, who loves to sing
and has a smile that lights up the room.
May your heart always be in harmony
with our Lord Jesus.
Love, Grandma

Chapter 1

"Marissa, did you put lead inside Bertha the Beast tonight?" Tyrone teased as he hoisted the stand-up bass into the van.

Marissa giggled and looped her arm around Jason's. "Possibly. 'Night, all; I'll see you tomorrow at the studio." They headed out of the reception hall of the Miami Country Club. They'd been dating for awhile now, and the idea of the group growing with the addition of spouses increased Tyrone's longing to find just the right woman.

Tristan handed over his viola. "Guess we can't quite call ourselves 'the quartet who always plays at weddings but never participates in them' any longer."

Eva placed her arm around Tristan's waist. "True, but we're still a quartet, plus one now."

"Don't get me wrong, I'm happy for them." Tyrone straightened his back. The staging seemed to be getting heavier. "Seriously, I know my parents wouldn't mind me settling down. Mom's been giving me more and more hints."

Eva groaned. "Mine reminds me of my biological clock."

Tristan chuckled. "That's one advantage we have over you

gals. Me, I don't have a clock. I live in Miami. Can you say, Miami time?"

"Ticktock, ticktock. You'd better remember to wind your clock. Tomorrow at the studio will cost us if you come on Miami time," Tyrone quipped. Getting used to Miami time had been a problem, but after spending summers here for three years and having lived here for five, he understood it. He didn't agree with it, but he'd become more relaxed about the late concert starts. They'd show up on time to do a wedding reception only to discover they'd have to wait an additional two hours before the guests arrived.

"You don't have to remind me. I know exactly what that studio is charging."

"Well, I'm off. I'll see you two tomorrow." Tristan jogged toward his car.

"I better get going, too. I'll see you at the studio." Eva handed Tyrone her violin.

"Let me walk you to your car, Eva. I'm sure it's safe but—"

"Thanks," she interrupted, giving him a wink. "I love having a big brother."

"You're welcome."

Tyrone loved his partners. They'd become their own musical family since college. Strolling across the parking lot, he took the keys from her hand and unlocked the car door.

"You're the perfect gentleman, Ty. You'll make a great husband someday."

"Thanks, Sis. Isn't it strange how weddings compel us to talk about marriage? It's not like I'm unsatisfied with my life."

A quirk of a grin rose on her dimly lit face. "Yeah, maybe we should stop playing for them."

"Nah, it's good money." Ty winked.

"Oh, right, money, food, survival. . .I forgot about that."

Tyrone chuckled with her. "At least you've got a side job." Eva was becoming a fantastic violinmaker. His spare time, on the other hand, was spent working on a special project. He'd kept the details secret from the others, wanting to see how it developed before asking them to contribute.

She closed the door. " 'Night. See you tomorrow."

He waved her off and watched as she left the parking lot. *Always the last to leave,* he mused.

Tyrone headed over to his van. A real "grocery getter," as he would have called it in high school. Somehow, vans and station wagons were always identified in his mind with parents' cars. But someone had to be responsible for lugging the equipment back and forth. Generally, everyone would go back to their studio and help unload the equipment. Tonight was different. The van would stay loaded, and he'd drive it to the recording studio early and set up for their session.

He slipped into the driver's seat and headed for home. A new neighbor had moved into his complex, but he hadn't seen her yet. The local gossip down by the pool said she was a nurse. No one he'd spoken with knew her name. However, she worked the graveyard shift. Tyrone rolled his head from side to side, working the stiffness out of his neck and shoulders.

At his condo, he noticed a fancy sports coupe with a convertible top glistening in the moonlight in the new tenant's parking spot. "Not bad," he admired. *Must pay to be a nurse these days.* Most of the gals he'd known who'd studied nursing were headed for the mission field. Obviously, this gal wasn't. *Now that's not fair,* he corrected himself. He didn't know this woman, and what she drove was her business, not his. Not to mention, it wasn't his responsibility to judge anyone.

He took the steps two at a time and hustled to his own place.

❧

Cassandra held the door open to her apartment. "Good night, Harold." She motioned for him to leave. "Why does every guy think a woman is a plaything?" she muttered under her breath.

"Come on, Sweetheart," he purred. Her stomach felt like it was about to hurl.

"Good night," she said a bit firmer.

"Hey, I can dig it. You want to take it slow. That's fine with me, Baby."

Cassy was beginning to think not one decent, single man existed in Miami. "Please don't call, Harold. I'm not interested." He stepped through the open doorway, then started to turn around. "Ever." Cassandra slammed the door shut.

Never again would she go out on a blind date. They couldn't pay her enough. Harold thought he was God's gift to women, and then some. "That man's ego is bigger than his car. No wonder he owns a convertible."

"Vanessa, you're dead." She stomped over to the wall phone and tapped in Vanessa's phone number.

"Hello?"

"Vanessa, this is Cassy."

"So soon. Isn't he marvelous?"

"Girlfriend, did someone turn off your brain? His ego—"

"Cassy, you didn't? What did you do to the poor guy?"

"Nothing he'll ever notice. He's an octopus, all hands. No more dates, Vanessa. I've had it. I'm not interested." She had to stop Vanessa from trying to set her up in these unbearable situations.

"Come on, Cassy. They're just for fun. It's not like we're planning on marrying them."

Cassy collapsed in her circular rattan chair. "Try to understand me, Vanessa. I don't consider sex before marriage fun. I'm a Christian."

"No way. You're not one of those. You're too much fun."

Cassy thought of all the times at the hospital when she'd joked around with Vanessa. She'd never proclaimed her faith, but she hadn't hidden from it, either. "I believe in fun. But I also believe in the sanctity of marriage."

"Whatever." Vanessa snapped her gum. It was an annoying habit to Cassy, but much more tolerable than cigarette smoking, which Vanessa had given up six months ago.

"Promise me, Vanessa, no more blind dates."

"Yeah, yeah, all right. But I think you're crazy. It's not like we live in the Stone Age anymore."

Cassy wasn't in the mood to get into a deep theological discussion. She fired up a quick prayer, asking the Lord to make the right opportunity in the near future to share the gospel with her friend. "I'm beat. Moving is a pain."

"I hear ya, Girlfriend. Good night, and sorry about Harold. I thought the two of you would hit it off, him being a doctor and all."

"I'll survive; see you at work." They each hung up and Cassy headed for the shower. A late-night dip in the pool would be wonderful, but the complex had rules about no swimming past 10:00 P.M. She supposed it had to do with the way the complex wrapped itself around the pool. She liked the quaintness of the place, but it did have more rules than most. So far, she appeared to be the only Afro-American in the place. But, then again, she hadn't met many of her neighbors yet.

Rinsing off in a quick shower, she felt the unpleasant evening wash away. She dried off, dressed in her robe, and sat down on her darkened deck. Biscayne Bay shimmered in the moonlight. The high-rise condos lining the beaches across the bay lit up the Miami skyline. And a faint, mournful sound played in the night air. Cassy looked around. No other lights appeared on, on this side of the complex. She squinted across the bay, looking for the source of the low cries from some stringed instrument. Then, as mysteriously as the somber tones had captured her attention, a lively beat took its place.

She leaned back and closed her eyes. Classical music always soothed her. In fact, as happy as she was for her friend, Diane, getting married on Saturday, the only reason she had agreed to spend time at the reception was because they had hired a classical string quartet. One that Diane went on and on about. Not that she didn't want to be supportive of Diane's marriage. . .

The beat shifted yet again. Was someone playing an instrument, or was this some bad recording? Classical music should be something to savor. Didn't the person playing the music understand that? Probably not. It was probably some kid studying for a crash course on music to pass a class. She listened again. A cool breeze slipped behind her bare legs. *Definitely amateur.*

Who was she kidding? She hadn't picked up her flute in ages. She slid her eyelids closed and concentrated on the once again mournful sounds coming from the. . .the what? It was too low for a viola and two high for a bass. *Cello, it has to be.*

88

Her mind drifted to the music. The faint hint of a harmony line in flute took flight in her mind. Lost in the music, she drifted off to sleep.

❦

Tyrone moaned as he pushed himself out of bed. He'd stayed up too late, playing and replaying the piece he'd been working on. The psalms were difficult to set to music. He'd begun dreaming of doing this since first realizing they were originally sung in the Jewish temple. Perhaps it wasn't his place to put these originally stringed psalms back into music. Perhaps that wasn't what God intended. Many of the psalms meant for stringed instruments were songs of mournful pleas to God. And every time he lost himself in the compositions and the words of the psalms, he had to fight off the same depression the psalmist had written from.

He opened his refrigerator, pulled out a carton of orange juice, a couple hard-boiled eggs, and a bagel. Not the type of breakfast his mother would make, but it had the protein and the carbs he needed to start the day.

A thirty-minute period of laps in the pool came next. Every day he started with breakfast and followed it up with his morning exercise. If the quartet finished early this afternoon, perhaps he could get in a sail. He glanced at his sailboard lying on the dock. *You'd think living on the water and in a city of perpetual sun, you'd get to windsurf more often.*

Tyrone let out a deep sigh. Perhaps twelve years was too long to work on one concept. In reality, only the past year had he been working on it every free moment. Tyrone sat down on the white vinyl lawn chairs under the tiki hut. He glanced up at the thatched ceiling and marveled that the management had hired an Indian from the Miccosukee tribe to thatch it. For months, the other tenants had him convinced they'd hired Englishmen to come over and do the job.

The tropical blue water of Biscayne Bay worked its magic, allowing his mind to drift away from the various psalms to the majesty of God the Creator. *Lord, if I could create a fraction of what You can do, it would testify to You. I feel the words of the psalms, but they are so depressing, they even depress me. What am I missing, Lord?*

A pelican swooped down in the water and scooped up a fish. Tyrone stretched his neck and worked out the morning kinks. A deep sigh escaped. "Get back to work." He pushed himself from the chair and headed back to his condo.

Dry and changed, he sat down with the cello between his legs. It was a familiar feeling, a calming one. The cello seemed to be a part of him now. He remembered when he was eight and first trying to wrap his legs around the instrument. At the time, being short for his age, he ended up playing the cello standing up for the first year. As he grew, the instruments became smaller, more manageable. Now the cello embodied a lot of who he was. He looked at the beautifully carved wood and reflected on its hollow body. "Am I like the cello, Lord? Hollow on the inside?"

Tyrone stared at the cello in a way he never had before. "I have to stop this project. It's draining the life right out of me." He set the cello back in place and began to play a piece he hadn't played in years. He closed his eyes and allowed the music, the praise, to come from his fingers, from beyond his fingers, from deep in his soul. The place only God could unlock.

Away his spirit soared. The music grew louder, the intensity of the rhythm increased. Joy warmed him deep within.

A loud banging noise jerked him from his thoughts. A female voice shrilled, "Don't you ever stop?"

Chapter 2

assandra rolled over in her bed and covered her head with a pillow. "How inconsiderate," she muttered and pounded on the apartments' adjoining wall. As her mind cleared, she peaked beneath her right eyelid and looked at the clock. She groaned. It was 8:30, and not a totally unreasonable hour for one to practice an instrument. "Lord, You knew I needed a condo with quiet neighbors. I visited this place three times during the day before I signed, and every time it was quiet, real quiet. Why? I'm not trying to complain here. I mean, I know I am, but You know I need my sleep if I'm going to work the graveyard shift."

The music stopped. She felt a little guilty for being rude and just banging on the wall. But she needed to go back to sleep. And getting up, changing, going over to the neighbor's, knocking, waiting for him to answer, and reversing the process would have awakened her too much. Arguing with herself and God produced the same results. She tossed the pillow to the foot of the bed and stumbled out from under the covers. *Maybe I can get a nap in later,* she hoped.

Feeling convicted enough to apologize and explain her

situation, Cassy dressed to meet her new neighbor. With determined steps, she marched over to the next unit and rapped on the door.

No answer.

She took in a deep breath and knocked again.

Again, no answer.

Who is this guy? First he wakes up the entire complex with his playing, now he doesn't have the nerve to face his neighbors? Cassandra stomped back.

Betty Ann waved. " 'Morning, Cassy, how's the moving in coming?" Betty Ann's silver-gray hair glistened in the morning light. She worked at the same hospital and had been her lead on this prime location. Which this morning seemed a little less than prime.

"Good, I'm just about done." They met halfway down the exterior hallway toward Betty's condo. There were several units between them. Betty Ann owned the corner condo on the second floor that faced the bay on two sides.

"I thought you and Tyrone would hit it off. You just missed him. He left just a couple minutes ago."

"Tyrone?"

Betty Ann wrinkled her forehead. "Your neighbor. You were at his door. I just assumed. . ."

"No, I haven't met him. I was going over there to ask him not to play in the morning."

"Uh. He always plays in the morning. I am a bit surprised he didn't play for the full hour."

Cassandra felt the heat rise on her cheeks. "I might have been the cause of that. I'm not a morning person. I banged the wall and yelled at him."

"Oh, no. He's quite an accomplished musician, Cassy," Betty Ann said in Tyrone's defense.

"I could hear that. I went to apologize for banging the wall. But does he have to play so early every morning?"

"Well, I don't know. You'll have to ask him. It's his occupation as well as his passion. He and his quartet gave a free mini-concert last Fourth of July. You must have heard me mention it. The residence had more visitors than usual that fourth. When the fireworks grand finale was going on, they played the 'Star Spangled Banner.'" Betty Ann sighed. "It was truly breathtaking."

"I wish you'd have told me about—what did you say his name was?"

"Tyrone."

"Tyrone and his playing. I probably wouldn't have moved here. I need to sleep during the days and. . ."

Betty Ann reached out and patted the top of her hand. "I'm sorry, Dear. I wasn't thinking. I guess I'm so used to hearing him, it's almost reassuring. Although lately he's been playing some mighty depressing music. Never would have thought a cello could sound like it was in agony." She shook her head as if shaking off the memories of those songs.

"He must have been playing some of that last night." *I wonder if the tone of his music caused me to wake up in such a sour mood this morning?* "Well, I'll see how it goes, but I might just have to sell this place and move somewhere else."

"Or stop working the graveyard shift." Betty Ann winked.

Cassy grinned. "Someone has to do it, and it pays well." They chatted for a few minutes, then Cassy returned to her apartment. Two boxes remained in the bedroom to unpack.

Since she was up, she might as well work.

Sorting through the mail on the kitchen counter, Cassy found the wedding invitation from her former patient and friend, Diane Kelly. She reopened the ivory envelope and pulled out the misty-rose invitation. The wedding ceremony was private, but the reception was open to friends and family. Cassy sighed. Diane's fiancé, Ken, had not wavered from his love and support of Diane, even while she recovered from the accident.

She'd scheduled the evening off in order to attend. Cassy glanced up at the calendar. This Saturday. "Oh, no!" She ran to her room and retrieved her purse. "What should I get them for a wedding present, Lord?"

❧

"Tristan, I need your help, Man. My new neighbor hates music," Tyrone droned into the cell phone. "I just came from the supply store and purchased some acoustic tiles to put up on the wall."

"When do you want to put them up?"

"After rehearsal today would be good. I can't imagine not playing every day, can you?"

Tristan laughed. "Occasionally, I take a day off. Sure, I'll call my brothers and let them know I'm busy. Hey, why don't I convince them to help? You spring for the steaks, and I'll bring the laborers."

"You're on. Thanks, I really appreciate this."

"No problem. So, have you met her yet?"

Tyrone turned toward the local grocery store. He didn't have enough meat in his freezer to feed Tristan and his brothers. *This new neighbor is costing me.* "Nope, just heard her shrieking through the walls. With a temper like that, she must be ugly as sin."

"Or as tempting." Tristan chuckled.

Tyrone groaned. "I'll see you later. Thanks again."

"You're welcome. See you at two."

Tyrone clicked his mobile phone off and headed into the grocery store. He'd worked with Tristan's brothers before. They all had healthy appetites. Quickly, he made his purchases and unloaded them at his apartment, along with the tiles to soundproof the wall. He glanced at the mirror panels. They'd have to come down.

The elaborate wall clock, a miniature cello, played a single note. *One o'clock. I better get going.* Hustling out the door, he just missed a collision with a lady carrying a large bundle. "Do you need a hand?" he asked.

"No, thank you. I have it," she replied.

Not seeing the woman's face, he didn't want to press his luck. If it was his new neighbor, he wasn't certain she'd appreciate his gentlemanly offer.

He arrived at the studio half an hour before the rest, unloaded the equipment, and set it up before the quartet arrived. He tuned the cello. Tyrone moved on to Marissa's "beast," his affectionate term for her stand-up bass. With him and Tristan each being six feet or more, it still struck him as strange that a gal as short as Marissa was the bass player.

Next, he took the viola and found it still in tune. Finally, he reached for Eva's violin and marveled at the workmanship. Eva's talents with the violin didn't end with her playing of the instrument. She was rapidly becoming a fine maker of the instrument herself. He didn't know how long she could keep up her pace, working as she did in her family's restaurant as well as her hobby.

By five of two, all of the members had arrived. The studio engineer wasn't in the control booth yet to do a sound check. "Shall we warm up while we wait?" Eva asked.

"Sounds like a plan." Tyrone sat in the chair and set the cello in place.

Everyone took their spots. Today they were recording some additional songs to go with their second wedding CD. They had recorded one years ago, but this would be full of additional selections, most having been requested over the years.

They'd made it through the first song when the engineer came into his booth. "Sorry," the voice came over the speakers. "Let's do a sound check. The boss says you have an additional fifteen minutes if you want it."

Tyrone looked over at Tristan and winked. He'd appreciate the financial savings for the group.

The session went great, plans were made for the next—and hopefully final one—for this album. The young engineer gave them a freshly burned CD for them to go over. Tyrone slipped the CD in the cello case. He had the responsibility of checking the recording and making the decisions for the final mix of each album they cut.

❧

Back at the condo, the men went to work, first moving the furniture, removing the mirror panels, then scraping the wall, making it ready for the tiles. Soon the hammers, music, and laborers were in full swing.

"Tyrone, you have a visitor," Aaron, Tristan's brother hollered over the noise.

Tyrone jumped up and banged his head on the tray of the

stepladder. "Ouch," he yelled. "Who is it? Can it wait?"

"Ahh, I don't think so. It's your neighbor," Aaron offered.

Cassy sucked in a deep breath. The man was beyond handsome, from the top of his bronzed head to the richness of his deep plum lips. "I'm sorry," she apologized. "I was wondering if you could stop the noise. I'm a nurse, and I have to work tonight. I didn't get enough sleep this morning."

"I'm sorry I woke you this morning. I'm putting up a soundproof wall so I won't bother you again." He pulled his hand from his head. Blood.

"Sit down, let me look at it."

"No, thanks, I'm fine. I just nicked it on the corner of the ladder. I'm sorry about the noise, but after tonight it shouldn't be a problem."

"Fine." She wasn't going to stand and argue with the man. He obviously was in pain, and she'd dealt with too many patients with no patience when they were in pain.

She retreated to her condo, knowing sleep would elude her once again. "Lord, please make it an easy evening tonight."

He's building a soundproof wall just because I knocked on it? He's either very concerned about his neighbors or he absolutely hates to be interrupted. Given his state of mind when she came to the door, she assumed the latter.

Cassy put on her swimsuit and went to the pool. *Maybe I can get some sleep there,* she mused. Slathered with sunblock, she lay down. The sun and surf lulled her to sleep.

A shiver woke Cassy. The sky had darkened. She pushed herself up. *How long have I slept?* she wondered. She sat up.

"Ouch!" *A sunburn, great. Just great.* Her naturally dark complexion meant she'd suffered far less than some of her fairer skinned friends, but she obviously had spent too much time in the sun even with sunblock on.

The best solution was a cold shower. Aloe would help, too. She searched the bathroom cabinet. The bottle held less than a handful of the precious lotion. She chided herself and went into the shower. "Four days, Lord. Only four days and I'm not liking this new home." She lay back against the ceramic tiles under the refreshing pulse of the shower. At first her body wanted to protest. But soon the raw nerve endings allowed the cool water to stop the burning.

In the mirror, she caught a glimpse of her burned body. "Girl, you've got to be the only black woman in America to look like black forest cake." Thankfully, she knew if she treated the burn properly, she'd heal quickly.

❦

The burn helped her stay awake Monday night. Tuesday through Friday, she calmed. Her new neighbor had been quiet as a mouse. She couldn't imagine how soundproofing the wall could have such a positive effect. It then occurred to her, it had been rather nice last Saturday to listen to him play as she relaxed from her date.

"Admit it, Girl, you don't know what you want." She grinned at her reflection. Tomorrow was Diane's wedding. The gift was bought, her dress back from the cleaners, and the night off after seven nights on would be a welcomed relief. Oddly, she'd barely seen Tyrone Carver. His handsome face played through her mind more times than she cared to recall. No man should affect a woman like that. Especially not a man who had paid no attention to her. Dressed for work, she headed out the door.

"Good evening." A voice like rich caramel worked its way down to her toes.

She grasped the rail tightly. It was him, with his cello case in hand. "Hello, are you just getting in?" It was a dumb question to ask, but it slipped out anyway.

"Yes, we played at a dinner party tonight."

"A dinner party?"

"Yes. Once in awhile we're asked to do a private concert for some folks."

"I see." *So, he's one of those. Socially elite. Of course, he could afford a waterfront condo.* She had to sell everything she owned in order to get the down payment.

He stepped past her. "Have a good night tonight."

"Thanks, you, too."

Tyrone nodded. His keys jingled as he sorted through them with one hand, finding the door key.

She continued down the stairs, whispering a prayer, "Be still, my heart. Lord, what kind of temptation have You put in my path?"

Coming in early at work to relieve Vanessa, she found Betty Ann and got a rundown on the patients and their various needs. "So, have you and Tyrone made up yet?" she eventually asked.

"What are you talking about? We're just neighbors."

"Uh-huh. I've seen how you look at him when you think no one is watching. There are advantages to being in the corner unit on the second floor."

"Really, Woman, there's no harm in looking. But he's barely even spoken to me."

"Well, that's a start. What's he said?"

" 'Good evening,' 'have a nice night.' Nothing major. Besides, I don't have time for a relationship."

Betty Ann sat on the corner of the desk and braced the metal clipboard between her thigh and hands. "I'm not one to tell anyone their business."

Cassy laughed out loud. "Right."

"Well, maybe a little," Betty Ann acknowledged. "A good man is hard to find. And if you find one, you have to get their attention. Banging on his door and complaining about his playing isn't the way to do that."

"Look, I didn't know he was a musician. Besides, he woke me up. I do need to sleep, you know."

"And so does the entire complex. They're all afraid to breathe if they see your car in the parking lot."

Cassy swallowed hard. "I'm sorry. I'm looking for a new place. But it will take me awhile to find one and to sell this."

"Oh, fiddlesticks. People will get used to you and be their old selves soon enough. Tyrone would be good for you. And if I was twenty years younger, you'd be in stiff competition with me. The man is the perfect gentleman."

Cassy wagged her head. "I'm not interested."

"You do have a screw loose up there, don't you? First, you like this horrible shift, and now you pass up one of the finest specimens of Homo sapiens this side of heaven." Betty Ann leaned over and checked Cassy's forehead with her wrist.

The phone buzzed. Cassy picked it up. "Station four?"

"Cassy, this is Rita from ER. Is Betty Ann still there?"

"Yeah, just a minute." Cassy cupped the phone. "It's Rita from ER. She needs to speak with you."

Betty Ann took the phone. "Hi, Rita, what's up?"

Betty Ann paled. "Oh, no, I'll be right there. Yes, yes, he's my neighbor, I can vouch for him. Just treat the man, I'll be right there."

Chapter 3

Ty moaned. His body ached from head to foot. He felt like he'd been hit by a large truck. Then again, a good-sized motorboat was probably more comparable. Thank the Lord they brought him to Aventura Hospital where his neighbor, Betty, worked. One didn't bring their wallets and personal identification sailboarding.

"Tyrone, what happened?" Betty Ann stood beside his bed, reaching for his wrist.

"I tried to get in a short sail this evening, and some kids weren't watching where they were going."

"You're lucky to be alive."

"It's only by God's grace."

"Well, we can thank Him for that." She placed his hand beside him on the bed after checking his pulse and carefully examined his head wound. "Concussion?" she asked.

Ty fought to focus. Her soft image blurred. "Yeah, I believe so."

She grabbed his chart. "Are they keeping you for observation?"

Ty attempted to speak. He closed his eyes and drifted off to sleep. Then he was aware of voices around his bed. He forced his eyes open. "Hey, Man, what were you thinking?" Tristan stepped a bit closer to his bed.

"It wasn't me."

"Yeah, I heard. Thank God, you're still alive."

"Amen." Tyrone couldn't have been more pleased to see his best friends and business partners beside him. The girls huddled up closer. "How'd you guys hear?"

"Your neighbor called," Eva offered.

"Ah. Thanks for coming."

Marissa held his hand. "We're calling around for another cellist for the wedding tomorrow. You rest."

"Nah, I'll be fine." Ty tried to sit up. The room spun. "Maybe not."

"I went to your place and retrieved the keys for the van, your wallet, and some clothes," Tristan said. "I've settled up with the accounting office. They have all your insurance information. The police need a statement. Although the kids on the boat admitted they weren't paying attention. It's a good thing too. From what I hear, they're the ones who pulled you out of the water and rushed you to shore."

Ty nodded his head slowly.

Tristan continued. "The doctor says you've got a mild concussion and you'll be fine. No broken bones or internal injuries."

"I tried to dive away from the boat."

Tears rimmed Marissa's eyes. "Don't scare us like that again."

Ty swallowed down his own. His mouth dry, he asked, "Is there any water?"

Eva quickly poured him a glass and helped him hold it. When his hand steadied, she backed away. "Thanks."

A male nurse walked in with a small basin. "Excuse me,

folks. You'll need to leave. It's time for the patient's bath."

Ty sat up. "I'll take a shower."

"Are you up for it? Any dizziness?" the nurse asked.

"I'll stay with him while he showers," Tristan offered.

The girls left along with the male nurse. "Thanks."

"No problem. Come on, let me help you to the showers. It'll remind us of college years."

"I am dizzy," Ty admitted.

"I could tell."

The next hour Ty spent getting showered and settling down for an evening's rest in the hospital. Every muscle in his body ached. He and Tristan talked about tomorrow's wedding. So far, the girls hadn't managed a replacement. Saturdays were hard to find a fill-in. And Tyrone only once had to bow out of a concert because of family needs back home.

"I'm feeling better," said Ty. "I might be able to play tomorrow."

"We can play without you. We'll just pick some other pieces."

"Seriously, I think I'll be all right."

"Okay, why don't we just wait until tomorrow to decide. *If,*" he emphasized, "we don't find a replacement."

"Sure." Ty wasn't going to argue.

"Well, do you need me for anything further?"

"No, thanks. I'd like to get some sleep."

Tristan looked at his watch. "Well, I've kept you up long enough, so I guess you can sleep now."

Ty raised his eyebrows.

"Doctor's orders."

"Ah. Thanks again."

"No problem, Brother. That's what we do for one another."

Ty's chest swelled with healthy pride. It was so good to be a part of this family. God's family. Within minutes from Tristan's departure, Ty found himself falling asleep.

⌦

Cassy stopped by her neighbor's room to check on him before she returned home. She tapped on his doorway. "Hi."

He pulled the covers up to his chest. She held back a chuckle. "Hi," he replied.

She took a step into his room. The bed beside him was empty. His hazel eyes and hazelnut skin tone set the man apart. "Betty Ann said you came in last night, so I thought I'd check on you before I went home. Need anything?"

"No, thanks."

"Hey, Ty."

Cassy turned to see a man with olive skin and black hair walk into the room. He turned to her and extended his hand. "I'm Tristan, Ty's partner."

Cassy took the proffered hand and shook it. "I'm Cassandra Jones. I just moved into the same apartment complex."

"Ah, the neighbor we built the sound wall for."

Cassy looked down at her feet.

"I'd been meaning to build one anyway," Tyrone offered.

Cassandra nodded and headed for the door. "I'll see you around. Bye."

She marched to the elevator and pushed the button. Why had she bothered to visit the man? Naturally, his only memory of her was her rude thumping on the wall and then complaining when he put up a sound wall she hadn't even asked for. And Betty had said everyone in the apartment complex was nervous around her for that. *I'll just move again,* she reasoned. *Maybe I ought to just buy a house and not worry about neighbors.*

At the apartment, she took a warm shower and readied herself for bed. She'd need a good rest before the wedding tonight.

Later that day, Cassandra slipped into a layered dress. The lower layer was a nice blend of satin in a rich plum color, the upper layer of fine, handmade, antique lace. A replica, of course, but nonetheless exquisite in its ivory design. She placed a teardrop pearl necklace around her neck and added the matching earrings. She let her hair down for the evening. Normally, she wore it in a tight bun or braid. It was easier that way when she was working. Tonight she was bound and determined to have a good time, giving no thought to neighbors or the problems she had with them, self-made or otherwise.

She should have gotten a date. The wedding invitation allowed for her to bring a guest but. . .who would she have asked? The only man that got her attention of late was her neighbor, but the first impression she'd made on him had been—well, less than perfect.

Cassy took one final glance in the car mirror and willed herself to enjoy the evening. In the hotel lobby, she followed the signs for Diane and Ken's wedding reception. The hall was lavishly decorated with white fences covered with ivy and small white roses. Strings of miniature white lights draped around each section of fencing. Each table was elegantly set with fine white china and silver, with a centerpiece of off-white candles on a mirrored surface. Cassy sighed. *It's beautiful.*

She heard the stringed quartet playing softly in the background and took her assigned seat. Others seated at the table made their introductions. Soon, she found herself engaged in light conversation and no longer felt out of place. When the bride and groom entered, Cassy stood and scanned the room. The quartet was dressed in black tuxedos and played the wedding march. Cassandra's eyes stopped on the cellist, along with her heart. Tyrone, her neighbor. She scanned the other members and discovered Tristan was playing the viola. Her palms began to sweat. *Oh, this is foolishness. You knew he was a musician. Tristan introduced himself as Ty's partner. So why are you so shocked?* she chided herself.

Reseated, she tried to get back into the table's discussion, but her mind and her eyes kept returning toward the quartet. "They're marvelous, aren't they?" Mildred, an older woman who sat to her right, commented.

"Yes. They are."

"I've purchased a couple of their CDs. I've been waiting for their newest."

Cassandra focused on her tablemate. "CDs?"

"Oh, yes. I've been listening to Classical Strings Quartet for the past eight years." She straightened in her chair. "I hope I played some small part in their staying in Miami after they finished their European tour."

Cassy blinked. Hadn't he sounded like an amateur the first time she'd heard him?

Mildred rambled on for a bit about Classical Strings Quartet, and Cassy found herself caught up in the woman's enthusiasm.

Suddenly there was a crash from the direction of the musicians, and the room let out a collective gasp. Cassandra ran over and discovered Ty lying on the floor. "What happened?" she asked.

"He passed out. I knew he shouldn't have been playing."

Cassandra took charge. She asked for a private room, and Tristan escorted the semilucid man to the secluded area. Cassy examined him as best she could. A doctor attending the reception came in and gave him a more thorough exam. "You say he was released from the hospital this morning for a concussion?"

"Yes," Cassandra and Tristan answered in unison.

"He appears fine, but you'll want to take him to his physician if he passes out again."

"Thank you." Tristan turned to her. "I hate to ask this, but could you stay with him? I'll need to go back to the reception and let everyone know he's all right. We should probably play a few numbers, also."

"No problem. I'd be happy to." Cassandra glanced over to her patient.

Embarrassed, Ty tried to sit up.

"Stay down," Cassy ordered.

"I'm fine," Tyrone weakly defended himself.

"I'm sure." Her voice softened. "Rest a bit longer. I'll take you home, if you like."

He liked the way "home" rolled off her lips. The woman was drop-dead gorgeous. Perhaps having a pretty nurse wasn't all that bad. He lay back down on the sofa.

"What?"

"Nothing."

Cassy chuckled. "I've seen that look more than once," she said, blushing. "I'm sorry we got off on the wrong foot. I love your quartet and how you play your cello. I miss not hearing it."

Tyrone smiled. "I'll open the slider when I play."

"Thanks. Although there were some awfully depressing sounds coming out of that cello. What were you playing?"

Ty closed his eyes. "Something I'm working on."

"It shows." She covered her mouth. "Sorry. I'm always doing that, speaking before I think."

"You're forgiven. And you're right, they are mournful sounds. It's hard to reflect the words and not reflect their meaning in the piece."

"Are you putting something to music?"

"Yes. But it's a secret. I haven't even told the others what I'm working on, not until I'm content with its structure. Then they can give me additional input."

"Ah. Well, I'm no musician. I played a little flute while I was in high school and less while I was in college. But I certainly never tried to compose."

Ty found himself liking this beautiful woman, even with her no-nonsense straightforwardness. After several minutes of conversation, he asked, "Can I sit up now?"

"You sound more alert. Let me check your eyes."

He found himself looking into her auburn brown eyes and caught a spark of passion. "Cassy. . ."

"How's my patient?" The doctor came back into the room. Tyrone didn't know if he was grateful or angry—maybe a mixture of both. Cassandra popped up and took a step back.

"Fine," Tyrone answered.

"His eyes are clear and his conversation has become quite lucid."

"Good, go home and rest, young man. You overdid it," the doctor commented and exited the room.

An awkward silence fell between the two.

Cassy cleared her throat. "Would you like me to take you home?"

"I need to pack up the equipment."

"I think Tristan can take care of that. You, Sir, need to rest. Doctor's orders."

What he wanted to do and what he should do were two different things. They had chemistry. Should he pursue her? "I'll let the others know I'm going home."

"You sit, I'll take care of it. I need to grab my purse anyway."

Ty sat with his head back on the sofa. He had to admit his entire body still ached from the impact. He'd been sweating just before he passed out. No doubt the exertion to stay focused on his playing and not on his body caused the overload. *Father, I hope the wedding party isn't upset by this.*

Classical Strings Quartet had a good reputation in the area. Always on time. Always professional. He should have let them go on with only the three of them and given the wedding a rebate.

Cassy returned and strolled up beside him, extending her arm. He latched on. Her strength startled him. Of course, she was a nurse, and helping patients up and down was part of her job.

They started home in relative silence. Her car was not the same one he'd seen in her parking space the first night. "I'm sorry to take you away from the reception."

"Diane was a former patient. But I didn't know anyone there. . . ." She halted her words. "It's not a problem."

"You worked seven days straight this week. Is that normal?"

"No, normally. . ." She paused. He caught a glimpse of her staring at him. "Normally, I work five days on, two off."

"Oh."

"I had to adjust my schedule this week to get Saturday off for the wedding."

He felt like a heel. She should be back at the reception. "Perhaps you can return after you drop me off."

"I'm fine. I wouldn't have offered if I didn't mean to."

"All right, thanks."

"You're welcome. Now tell me how you're feeling."

"Sore. I think trying to sit up straight to give the impression I was fine while playing exerted more energy than I expected."

"You're probably right. Betty said a boat rammed you when you were sailboarding in the bay."

"Yeah. A couple of kids going too fast and not paying attention. Tristan said they pulled me out and brought me to shore. Not only that, but they called the paramedics."

"You're fortunate."

"Very. God was looking out for me."

"You're a Christian?"

"Yes, the entire quartet is. We met at college."

"That's great. One of the women at my table was raving about your quartet, said she had a hand in getting you established in Miami."

Ty chuckled. "Mildred. She's a sweetheart." The woman told all her friends and insisted if they wanted the best, they should hire Classical Strings Quartet. With her connections in the upper class on the beach and in Aventura, she had helped them move forward quickly.

Cassy pulled into her assigned parking space. "We're here. I'll help you up to your place."

"Thanks, but I think I can handle it."

"Nonsense. I live next door. I'm going the same way anyway," she argued.

"You've made your point." Besides, wrapping his arm around this beautiful woman comforted him.

At his doorway, an awkward moment passed. He pulled out his keys and said, "Good night."

" 'Night."

Inside his apartment, he opened the slider and allowed the gentle breeze from the bay to wash over him. The moonlight shimmered on the water. "She's nice, Lord."

Crash. Something broke on the patio floor next door.

Chapter 4

Okay. Cassy leaned back from the bathroom sink. "He's a Christian. He's handsome. And he's everyone's dream musician, according to Betty Ann and others." She wagged the hairbrush at her mirrored image. She had to admit his quartet was superb. If Vanessa had anything to do with her getting this new condo, she'd be certain she was headed for another blind date. But Vanessa didn't know anything about Tyrone or this condo, so she hadn't been set up.

Cassy closed her eyes and pictured her handsome neighbor. Hazel eyes on a sea of mocha coffee with rich cream had invaded her dreams all night. She moaned, opened her eyes once again, and worked the brush through her hair. Noticing the kinky new growth, she decided she'd have to get a perm.

With will and sheer determination, she dressed for church. Letting her mind run through frivolous thoughts was a useless exercise and only ended in disappointment.

She grabbed her keys and headed out the door.

"Good morning." Tyrone grinned. His bronzed skin shimmered with droplets of water.

"Hi," she fumbled.

He scanned her from head to toe in one swift gaze. "Church?"

"Yes."

"I'm running late, myself. I overslept this morning."

"Are you feeling okay?"

"Fine. My head still has a dull ache. I worked most of the stiffness from my body with a swim this morning."

"You need to be careful. Don't overdo it."

"Yes, Doctor," he said and saluted.

She thought of giving him a lecture, but what would it matter? He was obviously noncompliant. Thankfully, he wouldn't be assigned to her floor. Well, her floor at the hospital. "I need to get going. Our church is hosting a special concert this morning."

"Really, which church?" he asked.

"Christ Community, near I-95."

Ty gave her a quirk of a smile.

He couldn't be, could he? Did she dare ask? Nah, he couldn't. He wasn't even dressed or ready for church.

"Yo, Tyrone, what's taking you so long?" Tristan yelled from the lower level entryway.

"Sorry, I'll be right down."

Unsure of how to depart, Cassy gave a slight wave and bounced down the stairway.

All through the church service, Cassy kept hoping to see Tyrone and his quartet appear on the chancel. But he didn't, and while the concert had included a wonderful testimony of what God was doing in the performers' lives, the music lacked the classical flare, which Cassandra adored.

Before leaving, the pastor came up beside her and asked if she'd be ready to share in music in two weeks. She'd been putting off polishing up her flute for ages. But having heard

Tyrone play the other night, the long hidden pleasure of playing her flute had resurfaced. "Yes, Pastor Paul, I'd love to."

"Great. I'll put you on the schedule."

She mingled for a bit longer, talking with old and new friends, then returned to her condo.

Over the next couple of days, she'd bounce into Tyrone and wave. They'd share light chitchat. Finally, after a week, she no longer felt weak in the knees when she saw him. Toward the end of the week, she found him sitting under the tiki hut. Boldly, she came up beside him. "Hi."

"Hi. Isn't this gorgeous?" He indicated the moonlit, peaceful bay with a sweep of his hands.

"Yes." She hadn't taken her eyes off of him.

He glanced up at her. "Do you have a night off?"

Cassandra pulled up a chair and sat down beside him. "As a matter of fact, I do."

"Me, too. I was planning on working on my project. But sometimes it's far too depressing."

"What are you working on? If you don't mind me asking."

He took in a deep breath and sighed. "I've been praying over the matter. I haven't liked how the music has made me feel. I was trying to put the psalms that are specifically mentioned as having been written for string instruments to music."

Cassandra thought it a wonderful idea, but hesitated telling him so. She could see the frustration etched on his forehead. "What's wrong?"

"They're depressing psalms."

"How so?"

"Most are written in anguish, grasping for the Lord as the world hits the writer. Usually there is a verse that reminds the reader that God is there and He cares, but it's generally a single verse and often followed with more cries of anguish."

Cassandra reached over and touched his forearm. "Why do you want to put these particular psalms to music?"

Tyrone leaned back in the chair. "I was a kid when the thought struck me. I was still in high school. It's never left me. But now that I've decided to buckle down and write it, it's been depressing me, and I don't like it."

"I'm no expert, but I do love classical music. If you'd like to play them for me, I'd be happy to give you my input. If you think it would help."

Tyrone's smile was like liquid gold and sent shivers slipping down her spine. *Lord, help me, I could fall in love with this man far too easily.*

"I have a better idea. Why don't I take you out to dinner? I mean, if you're free. I'm sorry. . .I don't know if you're involved with anyone or. . . ," he fumbled.

"I'm unattached, and I'd love to go."

"Great." He looked down at his swimming trunks. "I'll need to change."

"How shall I dress?"

"Comfortably casual," he said.

Cassy took Tyrone's hand as he helped her out of the chair.

"Shall I pick you up in fifteen, thirty minutes?"

"How about forty-five?"

His smile sent a shiver of excitement through her veins. *Lord, protect my heart from falling too hard and fast for this man.*

❧

"Tell me about yourself," Tyrone asked as he opened the door to the van for Cassandra.

"Not much to tell. I'm a nurse, work nights, and that's about it."

Ty shut the door and jogged around to the driver's side. "Come on," he said as he slid behind the wheel. "There's got to be something more. What's your favorite food?"

"Anything. Well, almost anything. I'm not a fan of sardines, anchovies, or any other slimy, crittery thing."

Tyrone chuckled. "Okay, no anchovies. Are you in a beef mood? Chinese? Cuban? Thai? We have it all down here."

"A simple steak dinner would be nice."

"Steak it is." He headed north on Biscayne Boulevard toward Aventura. "What excites you about nursing?"

"I like helping folks."

He looked into the side-view mirror and pulled into the middle lane. "Why the night shift?"

"It pays well, and I'm single. Few nurses want to give up their family time for that shift."

"Makes sense." They drove to the restaurant and continued their light chatter.

During dinner their conversation turned from friendly "I'm your neighbor conversation" to more pointed topics about their pasts, goals, and relationship with the Lord. Tyrone found himself wanting to know more and more about her. Their meals finished, desserts ordered and eaten, Tyrone searched for another reason to keep their conversation going.

"What made you decide on our complex?" he asked.

"The quiet. I'm sorry about the time I banged on your wall."

He raised his hands. "You've already apologized."

"I know, but I felt terrible. My girlfriend, Vanessa, had set me up on one of the worst blind dates the previous night and, well, I just wasn't in a very good mood."

"I should have checked with the new neighbor before playing."

"For what it's worth, I do enjoy your playing."

"Except for the psalms written for stringed instruments," he added.

"Right. Why are they so depressing?"

"They're moments of anguish where people are calling out to God."

Cassandra moved the empty dishes from in front of her and placed her elbows on the table. "You know, that first night, I had this melody come into my head. It was really strange. It had an unusual tempo, even, and was meant for a flute."

"Tell me more." Tyrone shifted closer.

Cassandra went on to explain how in her mind the flute's melody line was soft, but peacefully woven in between the mournful strains of his melody.

"Interesting, a contrasting melody line. Would you be willing to play a bit for me so I can get a sense of what you were hearing?"

"I'm not very good, and I don't know the first thing about writing music. I'm not sure—but I'm willing to try."

"Great." Ty jumped up from the table, laid a few bills down, and reached for Cassandra's hand. "Let's get started."

"Now?" She glanced at her watch. "It's nearly eleven."

"Oh. I suppose it could wait 'til morning. I just thought. . . since you're used to being up in the wee hours. . ."

Cassandra chuckled. "Lead the way. I can see you won't sleep tonight if I don't give you something to work with."

"Woman, I like your style." He winked.

"I can honestly say, I've never been asked to come to a guy's apartment to play my flute before."

Tyrone chuckled. "I'll spring for the coffee."

"You're on. But won't we keep the others up in the complex?"

"True. Okay, tell you what. I'll play the tape of the last recording I made of the Fifty-fifth Psalm and we can wear the headsets." She looked at him quizzically. "I have a unit with dual outputs."

"Oh."

&

They were back in the van and headed toward their condo in no time. Cassandra went to her apartment and picked up her flute. Ty set up the cassette and had everything in place by the time Cassy came back.

"I really appreciate this." He took the light box from her hand and escorted her into his condo.

She scanned the room. "I like what you've done with your space."

"Thanks."

"I think I might like to take down the wall in my kitchen. I like the effect of the island between the two rooms."

"Come over here." He led her into the living room. "I've set up the tape deck."

Cassy chuckled. "You really do seem to get into this stuff, don't you?"

"Afraid so." Tyrone found himself captivated by her smile. Was he really interested in hearing her idea or simply interested in spending more time with her? *Both*, he mused.

After a few minutes, Cassandra picked up her flute and tentatively played a few notes. Tyrone watched as her hands shook while playing for him. He'd seen it before when teaching music lessons. Lately, he'd been too busy to take on students. He closed his eyes and tried to picture the melody line she was trying to play.

"I'm sorry, I'm horrible at this. I can't believe I let my pastor talk me into doing special music in two weeks."

"No, you're doing fine. I'm catching a glimpse of the music."

"Seriously? I was thinking—with your psalms, if you added a gentle, secondary melody that eventually took over the piece when you met up with the positive verses of reassurance of God's love and grace, you might have a powerful piece."

"That's it." Ty jumped up and went over to his desk, riffling through the sheets of music scores. He sat down and went to work. At some point, he mumbled good-bye to Cassandra. At least, he thought he had. He hoped he had.

❧

Cassandra huffed as she made up her bed. She didn't know whether to be upset or excited about her time with Tyrone last night. Memories of their conversation flooded her with joy. Memories of working on his music with him also brought some satisfaction. However, the way in which he plummeted into his work was downright obsessive. *I doubt he even heard me leave, Lord.*

Not that she'd gotten her hopes up that they could possibly begin a relationship. "Friends, that's all I want in my life, right now, Lord. Just friends."

The doorbell rang.

Tyrone stood tall and dangerously handsome, offering a single yellow rose. "Peace offering," he volunteered.

"You didn't have to." She took the proffered rose. "But it's gorgeous. Thanks."

"My mom tells me yellow is the sign of friendship." He shuffled his feet. "In roses, that is."

"Your mother is right. Not that I'm an expert, but I've learned a little from all the bouquets that come into the hospital. Personally, I love orange lilies. But I've been told they are a sign of extreme hatred."

"If I ever buy orange lilies for you, please note it's because you like the flower and there's no hidden message."

"Noted." She took a step back into the apartment. "Would you like to come in?"

"I'd love to, but I stayed up most of the night. I need some rest before our concert this afternoon."

"Another wedding?"

" 'Tis the season." Tyrone stepped back. "I'll let you go. Thanks, and thanks again for the input last night. I think we might be on to something. By the way, you should practice your flute more often."

Cassy stiffened.

"No, no, I'm sorry. I was going to say because you've got the touch."

"Oh." Cassy relaxed her shoulders. *Why should I be so concerned about what he thinks of my playing?* She waved him off and leaned back against the counter as he shut the door. "Father, slow this thing down, and fast. I'm not good with sudden and quick decisions."

She looked down at the yellow rose and inhaled. "Hmm, yellow, friendship. Who's really speeding up this relationship?" she asked herself, looking straight into the reflection on the toaster oven. She didn't like the answer.

❧

For the next couple of days, she hardly saw Tyrone. He seemed to be locked day and night in his condo working on his project. "Definitely obsessive," she mused. She wanted to spend time with him. She wanted to get to know him. But wasn't it her own fault that he wasn't coming around? Wasn't it her own prayer? "Girlfriend, you don't know what you want."

Cassy poured herself a tall glass of iced tea and sat outside on the back deck that overlooked the bay. She loved this view and, admittedly, loved this apartment complex. It was quieter than any other place she'd lived. Taking in a long, cool sip, she leaned back on the chaise lounge and closed her eyes.

"Woman, you're too beautiful."

"Ty?"

Chapter 5

"Hang on, Mom, my neighbor just called me." Tyrone cupped the phone with his hand. "What do you need, Cassy?" He leaned out over the side wall so he could peak into her patio. She reclined there, intoxicating to the eyes.

"I'm sorry, I thought you said something to me. I didn't realize you were on the phone." She lowered her glance and avoided his eyes.

Ty held up a finger. "Hi, Mom, sorry about that."

"Was that the new neighbor?"

Ty slipped behind the wall and back into his apartment. "Yes, and I've been praying about her. It's too soon to tell if anything will develop."

"I'm glad to hear it. You know how much I'm looking forward to being a grandmother again."

Ty chuckled. "Not this week. Unless Denise is having another."

"Don't you be fussing with me. Back to what you were asking—I'll ship the box labeled 'high school scores.'"

"Thanks, Mom. I appreciate it. I'll let you know when I'm finished."

They said their good-byes and Ty went back out to the patio. "Cassy?" he called.

"I'm still here."

"May I come over?" Ty asked. He'd been fighting the urge to pester her. He liked Cassandra and wanted to spend more time with her, but he also picked up on the vibes from their one evening together that she wanted to keep men at a distance.

"Sure. I'll unlock the door."

Ty watched as she placed her glass of iced tea on the small table beside the chaise lounge. She had lots of plants on her patio. He glanced back at his own. A couple chairs and a table. Functional, not homey.

"Are you going to stand there all day, or are you coming over?"

"Sorry." How was it possible to have so many feelings for a woman he barely knew? *And how will she react when she knows? If she reacts, then she's not the right person for me,* he resolved. During high school and college it never seemed to matter until he brought Shawna home to meet the folks. Tyrone shook off the old memory and went to his neighbor's door.

Cassy opened the door for him. A sweet smile brightened her face.

"Do you know how beautiful you are?" Ty asked.

"Were you saying that to me or to your mother, earlier?"

Ty chuckled. "My mom. But you're beautiful, too."

"Come in, before the entire complex hears our business." Cassy stepped back and opened the door for him.

"Go out with me again, please."

She glanced into his eyes.

"You're as addictive as semisweet chocolate." He opened

his arms, and she took a tentative step closer. "Please, tell me you're feeling some of the same chemistry between us. You are, aren't you?"

She nodded.

He wrapped his arms around her and gently pulled her into his embrace. She felt wonderful. They felt wonderful together. *Lord, help me say the right things,* he silently prayed. "Cassy, I'm a Christian, and I take my Christianity seriously."

She gently made some distance between them. "Ty, what's happening here? I'm thinking of you night and day, and I barely know you. You've hardly spoken a word to me since we went out. I'm not sure where this is going or if I can deal with this intensity so fast."

Ty took in a deep breath. "You're right. I'm impulsive, and then shy away when I think I've been too forward. And I haven't managed to get you out of my thoughts, either. So where does this leave us?"

"How about we start as friends and see if we can get a handle on our intense attraction."

Ty stepped away and leaned against the kitchen counter. Cassy's apartment didn't have the open wall like his. The kitchen was a glorified hallway at best. "Okay, no touching."

Cassy wagged her head. "I didn't say that. After all, I rather liked being in your embrace."

Ty chuckled. "You're a breath of fresh air. I've never known a woman to be so honest. Please, don't stop. I like it. It lets a fella know right from the start where he is and where he shouldn't go."

"That quality has cost me more relationships and friendships over the years. 'I tell it like it is, Child,' my mama would always say. I guess I picked the trait up from her." Cassy opened the refrigerator. "Would you like some iced tea?"

"Thanks, I would. We'll need to figure out some times we can set aside for each other. Our schedules are so different."

"True, but I think we can work that out." Cassy poured and handed him a tall glass of iced tea. "So, do you always tell your mother she's beautiful?"

"Only when I'm flattering her. She's sending me some of my old scores. I've kept them in storage in my parents' attic. As you've learned, storage in Miami is the pits."

Cassy led them back out to her deck. Ty sat down in a chair across from her.

"So, you use flattery to get what you want," she teased. "I'll make a note of that."

"Only if it works." He took a sip. "Nice tea."

"Thanks. I added mango juice to it."

They talked about each other's families, where they were located, and how close they were with them.

"Mom's really pushing me to settle down," Ty said. "She doesn't realize how difficult it is to meet someone who's not. . . how do I say this? A groupie, I guess. It's not like rock and roll groupies, but there's a definite pattern. And, of course, many of the places we play we're surrounded by the older folks. They have the money and they have the time to appreciate the music."

"My mother drummed it into my head, 'Get your education, Girl. Don't get serious with a man. Be a self-sufficient woman before you settle down.'"

"My folks were big on education, too, but being a musician—well, we just don't make money the same way other folks do. Classical Strings Quartet has been fortunate. We were able to get a couple of European tours in during our summer vacations before settling down in Miami after college. Thankfully, South Florida has quite a few regular European visitors throughout the year. With Marissa wanting to get married, I'm thinking we'll be doing fewer concerts during the week, and I'll probably start private lessons again."

"Speaking of lessons, I'm supposed to be practicing that number for my church."

"How's that coming?"

"Lousy," she mumbled. "I never should have agreed to it."

"Show me, if you don't mind."

"Do you know how hard it was to play in front of you the other night?"

"A little. Come on, you can trust me. I didn't say anything critical the other night, did I?"

Cassy consented and got out her flute. She sat down, went through the number, and waited. "Well?"

Ty chuckled. *You're as impatient as I am.* "Okay, you've got the technical part down. What you're missing is the feel of the music. And that's normal, because you're so nervous playing in front of me. Can I touch you?"

"Uh, sure, I guess."

Ty came up behind her and massaged her shoulders. At first she tightened, then slowly began to relax.

She closed her eyes and sighed. "You ought to work in a hospital. The patients would love you."

"My mother taught me. Dad loved good back rubs. Desiree and I were just toddlers when we began to learn how to give a good massage."

"Remind me to thank your mother," she moaned.

He whispered into her ear, "Now think about the song, the words, and its message. Now, play it again."

Cassy picked up the flute and played. The music wafted into the open air, fluid and light as the breeze. "That's wonderful. How'd you do that?"

"I didn't. You did. I simply helped you relax enough to let it come out of you."

She glanced up at him, then closed her eyes. "We have a problem."

"What?"

She opened her eyes and he saw the fires of desire. It ignited his own. He closed his eyes and stepped back. "I see what you mean."

"This is ridiculous. We're two grown adults, strong in our Christian faith and convictions. We shouldn't be having a problem with this. I mean if we had been together for awhile I could understand it. But this is so sudden and. . ."

Tyrone placed his hands back on her shoulders. "With God's grace, we'll work this out, Cassy." He massaged her shoulders again. "My folks always told me that when I met the right woman, my passionate personality would be hard to control. I thought I'd met the right woman once before. Our passions were high for each other. I believed so strongly in what I thought was our love for one another that I even brought her home. That brief visit was the end of our relationship."

Cassandra turned around in her chair and faced him. "What happened?"

Chapter 6

Cassandra had no trouble staying awake last night at work. Ty's pained confession about his old girlfriend, Shawna, and how horribly she reacted to his mother being white, was ridiculous. How many African-Americans have no white blood in them? By the same token, she'd seen prejudice on both sides, and the sin was just as evil whether it came from a white man or a black man. It was sin and destructive to God's plan of all men being created in His image. Few things got her dander up more than hearing something like this.

Tyrone's fairer black skin color made it obvious he had some parent or grandparent who was white. She remembered a friend whose mother used to put her on the fire escape when she was a baby in order to help her darken. Both parents were black, but their daughter was fairer than either of them. People often do foolish things, she knew, but to just dump Tyrone like that. . . Unfortunately, she'd had to dress for work after learning about Shawna. All night she had wanted to call Ty and reassure him that it wasn't a problem for her. But he also had an evening engagement, and she didn't know when he'd return.

She parked her car in the assigned slot and headed up to her condo.

"Morning."

Cassy jumped.

Ty handed her a cup of hot chocolate.

"You startled me."

"Sorry. I've been waiting for you. I wanted to apologize for telling you everything about Shawna and my folks."

"Not a problem. I can't believe she refused to walk into a white woman's home. What was she afraid of?"

Ty chuckled. "I don't know. I never thought to tell her because I always thought in terms of everyone knowing. I forgot that my parents weren't able to come to the campus very often, and even if they had, it was a large enough school that most wouldn't have met them. I grew up in a small town, and all my life people always knew about my heritage. It never occurred to me it might be a real problem. I'd been called names—but my real friends never seemed to be phased. So, it didn't phase me."

"Would you like some breakfast?" Ty asked.

"What are you cooking?"

"Simple feast of poached eggs on toast and a couple of microwaved strips of turkey bacon."

"Sounds wonderful. Let me change out of my uniform and I'll join you." Cassy handed him back the mug of cocoa and went to her apartment. *Lord, he's so incredible. How can we continue to spend time with each other and not let our carnal desires run amok?*

She slipped into a casual top and pair of shorts, removed her knee highs, and slipped on a pair of sandals. A finishing touch of a breath mint, and she was out the door and knocking on his in minutes.

"Come in, it's open," Ty called out.

"Hi." Tristan stood on the other side of the half wall that doubled as a breakfast nook.

"Hi." She blinked. His presence would certainly help with desires running wild, she figured.

"Tristan generally joins me for breakfast on Saturdays so we can go over the business's schedule and finances."

"I'm sorry, I can take a rain check."

"Nonsense. I invited you, and we're more than happy to have a pretty face to look at." Ty winked.

"Hmm, I'm not sure how I should respond to that."

"Trust me, it was a compliment," Tristan offered.

Cassy found she liked Tristan, and she enjoyed the friendship of the two men. Before long, the weariness of the hour was getting to her and she began to yawn. "I need to go, guys. I've got a shift tonight and church in the morning."

"I understand, and thanks for joining us." Ty walked her to the door.

Cassy went home and dressed for bed. She closed the drapes and darkened the room. She had probably eaten too much to go to sleep on, but if she stayed up to do some sit-ups, she'd wake herself up for another couple hours. No, she'd deal with the extra pounds another day. Sleep. . .she needed to sleep.

Tristan whistled. "You've got it bad."

"Tell me about it. I barely know the woman, and yet I can't spend enough time with her. It's scary. I've never fallen this hard for anyone, not even Shawna."

"Talk about a disastrous relationship. I still can't believe she went ballistic on you and your mother."

Ty shook his head. "I still can't believe I didn't see it in her. I mean, she hung out with the quartet, and there was never a sign of a problem."

"She was a peculiar one, for sure. But let's get back to the present. We've done all right meeting expenses and salaries this quarter, but the cost of the album production cut into the profits. I don't see a problem making up the revenues within the year."

Tyrone lifted the dirty dishes from the table and brought them to the sink. "By the end of the year we should have more than covered the expenses. Look how well the first wedding album continues to sell."

"I agree. Marissa asked me to mention the staging under her. She thinks a few boards might need replacing."

Tyrone filled the sink with warm soapy water. "I'll check it out. With Marissa getting married, I've been thinking about taking on students. I can't imagine us keeping this schedule and her having time for her husband."

"Agreed. I was thinking along the same lines. Perhaps we should consider a different shop. Perhaps a storefront. Something where we could give lessons."

"It should have good lighting and security for parents transporting kids to and from."

"Agreed. Should we ask the girls to start praying about this?"

"Yeah, I think it's something all of us should be praying about. I know we've talked about the quartet staying together even after Marissa marries, but what happens when she starts having kids?"

"Let's cross that bridge when we come to it. I can't imagine it not being the four of us. We've been together so long." Tristan finished off his coffee, then glanced at his watch. "I need to be going. I promised my brothers I'd hang out with them today."

"No problem. Oh, by the way, my mom's hinting about how long it's been since she's seen me."

Tristan raised his hand. "Say no more. A few days off would be wonderful. Mention it to Marissa and let her know I think a few days off would be good, too."

"Will do. Take it easy."

Tristan headed out the door, and Tyrone finished picking up from their breakfast meeting. His apartment cleaned up, he headed to the pool to put in some laps. He hadn't replaced his sailboard and still wasn't sure he would. *A larger vessel might be in order, but who has the time for the maintenance?* On the other hand, windsurfing had a definite downside.

Later that evening he heard Cassandra playing her flute and could hear the nervousness in her playing. Ty left his deck and went through his apartment to knock on Cassy's front door. "Hi."

"Hi. Am I disturbing you?"

"No. But if you don't mind me saying so, I could hear your fear."

Cassy closed her eyes. "I'm about ready to call Pastor Paul and let him know I just can't do it."

"Can I help?"

"Are you busy tomorrow morning?"

"No, but I wasn't offering to take your place." Ty grinned.

Cassy stepped back, allowing him to enter her apartment. "Oh, come on, you'd be wonderful. The church would be so blessed."

"Play the piece again for me."

"Only if you work your magic fingers on my neck and shoulders," she teased.

"Not a problem."

Cassy sat down and positioned herself with the music. Ty worked her stiff muscles. "Why are you so afraid?"

"Stage fright, I guess. It's probably why I never went further with music. I love it, but I'm terrified playing in front of people."

"I'm obsessive in getting a piece just right. Ask the quartet. They'll all agree. I've held back on playing pieces for events if I didn't feel we were at a certain level. Of course, all of us have that in us to some extent."

"The four of you are really close, aren't you?"

"Yeah, kinda like an extended family."

"Ty, would you please play with me tomorrow?"

"But we haven't practiced together."

"Please. I know I'll be more confident playing with someone than by myself."

Tyrone gazed into her auburn eyes and saw her sincere pleading. "All right. Let me get my cello and see if we can work it out well enough to perform together."

"Thanks."

What had he agreed to? Hadn't he just told her he was a perfectionist when it came to performances? Was it possible to play together with only one rehearsal? He stopped himself at the door. "On second thought, bring your flute to my place. A flute is a lot less to lug around."

Cassy chuckled and grabbed her music. An incredible urge to pull her into his arms and kiss those sweet lips rushed over him. *Lord, give me strength.*

They played "Amazing Grace" over and over for an hour.

"I need a break," Cassy said.

"No problem. I think we've got it down pretty well."

"You weren't kidding when you said you were a perfectionist."

Ty placed the cello in its stand. "Sorry."

Cassandra rubbed her cheeks. "No, it's okay. I'm obviously not a professional. Thanks for being so patient with me. So often I just wanted to put my flute down and listen to you."

Tyrone chuckled. "You did."

"Oh, sorry."

He loved the playful banter that played out when they were together. She was so comfortable to be around. "As you can tell, I've played the piece many times before. But I do like the difference of the string and the wind instruments together. It's a nice sound."

"I was noticing that, too."

He wondered how well the rest of their lives would blend together. "Cassandra, I'm not sure how to ask this. I like you. I'm attracted to you. But I don't really like the dating scene. And I'm a man who, well, once I've made a commitment to go out with someone, it's exclusive. I guess what I'm trying to ask is if you'd like to go out with me on a regular basis."

"Go steady?"

Ty hadn't heard that term in years and chuckled. "For lack of a better term, yes."

"When you obsess you obsess," she quirked a grin. "Wasn't it just yesterday we decided to take it slow and begin as friends?"

Ty inhaled and let out a slow sigh. "You're right. I'm sorry. It's hard to believe that was only yesterday. It seems like weeks have passed. Well, maybe not weeks but. . ."

She stepped up to him and placed her finger to his lips. "It's all right. I feel the same things, too. I think we were right yesterday about our friendship, but I also think we have to be honest about our growing attractions."

He wrapped his arms around her and held her close. Cassy wanted to protest because she wanted him too much. She closed her eyes and prayed for strength. "Ty," she whispered.

"Yes," he purred.

That was all it took. She pushed herself away from his embrace.

"Sorry," he mumbled.

"Let's talk on the patio," she suggested. It was dangerous to be alone in a secluded place with him.

"Wise woman." Ty escorted her outside.

She loved being in his arms. She ached to be there right now. "How do we control this?"

"You've got me." Ty sat down on a patio chair. "Maybe we should talk about some neutral subjects, say, like baseball or something."

Cassy giggled. "Have you been to a Marlins game?"

"A couple times. It's so hard with the team struggling so. You?"

"Same. What about the Dolphins?"

"Now football's another matter. I've gone as often as I could reasonably afford it."

"How does the quartet survive financially?"

"Right now, we're doing well. We don't need second jobs. But with Marissa getting married, I foresee the day when our schedules will have to lessen and we'll be faced with a need to earn some money apart from the quartet."

"Ah." *I wonder if he can afford a wife and kids.*

Wife? Kids? And I think he's *obsessive.* She groaned.

"What?" he asked.

"Nothing."

"Cassy, be honest, what went through your mind?"

Honesty, something she prided herself on. "I wondered how you could provide for a wife and children."

Ty blushed. "I'm doing all right. I've tried to make wise investments. But, admittedly, the first two years out of school, I spent far more than I should have. Now I'm saving for the rainy day and preparing for my future. If I find the right house, I could provide well for a family at my current income."

"I'm sorry, I didn't mean. . ."

He cut her off. "It's okay, your thoughts haven't gone anywhere that mine haven't. Isn't it odd that we barely know each other, but when we sit down to talk it's as if we've known each other for years? And we've both admitted to our mutual attraction.

"I've been praying about us, Cassy. I know that's rather bold, especially since we've just begun to get to know each other. But I do want the Lord in our relationship right from the start."

Cassy smiled. "You don't know how long I've waited to hear that from a man. I've basically given up on dating also, especially after that blind date my girlfriend set me up with the night before I pounded on your wall—he was a real winner. She'd been trying to set me up for ages. Somehow, I agreed to that blind date. But I refuse to go on another one again."

"I don't have much free time for traditional dating. I'm generally the guy playing in the background for the romantic events."

"Well, if I can be so bold, I think it's time to come to the foreground and pick up a romance."

Ty got up and crossed the patio to her. "Are you serious?"

"Yes."

He pulled her up from her chair and into his arms. "Oh, Cassy." He covered her lips with his own. A wave of warmth flooded her body. She tightened her grasp of him and lost herself in the kiss.

Cool air flowed between them when he pulled back. Moments passed before she opened her eyes. Ty's beautiful hazel eyes gleamed back at her. "Wow," she managed to say.

Ty wiggled his eyebrows. "Wow back." He took her by the hand and led her into the apartment. Fear washed over her.

"Cassy, let's pray and ask the Lord for guidance."

Peace washed over her. "I'd like that."

He led them in a prayer. When it was over, she glanced up and noticed the clock on the wall. "Oh, no." She jumped up and grabbed her flute.

Chapter 7

W hat's the matter?"

"I'm late for work. I should have left a half hour ago."

"When are you due in?"

"Five minutes ago."

"Oh. Can I call work for you while you get dressed?"

Cassy gave him the numbers. She ran out, and he heard her banging drawers in her apartment. *Her slider must be open, too,* he thought. He'd have to remind her to close it. He called the hospital and let them know. He waited for her and caught her as she left. "Good night, Cassy."

" 'Night. I'll come by in the morning when I get home."

"Great." He hesitated. Should he kiss her?

She leaned over and gave him a quick kiss on the cheek. "I'll call you later from work."

"Thanks." He waved good-bye and felt like a seven year old. He shoved his hand in his pocket. Tonight was a rare Saturday off. If he hadn't been home, he wouldn't have heard her playing. And if he hadn't heard her playing, he wouldn't have agreed to rehearse with her. And if he hadn't agreed to play with her, they wouldn't have shared that awesome kiss. His pulse quickened just recalling it. Tristan's words came back to mind: "You've got it bad." Tristan had no idea how bad.

Over the next few weeks, Cassandra became a regular part of his life. He couldn't spend enough time with her. And she had admitted to him that she felt the same way. They worked their schedules out together. Cassy would come to any event that wasn't private, as her schedule allowed, in much the same way that Jason had when he and Marissa started dating. The quartet loved and accepted Cassy. Ty began to think in terms of marriage. *It's happened all so fast. Would she even consider it at this time?* he wondered.

His trip home to visit with his parents had been disastrous. He couldn't get his mind off Cassandra. He'd rung up more time on his cell phone than one should and dreaded the bill that would soon be arriving. He'd behaved so distractedly, his mother sent him home a day early.

Ty smiled after the thirteen-hour drive. He was finally home. The blue sedan sitting in Cassandra's spot heightened his excitement. Taking the steps two at a time, he passed his apartment and knocked on Cassy's door. Having driven all night, he tried telling himself he should be in bed, not waking up the one person he loved most.

Cassy opened the door, her hair mussed from sleep. "Ty?" Shock widened her eyes. She stepped back and closed the door.

"Cassy?"

"Ty, you should have told me you were coming home," she protested through the closed door.

"I wanted to surprise you. Cassy, let me in."

"No," she screeched. "I'm a mess."

Ty chuckled. "You're beautiful. Come on, let me in."

"No," she protested.

"How about a quick kiss? Then I'll leave you to your beauty sleep."

"No." He couldn't believe his ears. Hadn't she missed him just as much as he missed her?

"Cassy, open up," he pleaded.

A deep male voice answered. "She said no. Now beat it."

Anger burned like an ignited fuse throughout his body. What was a man doing in her apartment?

He heard some arguing going on behind the door. Ty shuffled back to his apartment, unlocked the door, and tossed the keys on the counter. "What just happened, Lord? Who is that man? And what's he doing in her apartment?" Ty held up his hands toward heaven. "Don't tell me; I don't want to know."

Thirteen hours on the road to surprise Cassy, and this. He pulled his grandmother's ring out of his pocket and tossed the velvet box onto his bureau. "So much for thinking she was the right one," he mumbled.

He set the headset over his ears and put on ten hours of classical music. Whenever stressed, he'd retreat to the music he loved. After an hour of pacing, he collapsed in his recliner and fell into an uneasy sleep.

Ty woke to find the sun setting. An orange hue blanketed the patio. Thoughts of Cassy emerged, and anger stirred once again in his body. How could he have been so wrong about her?

He dialed Tristan.

"Hey, Man, when did you get back?" he heard from the other end.

"This morning. I need to talk. Can you meet me at the shop?"

"Sure, what's up?" Tristan asked.

"I'll tell you at the shop."

"All right. See you in a few."

Tyrone hung up, packed an overnight bag, and headed to the shop. Once there, he paced the length of the room. At last, he heard Tristan's car pull in.

Tyrone met him at the door.

"What's up? You look horrible."

"Cassy." Tyrone sucked in a deep breath. "She had a man in her apartment this morning."

"What? No way."

"I heard him. She wouldn't let me in. And then he spoke up and told me to beat it."

"Sorry, Man, that's terrible. What happened?"

"What do you mean, what happened? I went to my place, put on my headset, and fell asleep. I called you when I woke up. I drove straight through the night to get home a day early, and this is what I find."

"There's got to be some mistake."

"There's no mistaking a deep male voice. I thought she was the one, Tristan. I really did. I'm wondering if I can bunk with you for a couple days."

"Couch is all yours. But shouldn't you talk with Cassy, find out what happened?"

"Maybe, but not now. I'll say something I'll regret."

"All right. But why stay at my place?"

"Because Cassy has the next two days off. We timed my return with her days off."

"Ah, I see." They made their way back to Tristan's place, each in his own car. Could he handle seeing Cassy again?

Could he handle seeing her daily? No, he didn't think so. At least not yet.

～

Cassy couldn't believe Ty's immaturity, not answering his door the entire day of his return. The van had been parked in his slot, so she knew he was home, avoiding her, like a spoiled child. It wasn't often her brother came for a visit, but when he did, he'd stay at her place. What bothered her more was that Ty had jumped to the wrong conclusion. Of course, she should have told him C. J. was her brother. But if he truly loved her, why hadn't he given her a chance to explain?

On the other hand, he'd never once said "I love you." In all their time together, those words never tumbled from his lips. And she, too, had held back claiming her love for him. How was it possible for an educated woman to fall head over heels for a man she barely knew?

She called his cell phone one more time and received his message center. She hung up, not bothering to leave another.

"Come on, Sis, the guy's not worth it. How about I take you out to dinner tonight, someplace special?" C. J. gave her an encouraging smile.

"I don't know."

"Come on, it'll be good for you. Besides, absence makes the heart grow fonder." C. J. wiggled his eyebrows.

Cassy chuckled. "Since when have you become an expert on love?" Her brother was more of the "love 'em and leave 'em" kind of guy. His relationship with the Lord, if he ever had one, ended when he was ten.

"Where would you like to have dinner?" C. J. changed the subject with little finesse.

"Houstons?" The restaurant sat on the water, not too far up the road from where she lived, and did not have classical music playing in the foreground. Though, to be honest, she knew Tyrone wouldn't be playing tonight since they had planned her days off to end with his trip home from seeing his parents. Perhaps she should have gone with him? It wouldn't have been too difficult to arrange for a few days off. Why had she resisted? Was she as afraid of commitment as her brother?

Dinner and her visit with C. J. had gone well the night before. But her mind kept going back to Tyrone. Where was he? He hadn't come home. She thought of tracking down Tristan Reuben, since he and Ty seemed to be fairly close. But her stubborn pride would not allow her to track the man down. If he loved her, he'd come to her and apologize.

Cassandra chewed her inner cheek. Her body was filled with tension. *And how do you eliminate tension if you don't have the opportunity to speak with the person you're upset with?* she asked herself. *God?* an inner voice whispered.

"Father, please bring Tyrone home so we can talk," Cassy prayed.

She dressed in her swimsuit and placed a white-laced beach cover on and headed for the pool. She'd been thinking about, praying about, and worrying over Tyrone since he'd knocked on her door. Grabbing her towel and slipping on her sandals, she made her way out to the farthest edge of the concrete dock that extended into the bay and sat on the bench. The sounds and sight of Biscayne Bay always helped soothe her frayed nerves. White-hulled boats glistened in the sunlight. The gentle waves rolled up against the concrete dock. Tropical fish swam below.

"I can't imagine what the crystal sea is going to look like if this is a mere faded reflection of heaven," she said into the onshore breeze.

"It will be awesome," Ty responded.

"Tyrone, where have you been? I've been worried sick about you!" She clamped her mouth shut. It wasn't wise to tell the man how greatly he affected her, she reasoned on second thought.

"I'm sorry I didn't return your calls. I didn't trust myself. It hurt to hear a man was in your apartment."

Cassy fought down her anger. "That man was my brother."

"Your brother?"

"Yes, my brother, C. J. And if you'd bothered to answer the door when I knocked on it ten minutes later, I would have told you."

Ty sat down beside her on the bench, clasped his hands together, and looked down at his feet. "I didn't hear you knock. I put my headset on and listened to music. It calms me. I'd just driven all night to come home a day early and, well. . .I'm sorry."

Cassy placed her hand on his forearm. "I'm sorry, too. I should have opened the door. But I was a mess, and I didn't want you to see me when I wasn't my best. I know it's silly but. . ."

Ty smiled. "Honey, you always look good." His gaze locked with hers. "I love you," he confessed.

Tears filled her eyes. "I love you, too."

He took her into his arms and kissed her softly on the lips.

Lost in his kiss, she leaned farther into his arms. She wanted to kiss him forever, or so it seemed. *Wait a minute, what about his assumption?* She realized she was falling for that old trick men use of persuading women by distracting them from the real issues. She pushed herself back from his embrace. "It won't work," she stammered.

Ty blinked open his hazel eyes. "Huh?"

"Kissing me is not going to distract me from my original anger with you."

Ty crossed his arms across his chest. "Oh?"

"Seriously, Ty, we've got a problem here. How can we develop a relationship if there isn't mutual trust?"

"You're right," he sighed. "I couldn't stop thinking or talking about you when I was with my folks. But as soon as you didn't respond the way I had been expecting, I jumped to the wrong conclusion."

"And you acted like a child, stomping off and not giving me a chance to explain. Why did you do that?"

Shrugging his shoulders, he got up and walked to the edge of the dock. "I don't know. I've never been this jealous before."

Jealous? Cassandra grinned.

Chapter 8

Tyrone watched the fish playing in the water, swimming in and out of the various seaweed-lined rocks. Cassandra had a point. They were easily upset with one another, and that wasn't healthy. Perhaps his desires to ask her to marry him had been too impulsive. He turned back to her. "You're right. We do have a problem. What do you suggest we do about it?"

She tapped the bench seat. He followed her lead and sat back down beside her. "I think we need to spend more time with each other and more time discussing our inner thoughts and desires. Not just our physical attraction."

"All right, where do we begin?" he asked.

Shaking her head, she asked, "Tell me about your trip?"

Ty went on to tell her about the past few days, how much he enjoyed being home but couldn't wait to get back to Miami. He'd missed her so much.

"I missed you, too," she whispered. "I know it was my vanity that wouldn't open the door. I'm sorry."

He placed his arm across her shoulders. "It's all right. I shouldn't have overreacted. By the way, don't be surprised if you get a call from my mother. She's quite curious about you."

"Oh?"

"Yeah. She's protective of her son and interested in the woman who's caught his eye."

"So, I've caught your eye, huh?"

"Woman, you have no idea." He laughed and kissed her again.

"Well, aren't you two giving the complex something to talk about." Betty Ann stood with her hands on her hips and winked.

Tyrone and Cassandra released each other at once. He'd forgotten the favorite pastime in the complex was gossip, and he and Cassy must have given them a week's worth with their kisses. Almost every condo in the place could see this spot of the dock.

"Nice to see you two getting along," Betty Ann said and chuckled. "Seriously, I didn't come here to embarrass you. The hospital called and was wondering if you could come in tonight."

Cassandra's glance caught his. He didn't want her to go to work, but understood they must be desperate to track Cassy down via Betty Ann. Ty released her hand and nodded his understanding.

Taking in a deep breath, Cassandra asked, "What's the problem?"

"Amy's got the flu and Vanessa's out of town for the week."

"Ah, I guess I have little choice."

"Oh, you have a choice, and I'm sure they'll find someone from some other floor, but you did mention wanting some overtime." Betty Ann cocked her head to the right. "Of course, I can think of another reason that might have a more desirable reward than extra money." Betty Ann flashed a smile at Tyrone.

Heat blushed his cheeks.

Cassy turned toward him. "Should I?"

"Honey, I'd love to spend the rest of the day and evening with you, but if you need the income, I certainly understand."

She'd have to go to bed soon if she was going to work the graveyard shift, he reasoned.

"We need to talk. . . ."

"I'll let you two discuss this in private." Betty Ann waved and retreated toward the condo.

Tyrone brushed the windblown hair from her face. "We have plenty of time to talk. And I promise I won't let my tiredness or foolish thoughts get the best of me next time."

Cassy chuckled. "Walk me back to my place?"

"With pleasure. Would you like to borrow my headset and CDs? You'll never hear a thing."

They slowly made their way down the dock holding each other around the waist. "Including my alarm. I don't think so."

"I'd be happy to wake you up. Let's see, I could take down the sound wall and bang on it with a hammer," Ty teased.

Cassy playfully swatted him on the shoulder. "No, thanks, I like my peace and quiet. Let's have breakfast together."

"I'll have it ready." He stopped outside her door. "I'm sorry, Cassy. I should have trusted you. I shouldn't have overreacted."

"You're forgiven." She leaned into him and gave him a quick kiss on the cheek. "I'll see you in the morning."

"Good night," he said, wanting to say more. Wanting to spend more time with her. But she needed her rest, and standing here, keeping her from entering her apartment, wouldn't let her rest.

" 'Night." She slipped her key in the lock and turned it to

the right. He waved, and felt like a child waving good-bye on the bus for the first time. Sucking in a deep breath, he marched over to his place. What would he do now? He ached to speak with Cassy. So much had been left unsaid. So many things yet to discuss. If he were to ask her to marry him, how could they merge their schedules?

Ty sat down with his cello and began to play. The words of Psalm 108:1 suddenly came to mind. "My heart is steadfast, O God; I will sing and make music with all my soul." He let the bow drop from its rightful position on the strings. He ached to spend more time with her and yet at the same time felt overjoyed in her proclamation of love. They had taken the next step in their relationship. Why was he nervous about the things not yet said?

Cassandra tossed and turned all evening. She wanted to be with Tyrone. She didn't want to go to work. But she did need the extra cash the hours would bring in. She'd set her mind on a special gift for Ty, and extra hours would help the dream become a reality.

Work dragged. By breakfast, she was ready to go home and crash for the morning. Tyrone had set a wonderfully romantic table, and she barely had the energy to thank him for it. Fortunately, she had remembered.

The next few days blurred into a series of a moment here and a moment there. As much as they tried to mesh their schedules, there always seemed to be a conflict. Cassy longed to find a way to make this work. *But how?* she wondered.

Cassandra looked down at her appointment book. She'd blocked in all of Tyrone's concerts and practice times. There were a couple of ways to arrange her sleep time if she worked from 11 P.M. to 7 A.M. One was to sleep as soon as she got home until midafternoon. The other was to stay awake until midafternoon and sleep the rest of the afternoon and evening. Cassy had always found the morning sleep suited her better. But with Ty's schedule, the afternoon and evening might be best. Would altering her schedule help? Or should they continue to try to line up days off? But that wouldn't work, since her schedule rotated between five days on and two days off.

Ty knocked on her door. "Come in," she called out.

"Hi. What ya doing?"

"Trying to figure out how we can spend more time together. It's been a horrible week."

"True, but it shouldn't be this bad all the time. I've just been putting in extra hours to set up the private lessons."

Cassy drummed her fingers on the countertop. "Even still, our schedules conflict most of the time. I'm sleeping when you're free. You're working when I'm sleeping."

Ty leaned back against the counter. "True," he sighed.

"I've been thinking of rearranging my sleep time. It'll take a week or so for my body to adjust, but it might be better in the long run."

"How so?" he asked.

She went on to explain the advantages and disadvantages of what she'd been trying to hammer out.

"I could schedule lessons in the afternoons while you're sleeping. That would leave the mornings free for us. How does that sound?"

"Worth trying." Cassy gave him an appreciative smile as she turned to meet him in her narrow kitchen. She really did like the way Tyrone had opened his wall up in his kitchen, making it feel less blocked in. "If you don't mind me asking, how much did it cost to open up your kitchen?"

"A couple thousand, because I replaced all the countertops and cabinets. Gradually, I've replaced all the appliances. These are great condos, but they are over thirty years old and minor adjustments are needed."

"I'd like to open up my kitchen, but I'm afraid it will have to wait for awhile."

"Let me know when you decide. I'll get Tristan and his brothers to help. We can knock it out in no time."

Cassy chuckled. "I imagine you can."

Ty stepped closer. "Are you free for a bit?"

"I can spare an hour. What's up?"

"We've found a new location for the quartet. I'd like your opinion. It's important to me."

"Sure. I'd love to."

Ty brought her to the possible new location. The place needed some work, but it had enough square footage, and parking space was more than adequate.

"What do you think? I know it needs paint and some remodeling but. . ." He left the sentence unfinished.

"I think you've picked a good location." Cassy looked up at the ceiling. "Will you need to put in some acoustic tiles?"

"Definitely. Here's what we're picturing." Ty went through the entire building and described some of the changes he saw taking place. "In the end, I think it will take us a good month, possibly six weeks to have it finished."

"You might want to work on a temporary front for possible passersby. You'll never know who might be going to the music

153

store down the block and notice your new construction," Cassy suggested.

"Good point. We've already thought about giving the music stores some flyers. At the moment, Tristan and I will be the only ones giving music lessons. But Marissa is looking forward to it after her wedding and honeymoon."

"I don't know much about business, and I certainly know little about yours, but I think you guys are making a wise decision."

"We've prayed about this. We really want to continue to play as a quartet, but we'll each have different needs." Ty looked down at his feet and coughed. "Well, you did say you only had an hour."

Cassy looked at her watch, "Right, thanks. And thank you for the tour. I can't wait to see it finished."

"Huh, you're going to help with the renovations." Ty smiled. "Oh, really?"

His voice softened. "If you don't mind."

Tyrone felt a little bad for being so forward in assuming Cassy would help. On the other hand, he needed to work on the studio and he didn't want to be apart from her more than he had to. Working together at the studio, playing together in his apartment, and working on his psalms compositions took up most of their free time.

He needed to do something special with her.

The doorbell rang and his door opened immediately. "Hey, got a minute?"

"Sure, I was just thinking about you."

Cassandra smiled. "Great." Her smile slipped. "Unless you're planning on working today," she quipped.

"No, but that is in part what I was thinking about." Ty walked up to her and grasped her hand. "I want to take you somewhere, anywhere. I was thinking we've had precious little time when we weren't working."

Cassy took in a deep breath. "Great minds think alike."

"What would you like to do?"

"Anything."

"How about a trip to the zoo?" he asked.

"I've never been."

"Good. It's been several years since I have. Date?"

"Date."

"Can you be ready in fifteen?" He asked. She did tend to spend a lot of time before going out on dates, he mused.

"For the animals, I can dress down and be ready. . ." She looked over her shoulder and whispered in his ear dramatically, "In five."

Ty laughed. He loved this woman. With each passing day, his love was growing. Their mutual respect and trust for each other was growing, too.

"Let me grab my purse and I'll be ready."

"Great."

Cassy left, and Ty pulled a couple of bottled waters, apples, and grapes from his refrigerator. He pulled a small blue-and-white cooler from under the sink and loaded it. He then selected some cheese and crackers to round off his impromptu picnic at the zoo.

The rest of their day was spent not discussing work or schedules or remodeling or even the psalms. Instead, they focused on each other, on memories from childhood. They admired the animals and simply enjoyed each other's company.

They stopped and sat down on a bench at a play area right after the elephant exhibit. "Thirsty?" he asked.

"A little," she replied.

"I've got some bottled water, but I'd be happy to buy you a soft drink or juice."

"Water's fine, thanks."

He pulled out a bottled water and handed it to her, then placed the small cutting board on the bench between them. "How about some cheese and crackers?"

Cassy's eyes sparkled. "You're a romantic."

"Sometimes. Most of the time I get too focused on the present and, well, my music."

"I've noticed."

"Sorry." He glanced away. "I know I'm a bit obsessive."

She laughed and placed her hand upon his. "Honey, it's all right. Just as long as you agree to my interrupting you from time to time."

"Please do." He placed some cheese on the cracker and handed it to her. "I love you."

"I love you, too."

He felt happy they had decided to take some free time with each other. Their schedules would definitely cause them problems. She seemed to like her shift at the hospital. But what if they were to marry? Would she still want to work those hours? Would they find themselves sleeping at separate times? Tyrone didn't care for that thought. Would she be willing to make that adjustment to her work schedule? His was set by the customers. There was little he could do. But if he had a wife, he certainly wouldn't want to keep the schedules they'd been keeping.

Wife? Jumping ahead, aren't you, Buddy? he silently quipped.

Chapter 9

Switching her sleeping hours had produced a little more time with Tyrone, but it didn't satisfy her desires to spend more time with him. They were quickly becoming the best of friends, seeking each other's advice, and working together on his project to bring music back to the psalms created for string instruments. The flute wasn't exactly a stringed instrument, but Ty easily converted the harmony for a violin.

Cassandra wiped the sweat off her palms. Today she and Tyrone would be playing his pieces for the quartet. This would allow the others to help fill out the musical structure of the various accompaniments. It was hard enough playing for Tyrone, but to be playing in front of the other three accomplished musicians seemed overwhelming.

She felt Tyrone's presence behind her before she felt his wonder-working hands on her shoulders. She closed her eyes and relaxed under his soothing ministrations. "Thanks," she mumbled.

"You're welcome," he whispered in her ear.

A pulse of electricity coursed through her spine. "I love you."

"I love you, too." He kissed the tip of her ear. "Come on, it's time."

The newly renovated storefront reflected the classical yet contemporary appearance of Classical Strings Quartet. Tyrone had picked up several students, and even the bookings for various functions seemed to be coming in more easily.

Tyrone cleared his throat. "Cassy's a little nervous and, admittedly, I am, too," he told the other members of the quartet who sat down in a semicircle, awaiting their private concert.

"I've had a dream since I was in high school," Tyrone continued, "and that was to score the psalms written for string instruments. It's been difficult, to say the least. Most of these psalms are referring to very hard, often mournful times.

"Cassy's helped me create a harmony to counter the mournfulness and use it as the answer that Christ gives us in our lives."

Cassandra gave a weak smile as all three turned their heads and looked directly at her.

"I'm figuring from what I've scored, the four of us can come up with some amazing pieces." Tyrone sat down. Cassandra stiffened and raised the flute to her lips. *Lord, help me.*

Before they began, Ty winked at her in his usual way and she relaxed. They made their way through the first number. Cassy only missed three notes. Not too bad, she mused. The others picked up their instruments and worked through the same piece, playing the scores Tyrone had written for them. Cassy sat back and enjoyed the concert, marveling at hearing the others never miss a beat.

Pleased with how well the others dove into Tyrone's creation, Cassy excused herself. After all, she needed to go home and go to bed. Maybe it was time to consider working another shift?

At home, she slept restlessly. She and Tyrone had been dating for awhile. Their relationship had developed, and yet she wanted more. She wanted to marry the man, have his children, and grow old together. She couldn't think of a more satisfying life. "Lord, is he the one I've been waiting for? I think he is. It feels like he is. From the first moment we connected, there's been an incredible bond between us. But Ty seems content with life the way it is. I don't want to push him, Lord. And, admittedly, we haven't known each other all that long but. . ." But what? What did she really want? A miscreant smile crept up her face. "To marry him," she sighed.

She looked over at a bow she had purchased for Tyrone. She prayed it was as good as she'd been told it was. A good bow was as important as a well-made cello. She'd looked long and hard to find one that would meet Tyrone's approval. She'd even gone into research, learning who made the best ones and why. She prayed she'd made the right choice. She couldn't afford the eighteen-thousand-dollar ones she'd come across and knew Tyrone would love, but settled for one slightly over four thousand dollars, a replica of a historical bow.

They'd made special plans for breakfast the next morning. In fact, they'd planned the entire day together. *That will be the perfect time. . . .*

Dressed for work, she made her way north on Biscayne Boulevard toward the hospital. She didn't know if she should pray for a calm night or a busy one. Both had their own advantages. A busy one would go fast. A calm one wouldn't wear her out for their special date. She decided not to worry about it and checked in at the nurse's station.

Everything went well until 3 A.M., when the quiet floor erupted in turmoil. The patient in 5B had awakened suddenly, disoriented and violent. She restrained him with the help of an orderly, then injected some medication to help him sleep. His stitches had torn, which required she report the event to the doctor on call. Fashioning some quick butterfly stitches over the aggravated area, Cassandra reported the incident to the doctor on call, not surprised he didn't come up to check on the patient. From that point on, Cassy watched the gentleman like a hawk. She wasn't going to allow a lawsuit to be levied against the hospital on her shift.

❧

Ty took the velvet box from the top of the dresser and opened it. His grandmother's ring sat cradled inside the dark velvet. The pink diamond had a unique Royal Asscher cut. If he remembered correctly, it was around two-thirds of a carat. "Lord, I love her with all my heart, and I know I want to spend my life with her. So why am I afraid?"

Tyrone closed the velvet box and placed it lovingly back on his dresser.

The phone rang and broke into his thoughts. "Hello."

"Hey, Ty, it's me." Cassy's voice warmed his heart.

He glanced back at the ring box. "It's good to hear your voice."

"I've got bad news. I need to work a double shift."

Tyrone's heart sank. "There's no one else?"

"I'm afraid not. I've personally called a couple of the nurses. I don't like my schedule, Ty. It's frustrating. We need more nurses, but budget restraints hold back on the hiring, and private duty nurses aren't always an option."

He closed his eyes. "I'm sorry. I know you tried to get off work."

"I don't give up our special days together easily. If it's any consolation, I'll have the next two days off. I already told them my phone will be disconnected. I'm working far too many hours. It's not healthy."

He had to agree there. "I wish there was something I could do."

Cassy chuckled. "Come to the hospital and join me for breakfast. I miss you."

"I'm on my way. I miss you, too." Making adjustments to his schedule, and her making adjustments to hers, was the only way they would be able to spend time together. *Cassandra is definitely worth the sacrifice, Lord.*

⬡

The highlight of Tyrone's day had been their breakfast together. Once Cassy returned home from work, she went straight to bed. He prepared a breakfast of fresh fruit and bagels. Today he would brave it and ask her the question. In a box on the counter sat fresh-cut exotic flowers, ones he believed would blend well with her natural color.

Next, he put on some classical music and lit the candles lining his apartment for the occasion.

The doorbell rang. He glanced over at the clock. Right on time. *Gotta love that,* he thought with a smile. He opened the door and she returned his smile. "Good morning, Sunshine."

" 'Morning. I'm sorry about yesterday."

"Shh, no problem. Work is work, and sick people need their nurses."

She looked down at her feet. "I almost quit. I told the hospital administrator he had to hire someone soon or I would quit. I also pointed out how much they were paying me and others in overtime by not hiring another nurse."

"Did it help?"

Cassy chuckled. "The bottom line with them is the money, not the patients. So, yeah, I think it worked." She looked to her left and to her right. "Do you think I might be able to come in?"

"Oh, sorry." Ty stepped back and let her pass before him.

"What's all this?" She gazed around the open room.

"I missed you."

"I missed you, too, but I didn't. . ." Her eyes fixed on the long white box on the kitchen counter.

"Do you have a tall vase?" he asked.

She hesitated. "Yes."

"I thought so. These are for you." He handed her the box.

She opened it. "They're gorgeous."

He liked pleasing this woman. And giving her simple gifts brought a deep, resounding pleasure and satisfaction.

"Since this is a day of gift giving, I have one for you. I'll be right back." Cassy fled to her apartment.

Tyrone paced, fingering the velvet box in his pants pocket.

Cassandra bustled back in through the front door. She held a long, thin, gift-wrapped box in her hand. "I hope you like it. If not, I can return it."

What had she purchased? He received the box in tentative hands. It was as light as a feather. His mind raced. Only one thing he knew came in a box of this size. "What did you do?"

Cassy smiled. "Open it."

Ty sat down. She shouldn't have. He ripped the wrapping off the package. The name of a well-known bow maker was on the outer box. "Cassandra, I can't accept this."

"You haven't opened it yet. How do you know?" she teased.

"I know the company, and they aren't cheap." His hands caressed the long box. "How did you come across them?"

"Well, open it before I explode," she demanded.

Ty chuckled.

"Trust me, it's paid in full."

"But, Honey. . ."

"Tyrone David Carver, open it and accept the gift as it's been given, with all my heart and love," she chastised.

"Yes, Ma'am." Inside he found what he'd expected. "It's beautiful. Thank you. But how can you. . ."

"Honey, I love you. I researched bows, and I felt I knew a little about your preferences, so I took a risk and purchased this replica."

"It's wonderful."

"Try it out. If it doesn't feel right or if it doesn't bring complete satisfaction, the company will replace it."

"I'm sure it's fine. I've been looking at this same bow for awhile now. It's perfect." Tyrone placed the bow on the coffee table. "I have another gift for you. Actually, it's more than a gift." He cleared his throat. "Come here. Sit beside me."

She took his hand and sat down.

"Thank you." He kissed her gently on the lips. "I love you, Cassandra."

"I love you, too."

He did not have a doubt of her love. Not because she'd spent far too much money on the beautiful bow, but because he could feel the honesty in her kiss. He could hear it in her voice, in the way she walked and in the way she moved. He loved her, and he knew she was the one for him. "Cassandra." He caressed her fingers. "I know our schedules will be a problem. But I want to spend every free moment I have with you. I want to rise with you in the morning and experience everything the Lord would have us experience together. I know we've spent few days together, but I know my heart, and I think I know yours. Please do me the honor of becoming my wife."

Gentle tears filled her eyes. Ty fought down the lump in his throat.

"Yes," she whispered. "I love you."

"I love you, too." He kissed her warmly on the lips. He pulled away and fumbled for the ring box in his pocket. "Honey, if you'd like to pick out a new ring, I understand. But my grandmother gave me this awhile ago. She didn't wear it any longer, with Grandpa gone, and she didn't feel safe keeping it with her in the assisted living facility." He popped open the box.

"Oh, Ty. It's beautiful. I've never seen a diamond like that."

"It's a Royal Asscher cut. Grandmother said it was first designed in 1902. It's also a pink diamond, which is very rare. My grandpa used to say 'it was a special ring for a special lady,' and I think I know how Grandpa felt."

Cassy's hand shook as she reached out for the ring.

Tyrone took her hand into his and kissed her ring finger. "I love you, Cassandra." He placed the ring on her finger.

"Oh, Ty, I love you, too." She tipped her head to the side. "Just how many kids did you say you wanted?"

Tyrone roared with laughter. "All in good time, my dear. All in good time."

Peace washed over them both. Ty clasped both of her hands with his and prayed. "Father, bless us and watch over us. May we remain true to you and true to each other." Then he quoted from Psalm 108, verses 1 and 2. " 'My heart is steadfast, O God; I will sing and make music with all my soul. Awake, harp and lyre! I will awaken the dawn.' "

"Amen." Cassy smiled. "I look forward to a lifetime of making music with you."

"We do harmonize well." Ty clicked off the stereo and picked up the bow. He sat down with his cello and played.

LYNN A. COLEMAN
Lynn makes her home in Miami, Florida, with her husband, serving the Lord as pastors of Christ Community Church. Together they are blessed with three married children and seven grandchildren. Lynn writes for the Lord's glory. She serves as advisor of the American Christian Romance Writers, an organization she cofounded. She loves hearing from her readers. Visit her Web page at www.lynncoleman.com.

Syncopation

by Bev Huston

Dedication

Thank you to the dedicated and talented musicians at www.viola.com and their E-mail loop, viola@yahoogroups.com. Your knowledge is impressive, your help appreciated!

Prologue

Tristan's eyes flew open. The room was dark. Fear gripped his stomach with an ironclad hold. A meaty hand covered his mouth while a strong force pinned his arms and legs to the mattress. His heart thudded against his chest.

"Tape," a gruff voice said to a dark, pencil-thin silhouette at the foot of the double bed.

Tristan blinked, struggling to force his eyes to adjust. Muffled cries of protest tried to escape his lips.

He caught sight of his alarm clock as it glowed like a neon greeting. Three in the morning. What was he thinking? Someone had broken into his condo and he wanted to know the time?

Today of all days.

Tristan recoiled at the rasp of tape tearing from the roll. The sound pierced the otherwise silent bedroom.

With experienced precision, the beefy hand slapped the tape down hard over Tristan's cheeks and lips. In an instant, they tossed him over onto his stomach and methodically tied his hands behind his back with itchy rope. He tried to catalog everything. Memorize each noise, hoping to abate his terror.

Someone wrapped a salty-smelling blindfold securely around

his head. They yanked him to his feet. As near as he could tell, there were three intruders. One like a beanpole, one like a grizzly bear, and one somewhere in between. Kind of like Laurel and Hardy with a sidekick. Could he hope this was all just a comedy of errors?

Probably not.

Unfortunately, he could not determine anything further about his kidnappers. Or his murderers? His body trembled.

A tight grip on his arms and a forceful shove at his back sent him forward. He shuffled along between two of the assailants. Tristan racked his brain trying to figure out what they could want. He was just a musician. And a violist at that. Did they think they'd captured someone famous?

Miami had its fill of rich residents, politicians, too. Now, they were big fish. Why not go after them?

His blood turned to ice.

Not the Amati.

He'd heard about private collectors stealing whatever they wanted. Many a priceless Stradivarius had vanished into unknown hands. Defiance surged through him. He tried to stop, but resistance was futile. They gripped harder and pushed him again.

Moments later they exited his condo and headed for the stairs. Tristan struggled to keep up.

Seven steps. Turn. Seven steps. Turn.

They were descending to the lobby. A breeze gently kissed his face as they left the building.

Another sharp jab in the back sent him forward.

"Get in!" The voice sounded disguised, but the man's impatience wasn't.

Tristan heard the engine roar to life just as one of his captors jammed his head down and shoved him forward. He landed on a soft surface. It smelled of leather.

The getaway vehicle.

You're watching too many cop shows, he silently chided himself. They would definitely be out from here on. He tried to pray, but could only come up with two words: *God, help.*

It felt like the thin man was seated beside Tristan. He assumed the other two were in the front.

Tires squealed when the driver lead-footed it away from his condo, causing Tristan to fall to the side. Probably onto his captor's lap. He tried to right himself.

"Stay down," one of the men barked.

Tristan did as he said.

Sweat beaded on his brow as he sucked in smoke-filled air. Stuck in an awkward position, he remained still and said nothing. Not that he could, with the strip of tape across his face. Thankfully he didn't play a wind instrument. He swallowed a laugh. Like it would matter now.

When it appeared that they would be on the road for some time, Tristan strained to relax his body, hoping it would protect his hands and increase the blood flow. Fear gripped his mind, causing his thoughts to crash like atoms into one another.

Twenty-nine today and what did he have? No wife. No children. Why even Mozart had over six hundred compositions before his death at thirty-five. How many did he have to his credit? He was a virtual unknown. Sure, the quartet played some of his pieces, but the Philharmonic Symphony wasn't breaking down his door for scores or clamoring after him to play. Why hadn't he listened to his mother and become a doctor?

"He has good hands," she always said. "Hands made for healing."

But from the first time he touched the piano, it gave him joy. Music was like a gift, a new present each and every day. God's blessing to him. No. He didn't regret his decision to pursue this love. But did it exclude too many other things in his life? Had he let everything slip away? How could he have ignored Marissa's or Tyrone's happiness when they'd each found their soul mates? What had this all-consuming pursuit cost?

Something's different.

The vehicle had stopped. Tristan cocked his head to listen. An ominous noise rumbled in the distance.

The car door opened and they dragged him out to his feet. Relief began to wash over him to some degree.

Then the sound grew louder. Building like a symphony crescendo. The earth bounced and rattled in response. Air ceased to flow through Tristan's lungs. He knew what was coming. A train!

They guided him around the back of the car, then hefted him into the trunk.

No! They couldn't do this.

Tristan's heart pounded like a jackhammer. His breath rasped through his nose. The lid slammed shut.

Outside, he heard them argue. "No scar! The boss said he had a long scar down his neck. I checked. Nothing." Tristan pictured the skinny guy shaking as he talked.

Someone cursed.

"Kill him," said a deep voice. Tristan figured this was from the hefty man who'd taped and tied him up.

"The boss only wanted the guy shook up." It sounded like

the sidekick was now speaking. His words were rough, like sandpaper on wood. "Can't get money from a corpse."

"We can't get nothing from this guy—he's the wrong man. I said kill him."

"I'm no killer," the sidekick argued. "I break a few bones. Collect a few debts. But I ain't rubbing anyone out. Get yerself a button man. . . ." His words trailed off.

Tristan strained but heard nothing more. Except the train. They had gone.

Help me, Lord. I need to escape. Somehow! he screamed in his mind. His thoughts grasped at threads of hope. *I'm going to die. I'm not ready. I have too many regrets. Like Cynthia. Oh, God, like Cynthia. I've never loved anyone the way I loved her. And I let her go. I can't believe I just let her walk away. Leave Miami. Leave me. Leave what we had behind. Six years wasted. . .*

A deep groan of regret burst in his chest.

Oh, God, if I had to do it over again, I'd have never let her go. Even if it meant following her to LA. I'm sorry. It's too late.

Please, God, help me and I promise I'll find her. I'll do what I should have done six years ago. Please, God.

The train whistle pierced his silent world.

Tristan tensed.

Chapter 1

Nikki Sears flipped her blond hair over her shoulders and adjusted her butterfly-shaped sunglasses, then glanced around the busy airport. MIA, as it was affectionately known. She'd never cared for the abbreviation since it made her think of "missing in action" instead of Miami International Airport.

Things sure have changed.

Well, what could she expect? She'd changed, too, in the six years she'd been gone. Was it for the better? She squared her shoulders. No, now was not the time to think about that.

Here she was, back home and with her star on the rise, this could only be like the proverbial cherry on top. A promotional boon if things went well. What would the headlines say?

She sighed, shoulders slightly lowered. With all her heart, she wished someone would understand the sacrifice, hard work, and loneliness that went into her career. But more than anything, she hoped Mama would finally be proud of her.

Resisting the urge to grab a strong coffee to calm her nerves, Nikki placed her face in her hands. Then she rubbed her fingertips across her cheekbones, just under her eyes.

Taking a deep breath, she started toward the doors where her driver had already exited.

Too bad she didn't want to see anyone while she was here. Except Mama, of course. And maybe Tristan. She shivered. All these years, and even now she wondered if she'd made a mistake leaving like she did. Wasn't she still chasing her desires like a mutt after a fox? A feeling of emptiness twanged in her stomach as she stepped into the Miami heat.

"Miss Sears. Your limo," the thin driver said as he gestured his hand toward the open back door of the long black vehicle.

She winced at the mention of her name, glancing around to see if anyone noticed her. A group of teen girls stared, then pointed. Nikki lowered herself into the seat, and the driver quickly closed the door. She could see out the tinted windows without a problem, but her privacy was intact. The girls she'd noticed earlier were now headed toward the car, screaming, but the driver skillfully pulled away.

Word would travel fast that she was in town.

In front of her lay a copy of the *Miami Herald.* She picked it up and flipped to the entertainment section, eager to see what they'd said about her impending arrival.

Nothing.

As she tossed the paper down, a picture caught her attention. She pulled it closer.

"Derelict hobo none other than missing musician." The warmth in the man's eyes tugged at her. Despite his disheveled appearance, he seemed familiar. She began to read the first paragraph.

A man found lost and confused not far from the rail

*yard claims to be none other than musician Tristan
Reuben, who had been missing for two days.*

*Reuben's parents notified police of his disappearance
when he failed to show up for a birthday bash in his honor.
A search of Reuben's beachfront condo showed signs of a
struggle.*

*Reuben contends that he was kidnapped, bound, and
blindfolded, then put into a car. He feared for his life when
he believed the vehicle had been left on the railroad tracks.
Moments after the train's whistle sounded, he states he was
pulled from the vehicle and tossed onto what he believed
was a railcar floor, which quickly began to move. He managed to work the blindfold off and eventually the rope from
his hands, then the tape from his mouth. . . .*

Nikki skimmed farther down the page.

*Reuben's brothers admit their prank went a little too
far when Tristan lost his balance and fell out of the railcar,
rendering him unconscious. David, Aaron, and Joel
Reuben had waited for their brother to disembark at the
next stop and panicked when he could not be found.*

*According to a family friend, this is not the first time
they've carried sibling rivalry a little too far. Two years
ago, they were responsible for circulating phony wanted
posters that ended with their brother's erroneous arrest.*

Nikki let the paper drop into her lap and leaned back in the
plush seat. She lowered the window for some air.

I sure could use a coffee.

The car slowed to a stop at a red light, and suddenly a crowd appeared beside her door.

"Nikki Sears!" voices screamed, while bodies pushed and shoved for a closer look.

She offered her star smile and celebrity wave as the driver inched away when the light reverted to green. She remembered a time when she would have loved such a welcome. Now, she yearned for something more. . .more personal, intimate. Tristan.

Nikki shook her head as if doing so could shake him from her thoughts and her heart. She had not returned to see him. She knew a relationship could not withstand the whirlwind lifestyle she now had. World tours, guest appearances on talk shows, radio spots, and commercials. Sometimes she could hardly find time for herself.

She gazed back out the now half-lowered window. Every man she saw looked like the tall, dark-haired, olive-skinned Tristan Reuben she'd left behind. The man who still held her heart.

Stop it!

"Miss Sears." The driver interrupted her thoughts. "There's a problem up ahead. Looks like we are being detoured. I know a back way to the hotel."

Taking in a deep breath, she squeezed the top of her nose, feeling her beating pulse. She told herself to remain calm. What she wouldn't give for a long soak in a hot bath. Then a thought came to her. "Driver, do you know where Venture Park is?"

"Yes, Ma'am."

"I'd like to go there, please," she said as she visualized their favorite place and hoped she'd find Tristan there. Like always.

You're so fickle, Girl.

❧

His mind felt thick, as if his head was filled with cotton balls. Tristan's brothers had reluctantly covered for his misadventure, yet the truth had shaken his world. His nights were sleepless, his days were fearful. Would his captors return?

"A five year old could do better," he muttered and tossed his pencil across the room. The modern, small studio seemed to have closed in on him. He needed some air.

At times like these, he found a walk to the park usually increased his creativity. It was where he went to clear his head, though lately it was where he went to think of Cynthia. Hadn't he made a promise when he thought he was about to die?

He stepped out onto the street and regretted his decision. He felt like the soup du jour. News of his kidnapping and homeless appearance had made him something of a celebrity—again. Albeit an odd one. He ignored their stares and unkind utterances and prayed the novelty would wear off by the time he played with the quartet at the Hammerstein wedding. Being in the limelight hadn't improved his career, nor his disposition in this instance.

He walked briskly, his right hand in his pocket jangling the loose change. He'd picked up the strange habit only recently, believing it had something to do with stress. He stilled his hand and pushed his thoughts to his current opus. Music filled his head as he hummed silently all the way to the park.

Once seated on a bench, Tristan became aware of a vague feeling of being watched. A shiver trilled up his spine. He looked around. The grounds had seen the last of noisy, joy-filled toddlers and their mothers this late in the afternoon. Only a few elderly people remained.

He closed his eyes and tried to remember the last time he and Cynthia came here. Somehow, just thinking about it still caused an ache.

"What do you mean you're going to California?"

"I need to do this, Tristan, and I thought you were the one person who would understand. Don't you see? If I don't find out what I can be, I'll always wonder. What if I settle for the way things are?"

He paced but a moment. "Is that what you think? Marrying me and living here is settling. . .compromising?"

"No, that's not what I meant." She began to cry softly.

He moved to the bench and seated himself beside her, wrapping his arms across her shoulders. "Don't cry, Babe. I understand what you're saying, but you're making a mistake. You need to just—"

"Don't, Tristan," she said, shooting to her feet. "Don't tell me what to do. All my life everyone has told me what to say, where to go. I don't even know who I am."

He cut her off. "That's ridiculous! Sure you've led a sheltered life, but those things don't tell you who you are. You know God has blessed you with a voice like an angel's, and I don't know anyone sweeter than you. Yes, you're vulnerable, but you're also a survivor. I love your generous and caring heart. What more do you need to know?"

"Plenty. What do I want out of life? I've always just fallen into things. I don't want to just fall into marriage, only to find out later that it's not for me."

He stood and glared at her, unable to hold his tongue despite the pain in her eyes. It had taken him years to realize she'd only been protecting him. "I guess I don't understand you," he'd replied in anger. "Just a few months ago you wanted to get married."

"And you didn't," she nearly whispered her response.

"I'm willing now—"

A sad laugh escaped her throat. "We never were in sync, were we?"

"Cynthia, haven't these past few years been. . .been good for both of us? You may have fallen into this relationship, as you put it, but it's lasted. God has blessed us. We like the same things, we can finish each other's—"

"Sentences. I know. But marriage is more than that. Don't you see? I just want to make sure. If God wants us together, it will still happen."

"Well, if you go, it won't happen. I won't follow you to California and beg you to come home." He knew he should stop talking now, but he couldn't. Her words had wounded him so much. And even though she'd never hurt him like this before, it was as if she had become another person. Someone he didn't even recognize. "If you go, you'll have to come back on your own. And, if things are as you say, then I suspect you'll fall into something else and forget all about what we have. If that's what you want, you can walk away from me right now."

He felt his knees weaken when she grabbed her purse, turned, and left without a word. Why had he said those things to the woman he loved? As everything in him seemed to crumble, he merely stood and watched her walk farther and farther away. He could tell she was crying. His heart said go to her, but his head said don't bother. That internal war had cost him everything.

By the time he'd listened to his heart, she was gone. From

that moment on, he buried himself in his music. His life revolved around the quartet, teaching, and composing.

A sudden shiver down his spine brought his thoughts to the present. He felt a cold stab of pain in his chest.

"Well, that was the past," he said to the air.

So why did it still hurt?

He scooted off the bench and spotted a long, sleek limousine pulling up to the curb on the far side of the park. He figured it was a wedding party since it wasn't unusual for couples to have their picture taken here.

Time to make an exit. The last thing he needed was a reminder of his loss. He'd never see Cynthia again. She'd left him and their life behind. In fact, she didn't even go by the name Cynthia Powers anymore. Now she was Nikki Sears. And if the buzz in the music world was correct, she was on a fast track to the top.

Guess his promise didn't matter now. Cynthia was lost forever.

Chapter 2

Mama!" Nikki hollered as she entered the old familiar apartment.

The faint smell of tea rose wafted to her. It was her mama's favorite potpourri. As Eleanor Powers entered the room drying her hands on a dish towel, Nikki raced like a little girl into her arms.

"Cynthia! Why didn't you tell me you were coming?" her mother asked as she took Nikki's hands, pulled back, and looked her over.

She could tell by her mother's reaction that she had not met with approval. No, Mama would never say anything, but the frown and moist eyes told her everything. She'd seen this same scenario all her life. Would she never measure up?

"I wanted to surprise you," she finally answered, amazed that she could choke back her emotions.

"Well, you did, Cynthia. Nearly gave me a heart attack."

How could she answer that? Was her coming home so bad?

"I go by Nikki now."

Mama nodded, her dark curls bouncing. "So, sit down. I'll make us some lemonade. Or would you like something else?"

"Lemonade's fine," she replied, following her mama into the kitchen.

The bright yellow walls she had loved as a child now seemed dull and lifeless. The blue accessories had paled as well. Or had they always been sad-looking and she'd never noticed? *Once this tour is over, I'm going to pay someone to redo this place,* she thought.

"Honey, did you hear me?"

"Sorry," Nikki answered, shaking the cobwebs from her mind.

"How long are you in town for?"

"Just a quick promotion to kick off my world tour. I'll be on *Miami Morning* tomorrow and a reporter from the *Herald* is going to do an interview at the hotel."

Her mama's brows dipped and narrowed over dark brown eyes, but her thin, pale lips neither frowned nor smiled. "Guess you're pretty busy with your career."

Did she detect a note of distaste in the way Mama had said "career," or was Nikki just being too sensitive? "Oh, it's getting there. It takes time. But this tour should be the thing that gets me noticed." She wrung her hands and wished for a cup of strong coffee.

"How do you survive out there, all alone? Or is there someone in your life?"

What a loaded question. How did she survive? She'd never felt so alone as the day she arrived at LAX. Well, that wasn't quite true. The day Tristan told her to leave and never come back had been the loneliest and saddest moment of her life. But LA was a big city, filled with the sounds of the great life, even if they weren't for her. "I used to be engaged, but it didn't work out," she admitted as she touched the chain around her neck.

How long would she have to wear this before it would be safe to throw it away?

"Engaged? And you never called to tell me or write?"

Why hadn't she? Had she known all along how it would end? Was she destined to relationships that lacked harmony, were full of discord and out of sync?

"I'm sorry, Mama," she said as she pulled out a worn chair and sat down.

Eleanor turned around and placed a plate of cookies on the old chrome table. "If I remember right, Cyndi-Ann, these are your favorite." Finally, a smile. A full smile. It reached all the way to Eleanor's eyes and brightened her pallid complexion.

Nikki winced at the pet name and squirmed under her mother's pleased gaze, then reached out for a cookie. Would she ever have the courage to tell her mother she hated oatmeal and raisins?

"You haven't lost your touch, Mama," she answered after taking a bite.

Nikki stayed only a short time. Her mother caught her up on all the neighbors, and then they seemed to have nothing to say.

"Will I see you before you head back to LA?"

"I'll try to stop by tomorrow. It's not easy sneaking out of the hotel. After my tour, I'll come back for a longer visit. You can stay in a hotel with me, and maybe we can go shopping and do some girl things. Maybe even go to Joe's for stone crabs and then the theater."

She fought back tears as she took in her mother's unyielding expression. Would they ever have a comfortable relationship?

"You need to save your money, Dear," Mama said with a determined tone.

A weight like concrete landed squarely on Nikki's heart. Nothing had changed.

"I've got money," she said, surprised at how young she sounded.

"Cynthia—"

"I go by Nikki now."

"I know, Dear. But that's when you're in California. You're just Cynthia to me," Eleanor said calmly as she reached out for a hug.

They embraced and Nikki left, a heaviness weighing her down. She felt isolated from her mama's world. Could things get any worse on this trip?

Darkness still hung in the sky when the white limousine from the *Miami Morning* show arrived. It was far too early to even consider a lively conversation with the host, Rex Leonard, but Tristan knew he needed to pull himself together and prepare. No doubt there would be questions about his latest adventure. What could he say that wouldn't be a lie? He'd have to keep Rex focused on the reason for his appearance and pray the host followed his lead.

His five-minute segment discussing his new teaching DVD, possibly throwing in a pitch for the quartet's latest CD, would go off without a hitch, he assured himself. When it was all over, he'd head home to crawl back into bed. Mornings had never agreed with him. He checked his appearance in the mirror as the limo made its way to the studio. Good thing he didn't look like he felt.

People were everywhere at the television station, rushing here and there. Voices sounded urgent, and those in authority gave directions. First, they ushered him to a dressing room, where they tried to make him look anything but like himself. Then, they put him in the green room to wait. He grabbed a cup of coffee off the table, two pastries, and some napkins. The couch looked comfortable, so he settled in.

A booming alto voice echoed through the halls.

"Hi there," Rex said, peeking in the room.

Tristan nodded. "Hi."

"Have they briefed you?"

"Yes," he answered, feeling a little out of his league.

"Nervous?"

"So far so good."

Rex roared with laughter. "I heard you play once. At a bar mitzvah. You've got real passion. You should ditch that sleepy group and go solo."

"Not much call for a violist these days. Now, if it were the 1700s, I'd consider your advice."

"They're waiting for you, Rex." A young woman interrupted their conversation.

"Thanks, Angela." He waved her away, then looked at Tristan. "Watch the monitor until someone comes to get you," Rex hollered as he walked away.

The buzz in the place reminded Tristan of a beehive. Everyone moved and talked fast. The producer was finishing with the audience members who were sufficiently pumped. Last-minute lighting and sound checks droned in the background, while someone shouted out the time like a newsboy calling out headlines. "Ten minutes, people."

Tristan flipped through an outdated *Miami Metro* magazine in an attempt to still his nerves. His stomach grumbled.

He hoped it wouldn't happen on the air.

He closed his eyes and willed himself to relax. This was just a short interview. Nothing to it. Pulling out the quartet's CD, he reviewed the song list. Funny how just reading the titles brought the tunes alive in his head.

Salut D'Amour. Eva's rich, majestic playing really seemed to be like a greeting to love. *Canon in D.* This was the song that always reminded him of Cynthia. The first time he ever laid eyes on her, she was singing it; not that it had words, it was a choral warm-up that made him think he was listening to a heavenly choir. *Morning Mood.* He chuckled to himself. Yes, he was in some mood this morning.

"Just in here, Ms. Sears," someone said as they neared the door.

Tristan stiffened. *Ms. Sears? As in Nikki Sears? As in Cynthia Powers?* He didn't have to wonder long as she stepped into the room.

"Ms. Sears, this is Mr. Reuben," Angela said, then left.

Silence echoed off the celebrity picture-filled walls as Tristan wiped sweaty palms on his napkin. His heart rate went from andante to presto and continued to thump wildly like a percussionist out of control. He stood as she stepped farther into the room and nodded a greeting. He didn't trust his voice.

For a split second she seemed thrilled to see him. Her eyes had instantly brightened, and he thought she was going to throw herself into his arms. Had he been dreaming? Now her smile seemed slight, and he barely heard her say hello. He watched as she quickly took a seat as far from him as she could.

He didn't blame her. Yet, while this was no place for a discussion, he did feel the need to say something. "It's good to see you, Cynthia," he squeaked out.

He saw a flash of something in her eyes. Was she glad he'd spoken to her? "Call me Nikki. You're looking better than your recent picture in the *Herald*."

He groaned. "Guess I clean up well."

"I was just going to say that," she said with a chuckle.

Could it be this easy to maneuver right back into their comfortable relationship?

"How have you been?"

"Things couldn't be better. What about you, Tristan?"

"Just fine. The quartet has really come together well. We've matured in our craft. Oh, and get this, Tyrone got married!" He was a babbling idiot. What a dumb thing to say to her.

He could have played several stanzas in the silence that ensued. Any chance of slipping back into that comfortable place had just hit *finis*.

Yet, his heart appeared to be thawing from looking into her sparkling green eyes that seemed to still be searching. Her rosebud lips, blushed with the pink gloss she always wore, begged to be kissed. Or was it just his imagination?

She glanced at the monitor, then picked up a nearby magazine and began flipping pages.

He continued his visual intake. Cynthia's dress hugged her curves and revealed too much cleavage, but the color complimented her creamy complexion. Her hair was perfect, in his unskilled opinion, save for one errant strand that she kept pushing behind her ear with her slim fingers. She glanced up, catching him staring at her.

"What?"

"Nothing. I just wondered if you picked out that outfit."

Mentally he shook his head. Just once, couldn't he not say what he thought?

"Yes, I did." She seemed pleased, as if he had complimented her.

Maybe she hadn't heard the condescension in his voice. Maybe he had time to recover. "It's rather revealing." And maybe he should just shoot himself now.

Her lower lip extended a little, and he knew his words had pained her.

"Two minutes," an ominous voice bellowed from the unknown.

Angela appeared in the doorway. "You're up first, Mr. Reuben. Follow me."

Tristan rose and offered Cynthia a look of apology, but she turned away and stared at the monitor, appearing totally uninterested in him.

❧

Nikki let the trapped air escape from her lungs. Tristan was the last person she expected to run into. She felt tongue-tied, wishing things had never ended so harshly. He brought so many buried feelings to the surface that her whole body seemed to be trembling. Would she be able to go out on stage like this? Could she get her mind off wondering if Tristan was married or had a significant other? After all, it had been six years. A lot could happen in that time.

When Rex called Tristan out, Nikki held her breath as she watched the monitor. Tristan moved on stage with ease, and she couldn't help but compare him to her former fiancé. Donald's blond hair, fair skin, and chiseled face paled, literally and figuratively, beside Tristan's dark looks and handsome features.

Height was something else Donald sorely lacked. While Tristan appeared intriguing and well educated, Donald was merely infuriating and ignorant. But Donald had one thing Tristan didn't.

She turned her attention to the last of the interview in progress.

"Now, I understand your viola is worth a lot. How do you keep it from being stolen?" Rex asked.

"I put it in a violin case," Tristan responded straight-faced.

Nikki smiled. Rex hadn't understood the old joke.

"I sense a bit of rivalry between violists and violinists. Am I right?"

"In all honesty, Rex, the viola ranks below the violin, even the cello. We don't get the limelight in performances. We're content to be the unsung heroes, kind of like the filling in a jelly donut, so we take a lot of ribbing as a result. But we can handle it."

"You mentioned people always ask what's in the case or make jokes. What do you reply?"

"Happens all the time," he said and chuckled. "I usually just smile, but once I couldn't resist a smart remark. An instrument can't be left in the car, as you know, and I had to meet some friends at a restaurant." Tristan shifted and scanned the audience.

Was he looking for someone? Nikki felt a strange feeling of jealousy sneak up on her.

"As I entered, the maître d' asked if I had a gun in the case. I replied, 'Here in Miami? Where they call out the National Guard for a six-year-old boy? I think not.'"

Rex roared with laughter and put out his hand. "Well,

thanks for being on our show today, Tristan. I know our viewers will be picking up your viola instruction DVD as soon as it comes out." Nikki watched as Rex held up the thin movie case.

"My pleasure, Rex," Tristan said while shaking the host's hand. As he slipped off the stool, he waved at the audience and flashed a smile for the camera.

Nikki's heart skipped a beat. She still loved him. Tears threatened and despair nearly choked her—for Tristan had not forgiven her. And he never would. He was not the forgiving type.

Chapter 3

"M s. Sears? Follow me." Angela interrupted her thoughts.

From the moment she came face-to-face with the audience, Rex Leonard put her at ease. Throughout the segment, he chuckled and appeared sympathetic in all the right spots when she talked. He almost seemed to be flirting with her, but she hardly noticed. Her thoughts kept drifting away. How she wished it were Tristan she was laughing with.

"Toccoa Falls College? Say, isn't that where our first guest Tristan Reuben went as well?"

Nikki flushed and merely nodded.

"So, do you know each other and I'm not talking in the biblical sense. We're not that kind of show." He winked.

Suddenly Rex didn't seem so warm and friendly.

"Actually, we were friends. Well, still are, I assume. But our careers took us in opposite directions."

"Surely he could have played his viola in LA?" The statement was laced with something she didn't quite understand. Was he baiting her?

"We were just friends," she said defensively.

"His loss, that's for sure."

Her eyes misted, and she fought to keep her chin from quivering. "Or mine," she said with a forced laugh, hoping to lighten the moment. She took a breath. "But I have someone pretty special in my life." Nikki hoped her words sounded convincing.

Rex seemed to ignore her last comment. "So, this world tour. How many countries will you be hitting?"

Nikki felt totally drained by the time she finished the show. It had been difficult in a few spots, but she knew her agent would be proud of her performance. When she sang "I'll Never Forget What We Once Had," her voice had caught with emotion, and she struggled to finish the song.

No, she'd never forget what she and Tristan once had, nor would she ever find it again. Of that she was certain. And even if, by some miracle, Tristan could find the ability to forgive her for leaving, he'd never be able to find that same grace for her once he found out what had happened to her in LA. She couldn't leave Miami soon enough. This was too painful. Maybe she could leave her feelings for Tristan behind, as well.

Relaxing in the limo, she cradled a cup of hot coffee like it had turned cold outside. Somehow the action gave her comfort. She even sipped with two hands while she thought about a line in the song she'd performed on the show. Though she sang with emotion, she'd never really paid much attention to this particular lyric before. Now the words stung.

"You've gone on with your life while I've lived alone in my world of hurt; you've found love, a wife, and I've only found my work." Even if Tristan had not found a wife, he was deeply loved by his friends, the quartet, and his family. He lived a rich, full life. She faced loneliness and a void daily. All the success and money in the entire universe couldn't hold her at night and whisper sweet words of endearment.

Her coffee had grown cold while she mused about her life. She needed to snap out of her melancholy mood and go visit her mama. There wouldn't be time tomorrow before her flight left.

"Driver, there's been a change."

❧

"Hey, the celebrity is here!" Tyrone teased as Tristan entered their practice studio.

"Yeah, Rex wanted me to do a solo act, so you'd all better treat me with the respect I deserve." He placed his viola case on the chair and turned to face three pairs of eyes staring at him. "What?" he asked, palms raised in surrender. "I didn't agree to it."

"That's not it, and you know it!" Rissa said, her hands akimbo on her hips.

"You'd better spill the beans, or we won't get any practicing done today," Eva teased as a grin spread across her face. "Besides, you're the one always making us unload our problems. Now you know how it feels."

Tristan turned to Tyrone.

"Don't look at me, I'm just as curious."

"Et tu, Brutus?"

Tyrone clutched his heart. "You wound me, Bro."

Tristan sighed. "She's back in town. That's all I know." Three sets of raised eyebrows and dagger looks told him he needed to elaborate. "All right. She appeared on the show. But we didn't talk. I made some sort of stupid remark and she got mad."

Tyrone shook his head while Rissa and Eva giggled.

"Have you learned nothing from the master?" Tyrone asked.

"Apparently not. Now, shall we get to work?"

Moving closer, Rissa studied him a moment. "You've seen her before the show, haven't you?"

He swallowed hard. "Well, yes. We sat in the green room together."

"How long has she been in town?"

Tristan shrugged. "I don't know."

"But you're seeing her again before she leaves, aren't you?"

"You know, I don't see a witness box nor did I swear on a Bible, so maybe can we adjourn the court and get to work?"

"Touchy, isn't he?" Rissa said to the others.

"Indeed," Tyrone and Eva answered in unison, then laughed.

"I'm pretty sure I'm right, though. Look at his eyes. He's packed for a European tour with those bags."

He should have known he couldn't get anything past them. Not only had he not been sleeping since the abduction, he'd been unable to compose. And there was only one reason this was happening.

Cynthia. Even before he saw her at the show, she'd invaded his thoughts again.

He felt so out of sorts. He liked his well-ordered life just fine. But what about his promise? It seemed like he had been given another chance. What was stopping him from following through? If he were honest with himself, he knew the answer to that question. He hated change. He wanted Cynthia and a family, but he wanted things to stay the same.

Fat chance, Buddy.

"Hmm, he does look pretty bad, gang, and I'm not even sure he's aware we're talking about him," Tyrone said with a gentle laugh. "Let's lay off. . .for now."

Tristan felt relieved when they called a halt to their good-natured ribbing. Normally, they didn't get to him, but Cynthia—or Nikki—was not a subject he cared to talk about. Especially since he had a feeling his lack of sleep and other problems had more to do with his promise than the abduction. After all, here she was. And he was doing nothing.

"Okay, back to work," Rissa said.

"I think I'm a little out of tune," Tristan said. "Who has a good A?"

As they rehearsed, Tristan's mind wandered back to the morning at the television studio. Cynthia's almost anorexic appearance shocked him. He hoped his reaction hadn't been noticeable. Of course, he'd never been very good at keeping his feelings hidden. Even before she left. And his comments about her dress only proved that.

In addition, he'd been jealous when he saw Cynthia flirting with Rex. Or, rather, him flirting with her. She could have at least put a damper on the man. He had turned away from the monitor, intending to leave in disgust when she stood to sing. Her voice had brought him to a halt. Maturity had brought a rich quality to her powerful, sultry sound. She sang with emotion. At one point, he worried she might even cry. He resisted the urge to wait for her to finish and slipped out before he could change his mind.

"What type of entrance was that?" Tyrone's voice broke through his daydreaming.

"Sorry, I just lost track of where we were." He offered a sheepish grin as an apology and flexed the fingers of his left hand.

Eva put down her violin, then said, "Why don't we take a break?"

Tristan stood and stretched, but remained quiet.

Leaning over the music stand, Tyrone stared at him. "Are you okay?"

"Sure," he answered too quickly, almost brightly like a girl.

"Sure," Tyrone said in a falsetto voice.

"Knock it off." He scowled.

Tyrone backed away, his smile quickly fading. "Sorry, Man."

"No, I'm sorry. You didn't deserve that."

Tyrone patted him on the back. "Wanna take a walk outside so we can chat without the snoop sisters?"

"I heard that," Rissa said as she flipped through some sheet music.

"Precisely," Tyrone replied with a smirk.

"Why don't Rissa and I go get us some lunch?" Eva offered.

With the girls gone, Tyrone dropped onto the small sofa in the corner. Placing his hands behind his head, he leaned back and waited.

Tristan shifted in his seat while formulating what to say. How did he feel?

"I don't think anyone could have been more surprised than me," Tyrone started, "when I asked Cassy to marry me. It's a big change, and I thank God He led me every step of the way. But it takes three to make a marriage. The bride, the groom, and God. Where do you think Cynthia is in her faith?"

"I'd say she left God here in Miami when she fled to LA."

"So, there's your answer."

"My answer?"

"Look, you love her, don't you?"

197

"I don't even know her. It's been six years. I hardly recognized her at first." Well, maybe visually, but his heart knew her instantly.

"Maybe that's a blessing. You don't want to spend time with her, falling back in love, if she doesn't share your beliefs. Right now it should be easy to walk away."

Easy. Yeah, it should be.

"On the other hand, we've been commissioned to preach the gospel in Jerusalem and in all Judea and Samaria and to the ends of the earth."

"And did you confuse the spelling of Samaria with C-y-n-t-h-i-a?"

Tyrone snickered. "Can you walk away if she refuses to hear?"

Could he? Could he walk away even now? *God, help me, please.*

❧

"What's this, Mama?" Nikki asked as she picked up a piece of paper near the phone.

Mama turned and faced her. "Nothing really. You know Dr. Leroy. Always wanting to do some test or other thing. Sit down, Dear. I think everything is on the table."

"It looks serious," she said as she pulled out the chrome and black chair and dropped onto the worn seat. "An EKG and an ECG?"

"Normal things to look at for a woman my age. Do you want some of my homemade bread?" Mama asked as she handed the basket to Nikki.

"Don't try to change the subject."

Mama seated herself and took a slice of the thick warm loaf. "I'm fine, Dear. This is just preventative."

"You sure?" Nikki asked as she held her knife and fork in

the air above her dinner plate.

"Of course."

Nikki watched as her mother looked away and started buttering her bread with vigor. Something didn't seem right.

"I think I'll cancel my flight and go with you tomorrow."

"That's not necessary," Mama answered without glancing up from her food.

"I'll be here in the morning. We'll go to the hospital together." Nikki attempted to keep her voice calm as she fought the fear that threatened to choke the air from her lungs.

She nodded. "Could you pass the salt, please?"

Were her mama's hands trembling as she took the small glass bottle from Nikki? She ignored what she'd seen. "Pass the salt?" Is that all she could say?

"You don't have to change your plans, Honey. I'm fine."

Does she not want me here? Before Nikki could speak, the phone shrilled.

"I'll get that," Mama said.

If Nikki hadn't known better, she would have thought her mother timed the interruption!

"Tristan, it's so good to hear your voice," Mama greeted, then paused. "Yes, I'm fine. And you?" Another lull as she listened. "I saw that. A DVD and CD. Your parents must be so proud of you."

What about me, Mama? I'm going on a world tour. Couldn't you, just for once, be proud or happy for me? Nikki bit back the painful thoughts while remorse ate at her for being so selfish.

"Why, yes, she's right here. Hang on while I pass the phone to her."

"Cynthia, it's Tristan," she said with a broad smile.

"I'll take it in the other room."

"Hang on, Tristan, while she picks up the extension."

Nikki went into the living room and leaned over the back of the faded and somewhat lumpy couch for the old green phone.

"Hello, Tristan."

"Hi, Cynthia." He sounded cheerful, and she didn't want to deflate him by asking him to call her Nikki again.

"I'm just calling to see if you might have time for dinner and a movie while you're here."

"I don't know. I had planned to leave tomorrow, but Mama has some tests so I'm staying until after that. If there is nothing wrong, I might try to make a red-eye to LA."

"Is Eleanor all right?"

She could hear the concern in his voice and loved him for it. "She says she is. I just want to be certain."

"You sound scared. Need a friend?"

She closed her eyes and pinched the bridge of her nose. Was that all Tristan would ever be to her now? Simply a friend? Well, in the scheme of things, it was better than nothing at this point.

"Cynthia, I could come over now if you need me," he offered with tenderness resonating in his voice.

She bit her lip. "No. Thanks. I want to spend some time with her alone tonight."

"I'm sure she'll love it."

I'm not so sure, Tristan.

"Cynthia, you still there?" he asked.

"No, she's not. But Nikki is."

He laughed. "Okay, Nikki. I'll try to call you that, but I make no promises. You'll always be Cynthia to me." He paused. "Now, why don't I pick you two up in the morning and take you to the hospital? There's nothing I'd like better."

She giggled. "If I remember correctly, you hate mornings."

"Not when I have two beautiful women on my arm. When should I be there?"

Now, she silently pleaded.

Chapter 4

I'm not joking," Eleanor said in response to Tristan's burst of laughter. "She really did insist on taking the dolphin home with her."

"Mama, I'm sure he's heard this story before," Nikki interrupted, wishing everyone would forget about the day they visited Miami Seaquarium. Even if it did seem to be making Mama sparkle with pleasure.

Tristan shook his head. "It's new to me," he said, leaning back in the hospital cafeteria chair and grinning like he wouldn't want to be any other place. His smile made her pulse quicken.

"When I asked her where it would sleep, she said she would share her bed. I told her the fish needed water. 'So, I'll get a waterbed,' she replied. 'That's what they're for.'"

Tristan laughed and slapped his knee. "So how did you get Cynthia, I mean Nikki, home?"

"The only way I could. I waited until she fell asleep."

Nikki rolled her eyes, knowing what would be next.

"I'm sure that didn't stop her."

"You know her too well." Eleanor laughed, then continued. "She wouldn't leave without rescuing that poor dolphin. When she woke up, she asked where he was. I told her that he'd slipped out of my hands while I was trying to carry her and it to the car and that he managed to get to the ocean safely."

"And she bought it? I'm surprised."

"Well, we didn't hear too much about it until that animated movie about a mermaid came out. Cynthia wanted to be one so she could go and make sure her dolphin had survived."

"And a lovely mermaid she would have made," Tristan said as he placed his palm protectively over the back of her hand.

Nikki watched as her mama's eyes lit up. In a quick motion, she withdrew from Tristan's touch and stood. She picked up Tristan's coffee mug and Mama's teapot and cup, added them to her tray of dirty dishes, and marched away. Maybe they'd get the hint that she didn't like being the topic of discussion. It was bad enough that her life was an open book with the press. All her mistakes were there in black-and-white for the world to judge without her mama being a turncoat as well.

When she returned, they were still enjoying themselves. No doubt at her expense. "Guess it's time to go," she said. "I've got a flight to catch back to LA, and you need to go home and rest, Mama. You look tired."

"I'm just not used to being up this early or having this much fun."

They walked out the automatic hospital doors into the bright day and headed toward the car. The warmth of the morning sun kissed their faces. The reason Florida was called the Sunshine State. Even the air smelled sunny to Nikki. It sure beat LA anytime.

As they stepped off the curb, Eleanor stumbled. Tristan caught her before she hit the road.

"Mama! Are you hurt?"

Eleanor didn't answer.

"Cynthia, I think she's fainted. Go back inside and get someone to help."

Without thinking, Nikki prayed. *Dear God, please help. Please don't, please don't. . .* Her words faltered.

❧

"We're just going to keep her overnight for observation," the doctor said while he leaned against the hospital bed footboard and perused Eleanor's chart.

His white medical coat was the same white as the bedding, the walls, and the curtains. Eleanor looked washed out against the color.

Tristan pulled Cynthia close to his side, his arm securely around her shoulders. Feeling her near gave him comfort. He hoped she would draw strength from him.

"So, there's nothing wrong?"

"Not that I can see at this point. We'll study her tests and monitor her for the evening. Is she under any stress?"

"I *am* in the room, Doctor," Eleanor said, her voice weak but determined. "And no, now that my daughter is home, I don't have a care in the world." She offered a weak smile.

"Maybe we should let you rest." The doctor flipped the chart closed. "I'll check back on you later." He turned to Tristan and Cynthia and said, "You two lovebirds need to go out and enjoy the day. She'll be fine here."

Tristan eyed Cynthia, wondering what she thought of the physician's comment. "I'll take that prescription, Doc," he said as he took her hand and led her toward the door. "Don't worry, Mrs. P, I'll take good care of her while you rest. Think it's safe to take her to the aquarium?"

Eleanor smiled. "I think so. Her heart belongs to someone else now that needs to be rescued with love." Slowly her eyelids drifted closed.

❧

"I called the church last night. Everyone is praying for her," Tristan said as they drove toward Rickenbacker Causeway. Out of the corner of his eye, he saw her nod. He reached for her hand.

Her hair bounced as she swung her head to look at him. *She's so beautiful, Lord. And so lost. Help me help her.* "You have to trust—"

"Please don't, Tristan. Don't talk to me about that. God doesn't always answer our prayers the way we think He should. Does He?"

"No. But you have to trust that He—" Tristan stopped. What could he say? This was not the time for platitudes and clichés. "You and I both think Eleanor should live forever. She's a wonderful person. Yet, God knows what's in store for her. If anything did happen, I'd like to believe it would be because it's for the better. He's a merciful God, Cynthia."

"Where was He when my father beat us? Or when I left Miami?"

Tristan swallowed hard and let the silence settle between them like a fog.

"Why don't you tell me what happened? I've wondered about you often, all these years." He stopped. He wanted to say and prayed for her as well, but couldn't.

"I don't think I can, Tristan. Not right now. My mind is on Mama."

"Would you rather just go home or back to the hospital?"

She nodded, then shook her head.

"Okay, was that yes to going home and no to the hospital?"

She shrugged, and Tristan resisted the desire to reach out for her. "I'll take you home. But first, let me get you some lunch. And while we're stopped, you can call and see how Eleanor is doing. Okay?"

"I'm not very hungry."

"You need to eat, to keep up your strength. When Eleanor comes home tomorrow, you'll want to pamper her until she's feeling stronger. Won't you?"

They stopped for a burger and fries and ate in silence. He didn't mind. He loved looking at her. Loved being lost in her apple-green eyes, even if they were sad. He longed to try to make everything right, but it seemed each time he opened his mouth, he said something wrong. So he settled for the quiet.

Eventually, he could prolong their time together no longer and they headed back to the hotel. He didn't like leaving her alone, but she insisted.

The crowd of fans had thinned, making it easier for them to slip in the back door and up to Cynthia's room. She inserted the key in the lock but didn't move.

"Want me to bring back some dinner?" he asked.

"I'll just order room service." A wisp of hair slipped forward on her face.

He brushed the wayward strand back, leaned down, and gently kissed her forehead, worried his actions would scare her away.

"I'm so glad you were with me today." Her voice was but a whisper.

"Me, too," he replied, pulling back before he found himself

in a difficult position. He yearned to comfort her, but knew it was dangerous territory. "I'll be praying for you. Call if you need anything," he said as he stepped away from her.

She nodded.

He turned and walked away.

He felt her eyes on him all the way to the elevator. How he wanted to turn back and scoop her up into his arms—promise her that everything would be fine. But that wasn't possible.

With a hand in his pocket, jiggling some change, he strode toward the elevator. Music blared from a nearby room. He recognized it immediately. Cynthia had sung it on the *Miami Morning* show. "You've gone on with your life while I've lived alone in my world of hurt, you've found love, a wife, and I've only found my work."

Tristan cringed as he remembered Eleanor's words. "She loves someone else." The thought caused a stabbing pain to his heart. And just like in the song, Cynthia had found someone else while all he had—would ever have—was his work.

❧

"Tristan. How sweet of you to stop by," Eleanor said as she pulled herself up in the stark white bed.

"I couldn't get anything done today until I'd made certain you were all right," he said as he leaned in and kissed her cheek.

"Go on with you." A faint blush rose in her cheeks.

"We prayed for you at rehearsal last night. Eva and Marissa will try to stop by to see you this afternoon."

"That's so sweet of them."

"So, where's your lovely daughter?"

"She called to say she's on her way as soon as she talks with her manager or agent or whatever he is."

"What's he like?"

"I don't even know his name. She never tells me anything, and I'm worried about her."

Tristan raised an eyebrow. "How so?"

"I know she's always been vulnerable and impressionable, but there's this sadness hanging over her head. If anyone's hurt my baby—" She stopped and reached for a nearby tissue to dab at the sudden tears in her eyes.

"Have you tried talking to her, asking questions?"

"I've never been one to pry, but I did find some newspaper clippings in a folder she left at the apartment. It hasn't been easy for her, and I keep hoping she'll trust me enough to share her problems."

Tristan nodded and waited for Eleanor to continue.

"In the few times I've heard from her, she's always promising to come back and take me shopping or spend the day doing things. I worry she's trying to buy my forgiveness, but there's nothing to forgive. From the moment our children are born, we raise them to be able to be independent and leave the nest. I knew she would go one day, I had just hoped she'd come home more often. I miss my baby."

Tristan felt torn as he saw the moisture pooling in Eleanor's eyes. He felt anger that Cynthia had hurt her so, but he wanted to be supportive, as well. Whichever side he chose, he would be a traitor. Might as well start calling him Benedict Arnold now.

"Eleanor, you need to tell her how you feel."

"And you need"—she looked up at him with her tear-filled eyes—"to take your own advice. You still love her, don't you?"

What could he say? Cynthia completed him. They were like bits of a jigsaw puzzle. No other pieces would fit together.

"You don't have to answer that. I can see it in your eyes. Every time you look at her. You love and adore her. Tell her. Tell her, Tristan, before it's too late."

"Tell me what?" Cynthia demanded as she rushed into the room and to the side of the bed. "Are you okay, Mama? What are you keeping from me?"

"Good morning to you, too, Dear." Eleanor reached for Cynthia and gave her a hug and kiss.

Holding back a smile, Tristan nodded his greeting. She sure looked especially beautiful this morning. She'd pulled her hair back into a youthful ponytail, and her flawless complexion held a natural creamy appearance. She looked like the teenager he'd fallen in love with.

"Sorry, Mama. But what do you want me to think when I walk in here and see you sobbing, begging Tristan to tell me something."

"Whoa, how do you know we were even talking about you?" He loved it when she blushed.

Cynthia gave him a pointed look, then turned to Eleanor. "So, you're okay?"

"Fine. I'm being released as soon as the doctor signs the orders."

Tristan noticed how Cynthia instantly relaxed. Her shoulders sagged as she took in a deep breath, then let the air escape in a sigh.

Lord, I wish she'd never left. We had something special.

Then why didn't you go after her? his conscience pricked at him. Why, indeed.

Chapter 5

"Stop fussing over me, Cyndi-Ann."

"I'll make you a deal, Mama. You stop calling me that. . ." Cynthia paused, placed her hands on her hips, and glared at Eleanor, who lounged on the sofa, surrounded by pillows. "And I'll stop being a mother hen."

Tristan saw the pain on Eleanor's face and knew it wasn't from anything physical. Cynthia's comment hurt. As long as he could remember, Eleanor called her daughter Cyndi-Ann as an expression of love. Cynthia had never understood and had rebelled, just before leaving, telling her mother she wasn't a baby anymore. How he wanted to help bring these two women back together, but if there was one thing he knew about himself, he always said the wrong thing at the wrong time. No matter how much he cared—even loved—those involved. Besides, he had family problems. If he couldn't fix them, how could he fix this?

"I'm feeling a little tired. I didn't sleep too well with the nurses checking me all night. Why don't you and Tristan go out for awhile?"

"Mama, I'm sure Tristan has other things to do today."

He couldn't miss the harsh tone in her words, yet he

thought he saw a flash of hurt in her eyes.

"You don't need to sit here and watch me sleep. Besides, you've been gone six years." She turned to Tristan. "Take her out and show her Miami."

"I'd be happy to, Eleanor. I'll leave you my cell phone number. If you need anything or just want some company, you call and we'll come right back."

"Now scoot, you two," she said with a smile and then laid back and closed her eyes.

Tristan took Cynthia by the hand and pulled her along to the door. "We won't go too far from the area," he whispered.

She nodded but didn't speak. Tristan gazed into her eyes and could see the moisture of unshed tears. He needed a straitjacket or some other restraining device now or he would take her in his arms. Something about this lovely creature exuded an air of vulnerability and a yearning for love. She was like that before she left to follow her dreams, yet now it seemed even more pronounced.

"The neighborhood still seems the same," he said, hoping she'd start talking.

"Why does she live there, Tristan? I could move her to a condo on the beach."

"It's home, I guess. Her friends are here, too. Though I know Eleanor loves the beach, so I'm surprised she turned down your offer."

Cynthia folded her arms and glared at him. What had he said?

"Why are parents so complicated?"

Tristan chuckled. "You're asking me? With my family troubles?"

"Oh, right. What *was* I thinking?"

"Exactly." They were silent as the noise of the traffic surrounded them. Tristan worried that Cynthia would withdraw again.

"So are you ever going to tell me about the paper?"

"Paper?"

"The *Herald*. Your kidnapping story. Not one of your better pictures, I might add."

He grimaced. "I think we discussed that photograph already, but that's my brothers for you."

"Your folks must have gone ballistic."

Oh, they'd gone ballistic all right and not at his brothers, this time. Should he tell her the truth or let the lie remain? He wanted to be honest with someone, but to do so might put their life in danger. He couldn't do that to Cynthia. "It was quite a scene."

"Of all their pranks, this has got to be the worst."

"I'd say. The snakes in my bed, the gelatin in my hair gel, and the wanted poster sure pale compared to this."

"Tristan, were you afraid?" she asked with wide-eyed innocence.

He wanted to say no, that he trusted God, but just thinking about those moments trapped in the car caused a sharp staccato beat in his chest. "I don't think there is a word for what I felt. Fear seems so inadequate. Stark terror comes close. Especially when I heard the train whistle and thought I was on the tracks."

Cynthia placed her hand on his shoulder. "I'm sorry."

"Why? You didn't do anything."

"I'm just sorry you had to experience that."

"I'd go through it again if it meant you'd comfort me," he teased.

She swatted him. "Oh, you men. You're all alike."

"And you women love it."

❧

"Tristan, you remembered," Nikki said as he turned into the parking lot at Castillo's Restaurant. It had been one of their favorite dining spots. She'd loved the romantic setting almost as much as the Cuban food. Her mouth was watering already for the *Flan de Queso*—a wonderful dessert with far too many calories for her.

"How could I forget?"

"Some of our best times were spent here," they said in unison.

And some of our worst times. She would always remember the night she'd told him she was leaving. The scene, like an old familiar movie, had never dimmed. She found it difficult to forgive herself for the pain she'd seen in his eyes or the hurt in his voice. Despite his anger. Their dinner had been perfect in every way, capped off with a walk around Venture Park. But the night ended as far from perfect as the sky from earth.

"Do you think Raul is still around?" It was a sneaky question, she knew, born out of jealousy. Had he brought someone else here? If so, it didn't matter because she was the one who'd left. She needed to remember that.

"He'd never quit," Tristan said with a laugh. "I can't remember the last time I came here, though."

"Really? You love this place."

"Guess maybe it had more to do with the company than the food, Cynthia," he replied in what appeared to be a tone of regret.

Nikki's heart ached for him. She didn't bother correcting him about her name. Especially since she felt responsible for his pain.

Tristan parked, and she waited for him to open her door. When he reached the passenger side, he leaned inside and reached for her hand, gently pulling her to her feet. She hadn't been treated like a lady in a long time, and it felt nice.

"Thank you," she said.

"Just one thing, Cynthia. Let's have fun. Let's forget about the past and just enjoy the moment." He placed his hand in the small of her back and guided her toward the restaurant.

She stopped and gazed into his eyes. "Why, Mr. Reuben, you make it sound like being with me is the most depressing thing on earth," she said in her best Scarlett O'Hara imitation.

"Frankly, my dear, we've both been pretty poor company." He winked and her heart did a hiccup.

Nikki cupped his jaw in her hand. "You deserve better, Tristan."

"Why don't you let me be the judge of that?" He guided her around and they entered the restaurant.

"Miss Powers, Mr. Reuben! It's like old times. I've the perfect spot for you," Raul greeted as he patted Tristan on the back.

"Good to see you," Tristan said.

"You haven't changed a bit," Nikki added.

Raul grinned. "But you have, Miss Powers. Who would have thought you could have become more beautiful?"

Heat rose in her cheeks. "I bet you say that to all your patrons."

"Just the female ones, at least," he conceded with a laugh.

Nikki noticed all heads turning as she walked to their table. *Please don't let anyone recognize me.*

Once they were seated, Raul leaned closer to her. "If anyone bothers you, I have a private room in the back."

So he'd noticed the stares, too. "You always know the right thing to say."

Her words brought a bright smile to his round, mustached face. "As do you, Miss Sears, er, Powers."

"Can anyone join this party?" Tristan asked.

"Forgive me. Such a pretty lady outshines everyone else in the room."

Nikki laughed.

"You speak the truth, Raul. Maybe we should take that private room."

"That's not necessary, Tristan."

"If you change your mind, let me know. Would you like to see the menu?"

Both of them shook their heads.

"The usual, then?"

"Yes," they replied in unison.

Raul placed the linen napkin in her lap, lit the candles, and bowed before leaving.

"He's the type of person I'd like my children to have for a grandfather," Nikki said wistfully, watching him as he walked away.

"You never knew your grandparents, on either side, did you?"

"No. I don't remember Mama's parents. I was only two when the fire broke out. I always doubted Daddy was an orphan, though, but I'll never know for sure now."

"They have programs where you could adopt a grandparent.

Maybe we should do that with Raul?" Tristan said with a chuckle.

"I'm a little old to be sitting on his knee, don't you think?"

"Well, yes, that's probably true, but you're never too old to experience the devoted love grandparents can shower their grandchildren with. I know my parents will probably spoil my children, but that's to be expected."

Devoted love. Tristan once offered her that, and she walked away from it. Had she made a mistake? If so, it didn't matter. It was too late now. She had a world tour coming up, and he would never leave Miami and the quartet. And she would never ask him to make such a sacrifice to be with her.

"If there is such a thing as drowning in love, I think that's what will happen with your children." Did she sound envious?

"Is that so terrible?"

"Probably not."

"I don't think you can love someone too much," he said thoughtfully.

Raul returned with their *Guarapo* and poured it into their glasses. "It's like old times, seeing you sitting here together with the fireworks going off." He laughed heartily.

She'd felt the draw—the current between them—but worried it had just been her imagination. Did Tristan feel it, too?

"We haven't started fighting yet, Raul, so it's not fireworks," Tristan said, then raised his goblet, filled with the fresh sugarcane juice. "But I will toast to old times and friendship."

"Is a good thing, Tristan," he replied.

Nikki watched as the two men talked for a few more moments, listening to the music playing. She recognized the song. *Con los años que me quedan por vivir: With the years I have left to live.* The lyrics spoke of a second chance at love. Was it possible for her and Tristan? Everything felt so right. Could it just be the familiarity of it all? Or was it something more?

Dinner ended all too fast, and soon they were back on the road. Tristan decided he wanted to show her the new studio he'd installed in his condo. It gave him the freedom to practice or work on composing, he had said, without worrying about disturbing anyone.

"They've painted." She noticed as he pulled up the gated garage.

"Yeah, our maintenance fee skyrocketed after they hired a designer for the common areas and outside."

"It's hard to tell if the stain is off-white or actually yellow."

"Bite your tongue!" he said as he cut the engine. "Nothing is just white or yellow. The exterior is Corinthian Column."

She giggled as he said the words in a foreign accent, obviously pretending to be the designer.

"I shouldn't joke. I liked her work so much I had her redo my place. I think she called it neoclassic or something like that. I call it dark and brooding."

"You don't like it?"

"I did, at first. The rich wood, the intricate designs and elegance of the massive pieces of furniture were so different from my modern look."

"Hmm, if I remember correctly, your 'modern look' as you call it, was really just your stark look."

"You wound me," he said, clutching his heart.

"A white couch, a glass coffee table, and an armchair, the color of which I can't even recall, do not make for a cozy home. I bet it looks inviting now."

"The only inviting part is my studio, in my humble, unprofessional opinion."

They stood waiting for the elevator without saying much. Tristan began to fiddle with some coins in his pocket and appeared to be watching an approaching man. If she had to guess what could be happening, she'd have thought he was suddenly nervous. But why? She'd seen his condo before.

Tristan nodded and greeted the man, but made no attempt to introduce them. When the doors swished open, he placed a hand on her elbow and guided her in. He pushed the button for the sixth floor and then for the seventh at the request of the middle-aged man whom Tristan seemed to be studying.

Before the elevator closed, three more men rushed to join them, with everyone shifting position. The heavyset man who had just joined them glanced at the buttons on the panel but did not push anything.

Tristan shivered noticeably. He stood behind the first man, staring at his neck. Then he glanced over at the trio. Sweat beaded on Tristan's forehead. She reached out to touch him just when the doors opened.

Instantly, Tristan gripped her hand and dragged her out as he pushed the man in front of them. "Hey, Pal, this is the floor," he said to the confused tenant.

The man turned, wide-eyed, and seemed to glance past Tristan. "Ah, yeah," he stuttered and moved quickly down the hall with them.

Tristan's hands trembled as he turned the key in the lock and glanced repeatedly back at the elevator. Once the door opened, he ushered them in quickly and closed it with force.

For a moment, they remained silent except for heavy

breathing. Nikki lowered herself onto the cream-colored linen couch, too shocked to really notice the new decor.

"How did you know?" he asked.

"The scar. The men. Your name's Joe, right?" Tristan answered breathlessly.

Joe nodded and pulled a handkerchief from his pocket and dabbed his face while he continued to glance nervously at the door. "Scar? Men? What do you mean?"

"Oh, what have I done?" Tristan mumbled. Then he looked at Cynthia. "What have I done?" he repeated and moved to her side. "Are you okay?"

"Yes, I think so. Just a little scared. What was that all about?"

"Forget about her, what about me?"

Tristan's eyes flashed with anger. He turned to Joe and said, "I just saved your neck. Probably at great risk to the lady here." He nodded in her direction. "If you can't appreciate it, there's the door."

"You're right. I'm sorry. Are you okay?" Joe asked her.

She merely nodded, too shook up to speak.

"What do we do now?"

"I don't know about we, but you, Pal, are going to call the police."

"I can't. Do you know what they'll do to me?"

"Then you'd better leave town. Because I'm going to make the call then."

"You won't live to see them in jail if you do." Joe's eyes narrowed, and his voice hardened with his words. "They'll kill her first." He pointed to Nikki. "And it won't be a pretty sight. Right now they probably think we're friends. I seriously doubt they'll do anything as long as we keep quiet."

She shuddered.

Tristan dropped to a nearby chair and lowered his head into his hands. She could tell this had shaken him. After a few minutes he looked up at her. "I'm so sorry, Cynthia."

Chapter 6

W hat's going on?" Cynthia asked.

Her voice sounded tender, and it made what he had to say all the harder. He studied her for a moment. She'd been quiet since Joe went into the studio to call the police. What could she be thinking? Better yet, what had he been thinking? How could he have jeopardized her life like this? A shock, like a broken viola string, hit his stomach. Was her life in danger now because of him?

"Are you going to answer me or just stare off into space?"

"I'm just trying to figure out what to do. You might be safer if you don't know anything."

"Safer? What do you mean? Are you into something illegal?"

"Me? No. Of course not. Is that what you think?"

"I don't know what to think. So, why don't you tell me," she said with a tremble in her voice. "I'm worried about you."

His heart soared, then plummeted. This was not the time. He needed to forget about his desires and do what would be best for her. He just didn't know what would keep her safe.

Cynthia moved to his side. "Whatever it is, it's eating you up. You need to tell someone. Have you spoken with Pastor Cole?"

"No. No, I haven't. I thought it was over."

"You can trust me, Tristan. I won't tell anyone. Maybe I can even help. I have friends in LA who helped me out of a jam once."

He sighed. "It all started on my birthday."

"Before or after your brothers' little prank?" she asked, sitting down beside him.

"More like during." He stood and paced in front of the large apartment windows. "My brothers didn't abduct me. I believe those three men in the elevator did. They were looking for Joe." He nodded his head toward the studio, where their guest was still on the phone. "When they figured out they had the wrong guy, they let me go. Only because the head guy insisted he didn't kill people for a living. I came so close to dying that night."

In an instant, she tucked herself into his arms. "Oh, Tristan," she sobbed.

He stared out the window as he told her about his experience, explaining how he noticed the scar on Joe's neck in the elevator and the weird feeling that overcame him when the three men got on the lift. "I guess what convinced me they were trouble was the guy with his hands in his pocket, jangling his coins—"

"You do that, too," she said in surprise as she pulled from his embrace.

"You noticed? I don't know why I started doing it, but once I saw that guy, I just knew who they were."

"I'm leaving town," Joe announced as he entered the room. "You both need to do the same. These guys play for keeps."

Tristan wanted to punch the guy, but Cynthia moved toward Joe. "Will you be okay until you can get out of here? I have a driver who could pick you up and take you to the airport."

"Thanks, Lady, but I've got it worked out."

"Cynthia, I think we need to stay out of this." Tristan stepped to her side and reached for the doorknob for Joe. "It's probably safe to leave."

"Yeah. Right. Well, ah, thanks," Joe said as he exited.

"Do you think he will be all right?" Cynthia asked as Tristan bolted the door.

"No. And I can only hope those guys thought we were friends like he said, or we might not be safe, either." He glanced at the clock and knew he needed to get Cynthia back to the hotel. "Let's wait a few minutes, and then I'll drive you back to the hotel."

"I'll call for the limo, Tristan." She pulled her cell phone from her purse and slipped a pearl earring off.

He didn't argue. He needed to try to figure out a way to tell her what had happened to him tonight. How worrying for her safety made him realize he loved her, still. It also made him realize how empty his life was without her. Just like when he'd been abducted. He'd made a vow then that he would change if given the chance. So, here it was. On a silver platter, no less. Why, then, were his feet encased in cement?

Cynthia hung up the phone and replaced her earring. "He's on his way."

She's incredible. She should be angry with him, but instead she looked at him with softness. She should hate him for putting her life in danger, and yet she was trying to make things easier for him.

"Sit down, Cynthia. I have one other thing I need to tell you."

She walked to the couch, never losing visual contact with him. He seated himself beside her and took her hands. "Tonight," he began then stopped. He took a deep breath and started again. "Tonight I realized something. Something very important."

She nodded for him to continue.

"I don't know how to tell you this or what you'll do—"

"I could never hate you, Tristan. Even if you were somehow involved in all this."

"You could never hate me, Cynthia, but could you love me?"

Her eyes opened wide.

Quickly he continued. "I realized tonight that I never stopped loving you. Even in the midst of everything, you were still concerned for that guy. You're more of a Christian than I am with your compassion and tender heart. I should have understood that when you left." The words poured out of him like a waterfall.

She blinked and looked away.

"Is there someone else?" Tristan asked, feeling like he'd just put his head under the guillotine.

He watched while she wrung her hands. "No. There's no one else, but we've been through this before. I live in LA, you live here."

"Lots of couples have bicoastal relationships. Can't we give it a try?"

"It's more than that, isn't it, Tristan? Let's be honest. You don't even know me anymore, and if I remember Tyrone and Pastor Cole, they won't be happy about this."

She had a point. And he loved her even more for it. Instead of taking whatever she could from him, she was still giving. Still ensuring he would do the right thing. "Why don't we forget about everything and start again?"

"That's hard to do since I'll be leaving tomorrow."

"Not hard at all. We have the Internet, phones, even cells and text messaging. We can be in constant touch. Let's see where this goes."

She nodded. "Okay, but no promises. If, for any reason, it doesn't work out, we just say 'we tried' and leave it at that."

"Well, it's certainly not as romantic as I had hoped, but at least we're giving our feelings a chance."

The intercom buzzed and Cynthia headed toward the door.

"Can I take you to the airport tomorrow?"

She smiled and his knees nearly gave way. "I'd like that."

He tugged her closer and barely touched her rosebud lips with his, totally aware of how high his heart now soared.

"Night," she said softly, then slipped out the door in answer to the driver's knock.

Tristan watched and waited until they entered the elevator, then stepped back inside his condo and bolted the lock.

"Thank You, Lord!" he shouted aloud as he headed to his studio. He knew just the thing he wanted to do. . .for Cynthia.

❧

Cynthia's three-day visit had turned into two weeks, and he was hoping she'd stay even longer. But when he got to the hotel for their breakfast date this morning, he knew she was leaving. How could this be? Things were working out so well, he'd been able to compose again. In fact, Cynthia had inspired a particular piece.

Plus, every night they'd gone to their old familiar stomping grounds. Places like Café Abbracci for salmon ravioli and Chef Allen's for steaks and homemade pastas. They enjoyed moonlit walks on the beach and spent time during the day with Eleanor playing backgammon and reminiscing. Cynthia had attended several rehearsals and the quartet's Friday night gig at Alono's Restaurant. It seemed like old times. Almost as if he'd never made the mistake of letting her go. They were back to finishing each other's sentences; she helped him with his search for some sheet music and even listened to his practicing. Plus, he was certain their relationship was the reason Eleanor was doing so well. Cynthia was happy, so that made her mama happy.

Now, if he could just sort out what to do. Cynthia had attended church with him on Sunday and seemed open to the gospel, but she'd yet to make a commitment. She'd scribbled down a verse from Philippians 4, and he knew it had special meaning to her. How he prayed that the peace of God would guard her heart.

Since she'd decided it was time to leave, he wondered if he should follow. His knees trembled at the thought. *Show me Your will, Lord.*

And so their last day together ended quickly. This was their final dinner together. Due to the paparazzi, they were dining in the hotel. Cynthia looked lovely in her classic white silk dress with a mandarin collar. A simple teardrop sapphire necklace twinkled against the fabric. He reached for her smooth hand.

"I've had a wonderful time while you've been home."

"Me, too."

"It's like you've never been—"

"Gone, I know. But I have," she said and looked into his eyes. "There's something you should know. Something I've never told anyone, and it would ruin everything if it got out."

"You sound worried. Don't you know there's nothing you could tell me that would make me love you less?"

"We'll see." She played with her napkin for a moment, then

continued. "When I first got to LA, I had a hard time making ends meet. Agents didn't like my squeaky-clean image, but I had bills to pay. I ended up doing odd jobs. Once I even agreed to deliver a package to the airport for a venue owner."

Already he could tell where this was going. Someone had taken advantage of her innocence and her vulnerability. Someone had abused her trust in them. He wanted to wring someone's neck. *Forgive me, Lord.*

"They arrested me," she said, staring into her water goblet.

"But you were innocent. You didn't know what the package contained."

"I received a lighter sentence, but I should have known. Ignorance isn't a defense, according to the judge."

"That's all behind you, Darling. I know you'd never get mixed up in drugs."

"Now who's trusting? How do you know I didn't get into that scene? It's tough to hold out, you know. People think it's funny to put stuff in your cola and see what happens. I needed to eat, too. Sometimes it seemed like life would have been easier if I just forgot my morals and ethics."

"Did you?" He had yet to let go of her hand.

"No, but that doesn't mean I wasn't tempted. It's lonely out there. I'm ashamed to say I went to a lot of parties hoping to catch a promoter's attention—and consider myself lucky that I made it home safely."

"I wish I'd known."

"Why? You wouldn't move to LA."

She'd never accused him of anything before and so her words stung.

"I might have. I still might."

"You have your career. It looks like the CD is selling well. And Marissa said you're booked for a movie that's filming here in Miami."

"So, I won't always have commitments here. Or maybe you won't always have commitments in LA. We're just taking it one day at a time, aren't we?"

She grinned. "Sounds like some sort of twelve-step program for Relationships Anonymous."

"Whatever it takes for us to get things on the right track, in sync."

Cynthia pulled back from Tristan's hold as the waiter placed their entrées before them.

"Do you mind if I say grace out loud? I've so much to be thankful for."

"That's just what I'm feeling. Mama is feeling better, and we're even getting along. Maybe there is something to prayer."

"Lord, thank You for this day and the fun that Cynthia I have enjoyed. We can see Your hand in everything and feel blessed. Please continue to watch over us. Bless this food and those involved in the preparation and serving of it. Amen."

"Amen," Cynthia said, then smiled up at him.

Just looking at her made his thoughts run rampant. He felt like gelatin. *I want to reach out and touch her, hold her, never let her go. I want to protect her. I want to be a better person for her. She makes my world spin on the axis of her love. Ugh,* he groaned inwardly. He should stick to composing music.

She hated saying good night to Tristan. It was their last evening together, and neither knew when they'd see each other again. Yes, they would e-mail and phone, but that couldn't replace holding hands along the sun-kissed beach.

At least she'd been able to get some of her past out in the open. If only she could bring herself to tell him about Donald.

She snuggled down under the covers and reached to turn out the light when the phone rang. Tristan. "Hi," she said softly.

"Cynthia?" a weak voice asked.

"Mama?" She bolted upright in bed, gripping the phone. "Mama, what's wrong?"

"Help."

"I'll be right there. I'll call 911 first. Hang on, Mama. I'm coming."

With trembling hands, Nikki threw on some clothes after calling for an ambulance and her driver. She ran down to the lobby and waited. As she paced, she held the bridge of her nose between her fingertips and sighed. When the limo arrived, she told him to take her home.

After all these years, she still called it home. Mama had made it a place of refuge for her. Why had she ever left? Why had she left the comfort of Tristan's love, as well? What could she possibly be looking for? Somehow she felt a little like Dorothy. She'd left in search of Oz, when everything she needed had been right here in Miami.

Oh, God, please keep Mama safe. Her sudden prayer startled her.

Traffic quickly thinned and her driver picked up the pace. She arrived at the apartment just as they were taking Mama out.

"Cynthia," her mother said through the oxygen mask.

"I'm here, Mama. I'm coming with you."

In the ambulance, with sirens blaring and lights passing in a blur, Nikki sat with her mother, holding her hand and praying. When they reached the hospital, an orderly and two nurses escorted the ambulance attendants into the ER. Nikki slowed her steps as they shouted orders for so many millimeters of a drug and demanded to know Mama's BP. It appeared so unreal. Everyone, except her, had an important role. There was nothing she could do to help Mama.

Time stood still as she watched the medical team work with precision. Sights and sounds floated around her, but nothing penetrated her thoughts. She felt frozen in time.

"Why don't you go out to the waiting room?" An orderly motioned toward her. "We'll call you as soon as she is stabilized."

Robotic feet carried her away from the dramatic scene. Somewhere a voice told her to stay, to insist they let her be with Mama, but her feet were moving. She couldn't fight them as they took her farther and farther away.

Chapter 7

Nikki jumped when a nurse touched her shoulder. "You can see her now."

She followed wordlessly back to the cubicle and sucked in a breath as she saw her mother, pale and fragile, lying in the bed.

"She's resting," the nurse said. "The doctor will be in to talk with you in a minute. You can stay with her as long as you like. We'll be moving her to ICU soon."

"Thank you," Nikki uttered, but the nurse had already slipped away.

When they came to move her mother, Nikki went to a vending machine to get some coffee. Her hands shook so badly she could hardly hold the cup without spilling.

She tried to calm herself. The doctor had said this was just a wake-up call for Mama and that he felt certain, in time, she would be fine. Nikki needed to cling to those thoughts. Yet, when she entered Mama's room, her whole world looked black with fear.

Tubes filled with air swooshed. Machines beeped or pumped, and her mama looked lost in the bed. Nikki moved cautiously to her side and took her hand.

"Oh, Mama," she whispered through tears.

Eleanor reached out for her.

They remained silent, clinging to one another. With her eyes misting, Nikki spoke impulsively from her heart. "I wanted to make you proud of me, Mama."

"Baby, don't you know?" her mama's voice rasped and halted. "I *was* proud of you the moment you took your first breath. You filled my heart and my life." She coughed and clutched her chest. "Is that why you left?"

She nodded, unable to speak while the tears pooling in her eyes escaped down her cheeks.

"Cyndi-Ann." Her mother paused. "You could be a homeless person or a poet laureate and I'd still be proud of you. It's what's in here," she said pointing to Cynthia's heart, "that counts."

Nikki watched as her mother struggled for life-giving breath. The machines whirled relentlessly in her ears. She didn't understand. How could Mama be so proud and yet criticize everything she ever did?

"Tell me," Mama whispered.

"Tell you what?" Cynthia leaned closer to hear.

"What have I done to make you think I didn't love you?" It wasn't an accusation.

Without thinking, she replied, "Like me taking you shopping. You didn't want to go. You told me to save my money. It seemed as though I was never good enough." She regretted the comment the moment it spilled forth. What if her mama died and these were the last words she heard?

Mama's eyes drifted closed, and for a moment silence

hung in the air like the calm before a storm. Nikki squeezed Eleanor's hand.

A solitary tear found its way down the side of her mama's face. "I didn't want your money; I just wanted to be with you. Nothing fancy. Just you and me," her voice faltered.

"I'm sorry I didn't call or write very much. I thought you'd. . . Well, it doesn't matter what I thought. From now on, we're going to be the best of friends. I'll stay here in Miami until you are better. And then. . .then we can think about moving you to LA."

Eleanor shook her head slightly. "It's okay, Baby. I know you love me." She coughed and winced.

"You need to rest," Nikki said, but her mother continued.

"And you need to know I love you."

A sudden alarm shrilled the small antiseptic room. As nurses and a doctor rushed in, Nikki backed away from the bed. She watched with horror as they struggled.

Lord, help her!

In that instant Tristan appeared in the doorway. He moved to her side silently and took her in his strong arms. He whispered in her ear, "Have you prayed?"

She nodded while uncontrollable sobs wracked her body. Tristan gently guided her through the doorway and down the hall to a small waiting area. They were alone.

She struggled to regain her composure as she dabbed at her eyes with a tissue Tristan had handed her. When there was nothing left but shreds, she reached for another one from the nearby box. "Thanks for coming. How did you know?"

"You're a celebrity, Nikki," he said softly.

Finally, after all her attempts, he stopped calling her

Cynthia. "Don't call me that. I wish I'd never—"

Tristan interrupted her. "Don't, Babe. Don't do this to yourself. Eleanor always understood why you had to leave. It was me who didn't. She supported your dream. Whether you made it to the top didn't matter to her. The fact that you were out trying, spreading your wings, is what made her so very proud."

"Don't talk like she's dead," Nikki yelled at him. "And don't tell me what she felt or thought. I've been gone for six years. How could she still love me?"

"The same way I still love you."

She stopped playing with the tissue and stared up at him. His eyes were warm and comforting, and she yearned to be back in his arms.

"Miss Powers?" the doctor asked as he approached.

She nodded.

"I'm sorry," he began, placing a hand on her shoulder and gazing at her with a look of concern. "She's had a serious attack this time. We'll need to try to stabilize her and keep her that way until we can operate."

Everything started to spin. Strong arms gripped her, but she could feel herself falling. Like Alice in Wonderland, the world blurred as she plummeted past it all. Fear sucked her breath away while she waited to hit bottom.

❧

Nikki sat straight-backed in a pew near the front of the sanctuary. Tears threatened to escape. The quartet had just finished playing "Ave Maria," her mama's favorite, and it had been lovely. Though Mama was recovering, the song brought renewed fears. It had been five days since Mama's heart surgery, and it looked like the crisis had passed.

Nikki moved over as Tristan and Eva slipped in beside her. Pastor Cole took the pulpit, but Nikki never heard a word he said. Suddenly, it was like she was all alone in the church. Just her and Jesus. Silently, she poured out her pain and hurt, knowing He'd never stopped loving her. The verse that Pastor Cole had shared a few weeks before had been a salve to her wounds. God had given them all a second chance thanks to Mama's close call. With His help, she was going to make things right between herself and Mama.

When the service was over, Tristan and Nikki left quickly for a brief check on Eleanor, who was to be discharged tomorrow. Her color was returning and she seemed stronger every day. After a short visit, Eleanor shooed them out of her hospital room, knowing it was her daughter's last day in Miami for awhile.

❧

"Where are we going?" Cynthia asked as they drove along South Dixie Highway.

" 'Tis a surprise, Milady," Tristan said with a wink.

She slid her butterfly-shaped sunglasses down her nose and laughed. "The festival?"

"Should I risk taking you there? Perhaps they will whisk you away as the most beautiful belle of the ball." Though he was teasing, in his heart he truly believed she would be the most gorgeous woman at the Renaissance Festival. The quartet had longed to play at Villa Vizcaya, but such a dream had never materialized. Still, the stunning Italian villa replica dimmed when compared to the many facets of Cynthia's personality.

"Hardly." She waved her hand in dismissal. "I've not the charm and beauty those ladies have."

"I beg to differ," Tristan said.

"Will we have time to watch the chess game?"

"Much awaits your pleasure."

The drive to Vizcaya was short. Cynthia jumped out of the car before Tristan could get her door.

"Wait," he hollered. "Or have you forgotten I'm coming?"

"You know how much I love this place."

Indeed he knew. The sights and sounds were like a buffet. What would they do first? Should they visit the tearoom? Or wander the gardens? Perhaps they'd listen to the music and watch the peasant dance troupe. No matter what they decided, Tristan knew nothing could spoil this day.

Hand in hand, they wandered around the grounds. Cynthia seemed happier than he'd ever seen her.

"Isn't this fun?" she asked as they stopped for a moment.

"I'm rather enjoying it." He pulled her into a quick embrace and then released her.

"Shall we head over to the chess game?" they both asked at the same time.

The human chess game, played out like a scene from a Shakespeare play, was popular with the visitors. Their performance, with replica weapons, must have taken years of practice to ensure no one was hurt.

"Is there anything else like this anywhere?" Cynthia asked, watching the heavyset black pawn pin his opponent to the board.

"I'm sure they take this show on the road. One can't make a living displaying their fine rapier wit once a year."

"And you thought I'd miss that line, didn't you?" she asked as she lightly punched him in the arm.

"Ow." He rubbed where she'd hit him. "What do you mean?"

"Rapier wit," she replied, pointing to the game. "They're using rapiers."

They laughed together.

"C'mon, let's get some food," Tristan said a short time later. They filed out through the crowd toward the court.

Once comfortably seated on the ground, they tore their bread apart and shared the cheese, sausages, and fruit.

"Mmm, you've got to try this," Cynthia said as she slipped a piece of cheese into Tristan's mouth.

"Yuck, what was that?"

"What? You didn't like it?"

He studied her for a moment and then said, "That'd be an understatement."

"Well, that's good that you don't like it. All the more for me."

"So, pray tell, is there anything here," Tristan said as he pointed to the array of food, "that you don't like?"

"Me and food are good friends, Sire. We won't be parting with nothing."

"Then I shall have to take what I want."

Cynthia leaned back in mock fear. "Oh, no!"

"I could be persuaded to leave the food in exchange for a kiss from your lovely lips." He puckered up.

She looked at the food, then at him, then back to the food. " 'Tis an easy choice, then," she said. "I shall have to resign myself to your tender lips, since not an ounce of food could I let leave my sight."

Tristan leaned forward to plant a little peck, and as he did, she slipped another piece of the disgusting cheese between his lips. He didn't know whether to swallow it or find some inoffensive way to remove it.

Cynthia held her stomach as she roared with laughter.

He finally swallowed. "You shall pay dearly for that." He leaned forward to embrace her, and she scooted backward. He fell onto the blanket and nearly landed on the food.

Immediately, Cynthia appeared contrite. He took advantage of the situation. "Oh, oh, my back."

"Your back?" she asked, scrambling closer.

"Oh, I'm in pain," he said with a wince for good measure. When she was close enough, he reached out and enfolded her passionately into his arms. "And the only thing that will take this pain away is the sweet kiss from the one who loves me."

Cynthia's eyes widened, but not a word of protest escaped her mouth. Probably only because Tristan had already claimed her lips. He felt her tremble. Aware of his own desires, he pulled back.

Silence hung in the air like a giant flag, limp from lack of wind. Should he apologize?

"I'm sorry," they both spoke at the same time and then laughed.

"We're always doing that," Cynthia carried on.

"It's normal when two people have been together as long as we have."

Cynthia stopped gathering their things. "But we've been apart longer than we were together."

A feeling of discord washed over him. What did her comment mean? Was he about to lose her all over again?

Chapter 8

Eventually, it was time to return Cynthia to the hotel. A mob scene with fans and reporters crowded them as they attempted to sneak in the back door. Funny, how the media didn't seem too interested in her when she first arrived, but now they couldn't get enough of her tear-stained cheeks and rumors of an unresolved rift between Cynthia and Eleanor. Gossip made the papers saleable. But at whose expense?

Tristan wanted to stay with Cynthia in her room while she packed the last few things, but he knew that wouldn't be wise.

"I'll wait for you in the restaurant. The maître d' has assured me no one will interrupt us at dinner."

She nodded.

He kissed her cheek and brushed his finger lightly down her nose. "I'm proud of you."

She turned away.

He knew his words had reminded her of Eleanor. "You've got to believe her, Cynthia. Eleanor is very proud of you. She understands you have to go. She wouldn't lie."

"You're right. It's just so hard."

"I don't know how either of us will survive until you come back."

"You'll manage. Just let her win one or two games of backgammon, okay?"

"Anything to make you happy."

❧

Tristan glanced at his watch. Just how long did it take to pack? Worry creased his brow. He stood to go check on Cynthia, but she appeared in the foyer of the restaurant.

He moved and held her chair out for her, pushing it in slightly when she sat down. "I ordered you an espresso."

"Thanks."

He watched her for a moment. She seemed pensive and wondered what sort of thoughts were running around in her pretty head. He picked up the menu. "Any idea what you'd like to eat?"

"Probably just a salad. I'm not very hungry."

He reached for her hand. "Why don't you stay a few more days until you're feeling confident Eleanor is better?"

"I can't. I've put things off long enough. I need to get back."

Should he offer to go to LA with her? Maybe it was too soon. And what about the quartet? He loved being a part of the group. Did that mean he didn't love Cynthia? *This is ridiculous.* Of course he loved her. So why couldn't he follow her? Because he hated change. He only knew the life he had. It was secure. Safe.

"Tristan, are you listening to me?" Cynthia's soft voice broke through his reverie.

"Sorry. I'm just trying to sort things out in my mind so I could go with you to LA." How could he have said that?

"With me?"

"Not tonight, but once I get everything settled here."

"Now's not a good time, Tristan."

"We don't have to get married right away. I just want to be there for you."

"We'll talk about this more later."

"You sound like you don't want me to come to LA." He hoped she'd help him understand why she didn't appear happy about his idea.

She seemed to hesitate.

"There you are, you tramp!"

Tristan spun around. An angry man reached for Cynthia's wrist, and she cried out. Tristan rose to his feet.

"I wouldn't if I were you." The man glared at Tristan. "The papers would just love to see us fighting over her. Or did she forget to tell you she's engaged?"

Cynthia started to cry.

He looked at her and then at the man who still held her wrist. Could this explain why she didn't want him to come to LA? Did she need to get rid of her fiancé first?

"Donald, please," she started.

"I don't see a ring on her finger, and it looks like the lady doesn't want to be disturbed by you. So why don't you just get out," Tristan interjected, wishing his sudden niggling doubts would disappear as quickly as they arrived.

"You think so, Bub? What does this tell you?" Donald reached for a chain hidden beneath Cynthia's collar. He pulled it out of her blouse. "This is my ring."

In a flash of anger, Tristan grabbed his wallet and tossed some bills on the table.

"Tristan," Cynthia pleaded.

He ignored her and walked out of the restaurant.

❧

Tristan folded the newspaper and threw it down. Cynthia's picture was plastered across the front with Donald gripping her wrist. But worse than that, an undisclosed source had revealed her drug arrest, complete with a mug shot. So much for the pure image her manager promoted.

He should never have walked out on her last night. He should have given her a chance to explain, but she didn't seem to be offering any explanations. Besides, she knew how to get in touch with him. He'd given her his E-mail address, and she already had his cell and home phone numbers.

So why hadn't she called?

Why didn't he call her? Because she was engaged. He didn't need a brick house to fall on him. She hadn't wanted him to move to LA. Now he knew the reason.

Chapter 9

"If your face gets any longer, we're going to call you hound dog," Tyrone said as he punched Tristan's shoulder.

"Yeah, well I seem to recall a similar expression when things were not going too well with Cassy, so a little understanding might be nice."

"Hey, don't remind me."

"Sorry. I just keep hoping she'll call."

"Has she ever before?"

Tristan shrugged.

"She's not the type. You've got to call her."

"I'm not the one engaged to someone named Donald."

"I think he's just yanking your chain, Bro. It's clear she loves you. And only you."

"She did nothing to clarify her feelings at the restaurant. And besides, I offered to go to LA and she refused. Why? Because of Donald."

"Did you ever think that maybe she knew your moving to California would not be a good thing? Maybe she wanted to go back and try to arrange it so she could live here or something just as romantic."

"Are those Cassy's words?"

Tyrone grinned. "Maybe."

"Let's change the subject. I finished that piece I've been working on. Want me to play the melody on the piano?"

"Sure."

When he hit the final note, he heard a small round of applause.

"That's incredibly beautiful," Eva said.

"Thanks. I don't know if it's suitable for the group, though."

Rissa leaned over the piano. "I think so. But the title makes me think it's actually for someone else."

Tristan grabbed the music and folded it over. "It's just a working title. We'll find something suitable once we fit it into the repertoire."

"Now I'm curious," Tyrone said. "What's the title?"

Tristan could feel his Adam's apple bobbing in his throat as he swallowed.

"It's for Cynthia, isn't it?" Eva asked.

He lowered his head and nodded.

Tension filled the air for a moment, then Tyrone said, "Okay, gang, we need to get practicing. We sure were sloppy at the Wallace wedding last week."

Everyone laughed. They'd played so well, they'd picked up two more gigs.

Tristan was grateful that Tyrone had shifted the attention off of him. Now if he could just shift his attention to his playing instead of trying to find a better title for his composition. "Cynthia's Theme" wasn't suitable.

❧

Nikki picked up the portable phone by her four-poster bed,

held it for a moment, then placed it back in the cradle. If Tristan had thought there was hope for their relationship, he would have contacted her. He wouldn't appreciate her calling him. Especially not now. It had been three months.

The thought caused a cold shiver up her spine.

Besides, she was certain, in his anger, he'd told the press about her arrest. She thought she could trust him, yet the minute things got rocky, he couldn't leave fast enough.

Of course, she really should thank him. Donald had held her little secret over her head for years. Even though she had psychologically departed the relationship long before she broke up with Donald, he didn't seem to get it and continued to threaten her.

Once Tristan leaked her arrest to the media, Donald had no more control over her. She'd thrown his stupid ring in his face and finally been free.

Only she'd trade it all for Tristan. When he'd told her he wanted to move to LA, she fell in love with him all over again. She could hardly wait to get back and cancel her world tour, sell her place, and surprise him by coming back to Miami. She couldn't take a year being away from Tristan right now, and she knew he couldn't leave the quartet. But all her dreams had gone up in flames.

She could forgive Tristan for giving the press the scoop about her arrest. She could forgive him for not sending Donald packing. But she found it hard to forgive him for not contacting her. Surely, he meant all those things he said to her about love. Or had she just been too trusting again?

The intercom buzzed.

"I'll be right down," she told the driver.

Well, this was it. She was leaving LA for good. Though it had never felt like home, she felt a twinge of sadness to be going. This was the school of hard knocks, and she'd passed. Where life would lead her from here, she didn't know. But God did, and that was all that mattered. It was time to return to Miami and work on her relationship with Mama before it was too late.

I'm so afraid, Lord.

She stopped and glanced around her apartment. Did she have everything? Everything but her heart. She'd given that to the only man she ever loved.

"No tears!" she told herself as she clutched the bridge of her nose and stepped out of the building.

Later, when the plane finally drifted high above the ground, Nikki let the tears slip unbidden down her cheeks.

God, I hope I'm doing the right thing.

Tristan scoured the papers on a regular basis for information about Cynthia. Her world tour—the one he'd known nothing about the night of the scuffle with Donald—had been canceled amid endless speculation. It had been costly to her career. So many times he'd typed a brief E-mail just to see how things were going, but always he deleted it before it could be sent.

As the weeks and months drifted by, Cynthia seemed to vanish from the media. He'd heard about a sold-out concert in Denver, but she'd refused any interviews before or after the show. She'd even canceled her appearance on a late-night talk show two weeks ago. Though the exposure would have been wonderful, Tristan felt it might be a good move.

He couldn't stop thinking about her, wondering how she was. So why didn't he call her?

He'd had a perfect excuse last week when the three thugs who'd abducted him were picked up on other charges relating to gambling. Guess that's what they wanted Joe for. A gambling debt. It would have made a good excuse to phone and tell Cynthia his life was safe again, please come home. But he didn't.

He felt like a heel. If the shoe had been on the other foot, Cynthia would have called him.

Chapter 10

Sitting in Venture Park, Tristan turned up the volume of his MP3 player. He wanted to shut out the world and listen to his heart. Cynthia had been gone three months, and he couldn't take it any longer.

What would it cost him to go after her? Did it matter?

The quartet could always find someone else. And anyone could do the books. Maybe not as dedicated to detail, but the IRS assured him he didn't need to do all the paperwork he did.

As for his family. . .it might be good if he got away for awhile. The difficulty with his brothers' jealousy kept rearing its ugly head. He didn't blame them. Sometimes he felt he understood the story in the Bible about Joseph better than anyone else. Sure, leaving would break his mother's heart, but they could stay in contact.

Two down. What next? Change. His ultimate fear. Could he face it? Could he embrace a whole new life somewhere so far removed from Miami?

Besides, it wasn't like he would be moving to California all by himself. Cynthia would be there.

He took in a deep breath. He knew what he needed to do.

He needed to go to LA and find Cynthia or Nikki or whatever else she might be calling herself these days.

He wouldn't be happy until he'd made her his wife.

Adrenalin pumped through his veins at high speed, along with his thoughts. First, he needed to put his condo up for sale. No, wait, first he needed to contact Cynthia.

Tristan flew off the bench and turned to rush home. He ran headlong into a young woman. He flipped the headphones off and reached out to help the girl to her feet. "I'm so sorry. I didn't see you and with these head—" He stopped.

She stood, never taking her eyes from his.

Hungry eyes, he used to call them. And they hadn't changed.

"Hi," she said softly.

"Hi," he replied, trying to still his heart rate.

"I thought you'd be at practice."

"I was but we broke—oh, Cynthia, I mean Nikki, I don't want to talk about mundane things. I was heading back to the condo to call you."

"You were?"

Was that relief that flashed across her eyes?

"Yes. I'm coming to California. If you get your tour running again, I may even go on that with you. Who cares if they call me Mr. Sears!"

"Was that a problem before?"

"No. I just thought I'd throw it in for good measure." He could hardly contain his emotions.

She giggled.

"Well, I don't think you can go on any world tours with me."

"Of course I can. I got my grandfather's inheritance, investments, and savings. I don't need to work for awhile."

"You can't go on something that's never going to be."

He reached for her hands. "So, we'll find something else to do in LA."

"Hmm, that might be a problem, too."

Was she smiling? How he wanted to swing her around with joy! "And why is that?"

"Because I just sold my apartment."

"So, we'll buy another—"

Cynthia giggled again.

"You sold your apartment?" He led her to a park bench and they sat down.

"What's going on?"

"I don't want to be Nikki Sears anymore, Tristan. My real love is writing lyrics. So I've hooked up with a new agent who loves my work. And the best part is, I'm writing Christian songs. I think this is God's will for my life."

"I don't understand. I thought you loved being a performer."

"I think I loved the thought of being a performer. Do you know how hard it is? I'm not going to have time for my children if I'm on the road."

Tristan felt like he'd been punched. Children? Did this mean she had patched things up with Donald?

"Tristan," Cynthia said, waving her hand in front of his face. "Is something wrong?"

"You're getting married?"

"Yes, that's the plan. You can't have children without a marriage, don't you think?"

A heavy weight pushed down on his shoulders. "I hope you'll be very happy."

"I hope so, too." She giggled again.

"What's so funny?"

"You! I would have thought you would have been a little happier."

"I am happy for you, Cynthia. I hope you and Donald—"

"Donald? You think I came all the way back to Miami to tell you I'm marrying Donald?"

He gulped. "You're not?"

She shook her head. "And I should be angry with you for breaking my confidence and telling the press about my past, but it saved me from him. He was blackmailing me. Even after I broke up with him, he wouldn't let me go. I had to wear his stupid ring around my neck like some sort of leash! But thanks to you—"

Tristan jumped to his feet. "But I didn't. I never told anyone."

She stood up and flung her arms around his neck. "You didn't?"

"Nope. So, is Donald out of the picture?"

"Oh, yes, thanks to whomever shared my mug shot with the newspapers."

Newspapers. Tristan figured he knew who'd been the one. Eleanor. She must have known what Donald was doing to Cynthia and stepped in to rescue her. He wouldn't tell Cynthia because he knew, in time, Eleanor would admit her involvement.

"I'm sorry."

"I'm not, Tristan. You helped me get back on track with my faith, helped me see Donald for what he really was, and you filled my life with your love. Plus you helped me see what's important."

"And?"

"Our relationship. What do you say? Want to make beautiful music together?"

"Is that a marriage or business proposal, Miss Powers?"

"Both."

He knew he was wearing a silly grin, but he couldn't help it. "It looks like we're finally in sync, doesn't it?"

"Yes, Darling. Syncopation."

"That's it!" Tristan shouted. "That's what I'll call my newest composition. 'Syncopation.' " He reached for her hands and twirled her around, then suddenly stopped. "We forgot to seal the deal with a kiss."

"I didn't," she said with a smile.

"Guess we're not quite in sync yet. But we've got a lot of years to get it right."

Cynthia nodded as Tristan leaned down and brushed her lips with a tender kiss.

BEV HUSTON

Bev lives in British Columbia—where residents don't tan, they rust—with her husband, two children, sister, and two cats, who give new meaning to the word aloof. Bev began her writing career in 1994 when, out of frustration, she wrote a humorous column about call waiting service, which sold right away. She is a contributing editor for *The Christian Communicator* and spent the last four years as the inspirational reviewer for *Romantic Times Bookclub*. *Syncopation* is her second novella, and she knows it couldn't have been written without the love and support of family and friends. Please visit her Web site and tell her what you think of her work: www.bevhuston.com.

Name That Tune

by Yvonne Lehman

Dedication

To Elizabeth and Adam
for their invaluable music information

Sing joyfully to the LORD, you righteous;
it is fitting for the upright to praise him.
Praise the LORD with the harp;
make music to him on the ten-stringed lyre.
PSALM 33:1–2

Chapter 1

On Friday morning, Eva Alono acknowledged Tristan with a "Hi," mingled with the other quartet members greeting him as he walked through the doorway of the practice room with the morning mail. Even when he said, "This one's from Vizcaya," Eva felt a sense of regret rather than hope. She remained seated and kept rubbing her horsehair bow across the rosin, preparing it for the practice session. Next, she'd make sure her violin strings were in tune.

Tristan walked closer. "Addressed to you, Eva."

"Me?" She quickly laid her bow aside and took the letter. Normally, since she'd contacted Vizcaya, they'd sent seasonal programs addressed to the Classical Strings Quartet, not her personally. One of her major goals was for the quartet to become recognized in their hometown of Miami. If their résumé could include having played at Vizcaya, they'd have made their mark locally.

She'd sent their press kit to the museum over two years ago and was left wondering if they'd trashed it. Excitement mounted as she held the envelope up to the light from the window, trying to see inside. "Is it an invitation? Or just more of their promotional material? Oh, I can't look."

Tristan laughed. "You'll never find out that way."

Rissa reached out her hand. "Here, let me."

"No." Eva lowered her arm and held the letter close to her chest.

Amid the sighs and head shakes, Tyrone drew out a low, plaintive moan from his cello.

Rissa turned away. "She's not going to open it. Let's get on with our practice. I have a date with my mate."

"Okay," Eva retorted. "I'll do it. Where's a letter opener?"

"On the end of your hand," Tristan said.

Eva shook her head. She couldn't open it with her finger and chance leaving a ragged edge. If this was an invitation or even a belated personal response, it belonged in the quartet's scrapbook and a copy in her personal one.

Rissa produced a fingernail file.

Eva read the letter, occasionally glancing up at the expectant faces. She tried to keep her own face straight. Finally she could stand it no longer. "Yippee! We've hit the jackpot. Who says a prophet's not respected in his own hometown?"

The group's excitement matched Eva's until Rissa asked the question, "What's the date we're to play?"

"During the Renaissance Festival."

"That lasts four days," Tyrone said.

"No." Eva shook her head. "They want us for only one day. They must have had a cancellation and chose us. You know they plan their programs long in advance."

"You're right," Tristan said. "The festival is only a few weeks from now. Cynthia and I are planning to set a wedding date, and we both have agreed it should be as soon as possible. We've wasted too many years apart already."

Rissa said what was on Eva's mind. "We've waited for two years just to get a response from Vizcaya. The date's not going to be negotiable."

Tyrone sighed. "You know, I have to check with my better half now before making any decisions."

Rissa cast a longing look at Eva. "We'll try our best, Eva." She glanced around at the others. "Won't we, guys?"

"Sure," both men replied and set to tuning their instruments.

The practice seemed like a waste of time to Eva. However, she inwardly praised herself for playing the required notes even if her heart wasn't in it. The entire group sounded dull and lifeless. Not long ago they would be literally jumping up and down at this opportunity. One day at Vizcaya could have lifelong career implications.

Now, it didn't seem to matter to her friends. She felt they were so caught up in their personal lives that they no longer cared about the quartet and its future.

By the time the practice ended, she felt like the letter had given her the emotion of a sugar high that had now plunged her into a deep low. The others said they'd get back to her about their schedules as soon as possible.

It began to look like one of her major goals might bite the dust. This was no longer a goal of the quartet, just hers alone.

"Let's go to lunch," Rissa suggested.

Both Tristan and Tyrone had other plans.

"How about you, Eva?" Rissa asked.

Eva shook her head. "Thanks, but I'm playing at the restaurant tonight. Mine and Grandpa's dirty laundry is piled up and so is my bedroom. Some other time, okay?"

"Sure." A light sparked in Rissa's eyes. "I can always run by SilkWood and see if Jason's free."

Eva was happy that Rissa and Jason had found each other, but she missed that closeness and time she used to spend with Rissa.

Rissa must have sensed her melancholy. "Oh, Eva. I know things aren't turning out the way we've planned for years. The quartet still means the world to each of us. It's just that right now we're caught up in having found our life's mate. You understand?"

"Sure," Eva said. "I'm okay." She forced a small laugh. "I just miss my friends."

Rissa hugged her. "We'll always be friends."

Eva nodded. "I know."

After the others left, Eva walked around in the workshop part of the basement, hardly aware of the familiar odor of wood, glue, and varnish. Her gaze swept across the repair section where some violins needed major repair while others needed only a new string.

In another section violins lay in varied stages of being made. Most of her work consisted of making the beginner violins. Some fit the hands of a small child, while others were for adults. Grandpa made most of the violins that would be played by the experts. But she was learning.

That idea didn't excite her today. She thought about how everything in her life was being turned upside down. Often, she thought about her three major goals in life that she'd planned out four years ago. One was to serve the Lord with her life and music, another was for the quartet to become known as professional in her hometown, and the last was to someday make a violin comparable to the Stradivarius.

"At least I still have the goal of serving the Lord," Eva said aloud to herself, feeling rather guilty that her tone of voice sounded resentful instead of joyful.

She walked over to the CD player where Mozart was ready and waiting since this morning, when Grandpa had listened to it. She agreed with her grandpa and former music instructors, who had said people who love Mozart's music regard it as the closest thing to heaven on earth. She pushed the Play button and welcomed the melodic tones of the great master.

As she listened, a nagging thought found its way to the forefront. Was she destined to be an old maid? She'd heard older people say they wanted to grow old gracefully. She was only twenty-six, but many people that age were married and had children. She hoped, if she must face life without a mate, she might do it gracefully.

A deep sigh escaped her throat. For a moment longer, she listened to the heavenly music while a sense of earthly loneliness wafted over her.

Later that evening, the front door of the restaurant closed behind the silhouette of a man, blocking out the bright sun that had caused Eva to blink against the evening's slanting rays.

"Welcome to Alono's, Sir. Do you have a reservation?"

"No, but I would like a table for one, please."

"I'm sorry, but tonight is reservations only. The house is filled."

He looked around. "Unless they're invisible, I would say the house is not filled and there are many available tables, Miss."

Eva took in a deep breath, steeling herself for whatever

reaction might come from informing him that the dinner hour was almost upon them and all tables were reserved. However, his head turned toward her again with a rather indignant lift of his chin. Her eyes had readjusted to the dimness of the restaurant, and her breath came out in a rush. The most telling sign was the realization that he held in his hand—a violin case.

"You're. . . ?"

Her gaze played over the dark hair that curled about his ears and down the back of his neck. Something about the curved shape of his nose and heavy eyebrows over piercing dark eyes was exactly like the newspaper picture she'd pored over not two hours ago—even to the dark suit and bow tie.

"If that means I may have a table, then yes, I am," he said.

His piercing gaze bore into hers as his chin lowered, as if he were a little boy pleading for a piece of candy. Was he flirting with her? Well, she'd encountered all sorts of guises patrons often used to get a table when none were available. She would say to him what she'd heard her parents say when some of their friends dropped in at the last moment.

"I will find you a table if I have to build it myself, Mr. Baldovino."

"You. . .own the restaurant?" he asked.

"My parents do," she said. "I'm Eva Alono."

That slight movement of his eyebrows up, then down in rhythm to his nod gave her the impression of a conductor giving his nod to the orchestra at the beginning of a concert.

Strangely, she could almost hear the music.

"Thank you," he said. "I'm Georgio to such a lovely young lady who appears to know me."

"Thank you," she said, not accustomed to such a compliment

from a famous violinist, or anyone for that matter, except maybe her grandpa. In fact, she'd never been face-to-face with such a famous violinist before. The newspaper articles and advertisements said he had been a child prodigy, the son of famous opera stars and musicians. He'd been the child actor in many productions of *Madame Butterfly,* accustomed to audiences and orchestras. In his teen years, he'd played the violin in the orchestra while his parents performed. Now, at only thirty years of age, he had become one of the most widely acclaimed violinists in the world and in a matter of weeks would be performing at the concert hall.

"I only know you from some of your publicity," she said. "I have already made arrangements for one of the best seats at your concert."

She thought he looked surprised, but he said, "I'm honored."

She smiled. "So, what can I do but offer you the best seat in our restaurant?" She picked up a printed program and stepped out from behind the partition. "We don't use menus on Fridays, we use a program."

He paused. "Is this a private party?"

"No," she said. "It's just that Friday nights are so popular, we insist upon reservations. Would you prefer a table up front?"

He followed her into the large dining area and looked around at tables where waiters and waitresses were ensuring their stations were properly set up. "Perhaps near the stage," he said, "at the side."

Eva felt like she was walking on air and at the same time was afraid she'd trip over her own feet or bump into a table. She felt sure he'd wanted to sit at the side so he wouldn't be in the light from the stage when the entertainment began.

The thought of that caused her heart to drop into her socks—except she wasn't wearing socks. How could she possibly play the violin with Georgio Baldovino listening?

Poorly, probably!

At least she was dressed elegantly in a Spanish-style red dress with a vee neckline and a multilayered gold necklace. She wore large hoop earrings, and her dark hair was pulled back into a twist, adorned with a gold clasp. On Friday nights, when her schedule allowed, she donned Spanish-style clothes and became part of the restaurant's entertainment. Tonight, the maître d' was delayed, so Eva was elected by her parents to seat any patrons with reservations who might come earlier than the dinner hour.

Georgio approved of the small table for two at the side, where he would have a perfect view of the stage. "Very nice." He stood holding on to the back of the chair. "Would you join me for a moment, or are you too busy making tables for your invisible guests?"

She hoped the dim lighting covered her blush. She did not respond to his request, being sure her imagination had conjured up the thought that he asked her to join him. Such a thing could happen only in one's dreams.

"I'll. . .I'll get your water." She laid the program on the table.

He nodded and pulled out his chair, sat, and placed his violin under the table.

Eva hurried into the kitchen. Marco, the waiter for the section she'd just left, followed her in and picked up a gold-rimmed crystal goblet.

"I'll take his water," she told him.

Marco looked dumbfounded, and the chef glanced up from where he was artistically decorating dessert dishes with strings of liquid chocolate.

Lest they think Marco had done something wrong, she quickly told them about Georgio Baldovino.

The chef seemed to think his chocolate was more important, and Marco shrugged a shoulder.

"Never mind," she said. "Just don't come near his table until I give the word."

Marco filled the goblet with water. Looking unhappy, he handed it to her.

Eva took a deep breath, left the kitchen, and walked toward the table, where Georgio was looking at the program. She was placing the goblet on the table when someone walked up beside her. Perhaps the maître d' had arrived. Just as she started to let go of the glass, the person in that deep baritone voice she'd never forgotten said, "Hello, Beautiful."

More startled than when she'd recognized Georgio Baldovino, Eva whirled around, despite telling herself to remain calm upon looking at that tall, blond man with the dreamy sea green eyes. Her emotions didn't obey, and her fingers loosened from around the glass. She felt it tip. Her head jerked toward it and she tried to reach it, just as Georgio tried. Their hands collided and the goblet toppled over. The fragile glass clinked against the table and shattered as if a soprano had sung her high C note. Water poured across the table.

Eva gasped as Georgio jumped up, jerked his violin from under the table, and stepped back, causing the chair to overturn and crash to the floor.

In horror, she stared at Georgio, who held out his violin

case and gazed at it as if someone had attacked his baby. He managed to mumble in a relieved tone, "It's not wet."

"Are. . .are you?" Eva stammered.

"No." He nodded toward the table with an expression of disdain. "However, you have a completely doused table and a huge puddle forming on the floor."

Jack Darren stepped closer and reached for the centerpiece on the table. "Eva, maybe you can find a sponge or something to clean this up." He moved the centerpiece to another table. "Speaking of sponges," he said in the manner of one telling a story, "have you ever wondered how much deeper the ocean would be without sponges?"

It took a moment, then a small chuckle sounded from Georgio. Eva felt relieved that he would laugh rather than storm out of the restaurant in disgust. Eva smiled after a fleeting glance at Jack, then at Georgio, who returned her smile, then laid his violin on a nearby chair.

Jack always had a way of putting people—except her—at ease. He could turn a sticky situation into a bearable one and make you see the humor in things instead of getting bent out of shape.

The water incident began to seem trivial. Come to think of it, although proving herself to be a total klutz, she felt rather good about being called "lovely" and "beautiful" by two different men in less than five minutes.

One was a man she wanted to know better. The other was one she had tried to forget.

Chapter 2

While Eva summoned a waiter, Jack introduced himself to the man with the violin and recognized the name of Georgio Baldovino. He quickly deduced that Eva hadn't met the violinist before and they weren't here together, otherwise she wouldn't have been bringing water to his table when there were numerous waiters and waitresses about.

It held to reason she was trying to meet this fellow. Spilling his water was one way to do it, but it was also taking a chance. Had the water seeped into his violin case, this restaurant could well be in for a lawsuit.

But he didn't think she did it purposely. He'd startled her. Had he been anyone but Jack Darren, he felt sure she would have remained as calm as a cucumber. He understood her reaction. He'd hoped she'd grown out of the resentment she'd had for him and the hurt she'd felt over the entire incident with him and her grandpa. Apparently, she hadn't. Perhaps she'd never expected, and never wanted, to see him again.

Eva returned, followed by Marco, who greeted Jack exuberantly, then set about seeing that a younger waiter, obviously being trained by Marco, returned the table and floor to its previous condition.

"Again, I'm sorry," Eva said, moving closer to Baldovino. "Please excuse me now. I play the violin at the beginning of the meal."

"How delightful," Baldovino said with exuberance.

"No," Eva contradicted. "Compared with you, I'm very much the amateur."

"Ah," he returned. "And compared with you, I am the rain and you are the rainbow. And you will return to me, no?"

"Thank you. Yes."

Jack realized Eva had a confidence now that she hadn't four years ago. He stepped over to Eva, feeling daunted by her indifference to him, and this. . .exchange. . .going on between her and Baldovino. Neither suggested that he join them. "Are your parents here?" he asked.

"Yes, and I just saw Grandpa go to the family table. Go on back."

After knocking on the Alonos' office door, Jack received the kind of "welcome home" greeting from Eva's parents that he'd desired. As he expected, they told him to sit at the family table. He got a cup of coffee and seated himself with Grandpa Al, across the room from where Baldovino now sat and where Marco was putting two place settings. As if sensing someone looking at him, Baldovino's gaze seemed to meet Jack's from across the room, which was beginning to fill with expectant patrons.

Jack quickly returned his attention to his coffee cup.

"So, you found yourself, huh?" Al asked in that blunt way of his.

Jack laughed lightly. "That is why I left, isn't it?" He looked at the wise old man. "I discovered I took myself with me. Couldn't escape him. And, too," he added on a wistful note, "I discovered I left a part of myself right here in my own hometown."

Al was nodding as he eyed the waiters taking gold-rimmed crystal goblets of water to the tables.

"And you're not surprised at that," Jack said, rather than ask.

"No." Al returned his attention to Jack. "You were sort of a lost soul after your parents decided to take their production tours abroad. Left you without a base."

Jack was nodding. "Thanks to you, I found that base. And I have it now no matter where I alight. Now I'd like to give others the kind of lifeline you gave to me."

Al reached over and grasped Jack's arm. "Good to have you home, Jack."

"Like the saying goes, home is where the heart is."

Al gave him that knowing stare, then focused on the stage when Roberto Alono announced, "Welcome." After a brief greeting and informing the patrons about their choice of two entrées, Roberto announced the protocol for the evening, although it was printed on the programs.

Jack knew the reason for the programs. Many patrons came to Alono's precisely for the opportunity to see Roberto and Beverly Alono and would seek autographs from the once-famous pair.

After adding his own words about the artists who would entertain between courses, Roberto introduced Eva. He said she was one of a string quartet of growing popularity and working with her grandpa in his business of violin making and repair.

"My lovely daughter, Eva Alono, will now play our invocation on the violin." A serious look crossed his face as he looked out at the guests and said, "Blessed be the name of the Lord."

Strange, how nothing seemed to change in four years, then again everything seemed to change. The routine was basically the same. Sometimes the Alono family had groups come in and perform. Jack himself had played the piano and sung many times.

Jack remembered his parents singing there one evening. His dad played the piano while his mom stood with her arm resting on it, looking at his dad while they sang, "So in Love."

Jack had glanced at Eva and saw a special light in her eyes as she gazed at him. He had looked away and dismissed it. He hadn't been ready to consider love on a serious plane.

Now, Eva coolly disregarded him.

The restaurant patrons became courteously silent as Eva stepped into the spotlight. She smiled briefly, lifted the violin to her shoulder, placed the side of her face on the chin rest, raised the bow, and with a professional expertise began playing the beautiful melody of "Let Us Break Bread Together."

Jack closed his eyes to concentrate, not on the woman, but on the words that included breaking bread together, drinking the cup together, praising God together, on one's knees. He knew the words and the meaning of the song, which was a traditional spiritual.

He felt the joy of the song about one facing the rising sun, imploring the Lord to have mercy on him. Jack had experienced it. He had even sung it here in this place, words that had been beautiful words, but not the priority of his life. The memory of it, and the Alonos, had drawn him back. . .back to his roots.

When Eva finished, Jack, along with the patrons, applauded as she made an appreciative bow, then left the stage to share a table, not with her family, but with someone who could possibly present the opportunity for her to have a much larger audience than she could ever have at Alono's.

After the salad course, Roberto Alono and his English wife, Beverly, who looked as Spanish as any other flamenco dancer with her russet-colored hair and dark eyes, wowed the crowd with their bright costumes and fancy footwork and the flirtatious glances between the pair.

They had been professional artists of the dance before retiring. They had canceled tours and settled down to raise Eva and help Al with the care of his ailing wife. They opened Alono's Restaurant. Now they danced only for each other and to the Lord.

After the dance, Beverly and Roberto changed into evening clothes and joined Jack and Al. Waiters brought out huge round trays balanced on their hands and shoulders, then served the chosen entrées to the happy guests conversing in lively tones.

Having read the program, Jack felt they, too, would look forward to the break between the entrées and dessert when the folksinging with guitar would be performed by several of the waiters and waitresses who were students of music.

"Well," Beverly commented, "looks like Eva is occupied this evening."

Jack explained the status of Baldovino.

Of course they had heard of him, and Al filled in the rest from what he'd known and read in the paper.

"Ohh," Beverly said with lifted eyebrows, while Roberto stared across the room. "Did you know about this, Al?"

His "no" was as drawn out as Beverly's exclamation. "She would have mentioned it or perhaps have shouted it from the rooftops."

A delighted little laugh escaped Beverly's exquisite throat. "Then perhaps this is rather like a director who drops in at a community theater and discovers a star."

They all laughed lightly while Jack pasted a smile on his face.

Later, after the performances ended and guests lingered over coffee while a pianist played, Jack noticed that Baldovino was showing his violin to Eva. Likely, it was a Stradivarius. Knowing how she felt about the violin, Jack knew that would impress her more than anything he could do.

From Eva's point of view, Jack had taken from her what she had considered a most valuable and desired asset—something he could not return to her.

And judging from her reticence tonight, she had not forgiven him.

Chapter 3

Eva couldn't wait to get Rissa on the phone.

"Oh, Rissa. Sorry if I woke you. But this couldn't wait. You'll never guess whose table I shared last night at the restaurant."

Rissa laughed. "Sure I can. This will pay you back for calling before I've had my morning coffee. It's Jack. He called yesterday to let me know he's back in town and said he would surprise you at the restaurant. Ha. Gotcha!"

Eva moaned. Her emotional balloon was momentarily deflated. "No, Rissa. I mean, Jack was there, but that's not who I'm excited about."

"Well, it sure used to be," Rissa reminded her.

Eva closed her eyes against that statement and the memories it elicited. She didn't want to think about Jack. She didn't want to talk about Jack. He was history. "That was years ago."

"Okay, without caffeine I couldn't possibly imagine who would make you chance waking me early on Saturday morning if it's not Jack."

Eva wished the name Jack was not in Rissa's vocabulary!

She said with the best Italian accent she could muster, "I met Georgio."

"Georgio? What is that?"

"A person," Eva wailed.

"Well, Georgio who?"

"Rissa. There's only one Georgio."

Eva could almost hear Rissa thinking. "Not. . .not the one in the newspaper article that you cut out and danced around with!"

"The one and only. Not only did I spend the evening with him. He's coming here at ten o'clock this morning."

Now, Eva could visualize Rissa sitting up in bed with her mouth wide open in disbelief. Eva laughed. "We ate together. We talked and he asked me to call him Georgio. Annnnd. . ." She stretched out the word. "He even said I was a lovely lady."

Eva forced away the word "beautiful" that Jack had said. But that was only a phrase. She'd often said, "Come on, Baby," to her cat named Scat. But Scat was still a cat.

"Eva! That's terrific."

"Woke you up quicker than caffeine, didn't it?" Eva laughed.

"I'll say," Rissa replied. "See how things can change? Lately, you've been concerned about being an old maid. Now, you're telling me you've got two gorgeous guys at your beck and call."

"Rissa, stop that. Jack has never been at my beck and call. He wouldn't help me start a band and he left. Stayed away four years, doing who knows what!" She took a deep breath, trying to stifle her resentment of having a keen idea of "what" he had been doing.

"Well, I think Jack came to his senses and that's why he came home. And you said you're going to see Georgio this morning?"

Eva sighed. "I guess I'd better be honest with you, Rissa.

274

Georgio came to the restaurant with a purpose. He had a problem with his violin. At the music store, he was told that Al Alono was a noted violin maker and repairman. The manager told Georgio if Grandpa wasn't home, he'd likely be at Alono's since it was Friday evening. After dinner, I took Georgio to Grandpa, and the appointment was made for ten o'clock this morning. And you can believe I'll be downstairs when he comes. That is, if I ever get off this phone."

"You go, Girl, and make yourself irresistible."

"I was that last night," Eva said in an exaggerated tone. "Today, I become plain ol' Eva again."

"Honey, you could never be plain. You know the Lord works in mysterious ways. I have a feeling this is going to lead somewhere special."

Eva inhaled deeply. "Oh, Rissa. I wasn't too realistic last night in that fanciful setting of candlelight and soft music. But in the light of this beautiful clear spring day outside my window, I have to face the fact he's just coming to get his violin repaired."

"Just be there," Rissa said. "Remember, not long ago I had no idea Jason existed. Now look!"

"Oh, why are we talking like this?" Eva wailed. "A famous violinist is coming to get his violin repaired and we're talking moonlight and roses. Last night I was just a distraction for him. Who knows, he's probably even married."

"Make sure you're down there to find out."

"Okay, gotta go. I'll let you know what happens."

Eva showered, then put in a CD and listened to violin music while she dressed. Applying makeup wasn't the easiest thing to do while envisioning fragile little fairies flitting around on gossamer wings in rhythm to the airy tones of a violinist.

Unless an emergency occurred, the basement shop wasn't open on weekends and Eva often slept in on Saturdays unless the quartet was away for a performance. Was it only coincidence—or divine providence—that she had nothing pressing for today?

Although they'd had many noted violinists come to Grandpa, and he'd been a noted one himself in earlier years, no one of Georgio's stature had come to their shop.

Food wasn't on her top-priority list at the moment, but a growling stomach in front of Georgio would surely be a discordant note. She toasted a bagel, slathered it with cream cheese, and downed a cup of coffee with it.

At 9:45 she switched off the music and descended the stairs to the basement shop. She floated down as if it were every day that she dressed in a silk blouse and dress slacks and took extra care with her makeup and hair. Although she'd switched off the CD, her senses could still hear the mellow strands of Vivaldi.

That is, until she walked into the basement and saw Jack tuning the object of her frustration.

✥

Jack smiled and said, "Good morning, Eva," just as Al said, "You going somewhere this morning, Hon?"

Eva hardly glanced at Jack when she responded blandly, "Good morning." She avoided looking at his violin and bow, which he laid on the partition near the front where customers entered the basement shop. Like last night, there was no hug for Jack, no special welcome. She gave her full attention to Al.

She laughed lightly. "I always go *somewhere* on Saturdays, Grandpa."

"Mmhmm." Grandpa gave her a sideways glance over the top of his reading glasses, which sat midway on his nose. "Beautiful day for going *somewhere.*"

"Right," Jack said. "Just look out there." He waved his hand toward the wide windows and French door. "A day without sunshine is like. . ."

He waited until Eva finally looked around at Al, and at him, before he finished. Her gaze questioned him.

"Well, like. . .night," he said.

At least that got a groan from her, accompanied by a thin smile. He'd already determined to pretend he didn't notice her reserve toward him and find a way to have her dispense with it. "Al and I are going to look at a shop I'm considering opening up as a music store. Come with us, Eva. I'd like to know what you think."

Her obvious reluctance to answer gave him a good indication of what she thought. She focused her attention on the child's violin on which Al, never idle, was affixing the chin rest that had slipped off. Al finished with the chin rest and moved away to place it with items that were ready for customers to pick up. Just as she looked over at Jack and opened her mouth to respond, a movement drew her attention to the entrance.

Jack knew, without looking toward the entry, what put the light in her eyes and the heightened color in her cheeks. It wasn't the sunshine—but the one and only Georgio Baldovino, with violin case in hand. The door music chimed as he came in looking almost like a regular guy in slacks and a short-sleeved shirt.

Last night at the restaurant, Al had offered to take the violin home with him and assess the damage so that Baldovino could get his Stradivarius back as soon as possible. Baldovino wasn't willing to let the Stradivarius out of his sight. Al understood that, and they'd arranged for the violinist to come this morning at ten o'clock. That's when Jack decided to come and reassure Baldovino that Al wasn't a mediocre repairman but as expert at making and repairing violins as Baldovino was at playing them.

After his warm and gracious greeting to a most-receptive Eva, Baldovino gave Jack a curious look, then a serious one as Al walked up to the partition.

Baldovino lay the case on the partition and opened it. "This is a Stradivarius. I'm sure you're competent, but I do need to know your qualifications."

"Absolutely," Al said, gently touching the violin as if it were a newborn babe. Eva looked at it just as longingly as Jack felt.

"How long have you been repairing violins?"

Al laughed lightly. "Oh, I started about the time God gave Moses the Ten Commandments."

Jack and Eva smiled, having heard that statement many times. Baldovino nodded, but they all knew that wasn't enough.

"Seems that long, anyway," Al said. "I studied violin making in LA, the oldest and most famous of such schools. I've been repairing them for about fifty years. I began making my own about forty years ago and now they bear my own name. A mentor and friend of mine worked with Mertzanoff."

"Mertzanoff?" Baldovino's eyes widened. "The research scientist who unveiled the secret of the Strad tone?"

Al nodded.

"The Alono." Baldovino gazed at Al with an expression of awe. "I didn't make that kind of connection last night. Forgive me."

Al raised both hands. "No. No. I need no praise."

"If it's true what I've heard, you deserve great acclaim. Is it true that a group of two hundred leading musicians met in New York to select the violin they preferred and yours was chosen?"

Al nodded as Baldovino added, "And a Strad was included in the competition."

That's why Jack determined to be here this morning. To confirm to the famous Baldovino he had no reason for concern about Al repairing his violin. Jack picked up his instrument and placed it beneath his chin, lifted his bow, and played chords that Mozart had written.

Baldovino sucked in his breath, then exhaled when Jack finished. "That's a Strad."

Jack shook his head. "It's the Alono."

Baldovino's laugh was one of disbelief. "May I?"

While Baldovino played the same chords that Jack had played, Jack's immediate reaction was envy. Jack had the gift of perfect pitch and knew when an instrument was off the slightest amount. Baldovino had the magic touch—an artist with a gift that went beyond any amount of training or practice.

"That was beautiful," Eva whispered when Baldovino stopped playing.

"I've had many great artists try out various violins in here," Al said. "But never with such beauty. I am honored."

"Could I take a picture of you and Grandpa to hang on the wall with the others?" Eva asked.

"Now I am honored," Baldovino said graciously, then he resumed playing until she returned from her office with the camera.

Jack watched as Eva positioned Al and Baldovino facing

the sunlight with the workshop background of musical instruments lying on tables and hanging from hooks and displayed on the walls. Baldovino lifted the Alono in a playing position.

"I don't suppose you would allow me to use any of these in publicity?" Eva asked tentatively.

Jack could do nothing but watch silently as Baldovino's dark gaze surveyed the beautiful Eva standing in front of the door. The backdrop of sunlight made a golden halo around her dark brown hair as it lay softly against her shoulders. The blue silk blouse caressed her mature figure with a soft glow.

A smile graced Baldovino's aristocratic face as he said what Jack thought. "How could I refuse the request of such a lovely young woman? Of course, I would want to approve any project, but for my personal pleasure, I would like a picture of the three of us, then. . ." He lowered his head and narrowed his eyes in what Jack supposed was a flirtatious gesture. His voice held a baritone quality. "I would like a picture of you and me." He took the camera from her willing hands and turned. "Jack?"

Jack didn't like this at all. He didn't mind snapping the three of them. But he didn't care for the duo in which Baldovino held the Alono while Baldovino looked into her eyes and Eva stared at him with open admiration. Her gaze reminded Jack of how he felt about Baldovino's short but masterful playing of a Mozart aria. However, he suspected Eva did not separate the man from the violin playing.

The picture-taking session ended and Al, who had examined the violin said, "This is your problem. There's a slight separation here at the edge. That gives your violin an inferior tonal quality."

Baldovino nodded as if that were no surprise. "That has

happened before. You think it's the glue?"

"No, I don't think so," Al said. "If the glue were stronger than the wood, that would result in mechanical stress leading to splintered wood and separated joints. Then repair would be very difficult." He shrugged a shoulder. "This is what you can expect from having a very old instrument." He laughed lightly. "Even if it is a Stradivarius."

"Yes," Baldovino said with complete confidence. "I'm convinced you know your business." He took a deep breath. "I will leave my Strad with you." He looked longingly at it like a mother might do when leaving her baby for the first time. Then he looked at Al. "Could I take the Alono while my Strad is being repaired?"

"It belongs to Jack," Al said.

The clatter of plastic against the hardwood floor turned their attention to Eva, who stooped to retrieve a CD case she'd dropped. Her quick glance toward Jack and the slight flaring of her nostrils as if she'd taken in a deep breath were the only indications of what Jack knew was resentment seething inside her. Al grimaced slightly as he turned again toward the Strad, closed the lid, and zipped the case.

Glancing at Baldovino, who looked from one to the other, Jack suspected the man guessed more than Jack cared to reveal. A sly look appeared in the violinist's eyes. "May I borrow your violin?"

"If you need to practice while the Strad is being repaired, you may do it here." He said something similar to what Baldovino had said the night before. "I won't part with my Alono."

Baldovino nodded. "I would like to play it for awhile. And if it has the quality it displayed today, then I would like to buy it."

For the first time since Baldovino walked into the shop, or even since he'd seen him at the restaurant with Eva, Jack felt in control. "It's not for sale."

Baldovino lowered his head slightly, and his brow furrowed. "I know the cost of great violins. I'm willing to pay the price."

Jack knew the cost, too. He knew that if Baldovino played the Alono for several days, he would sell his soul for it. He was almost willing to do that now. But he could only repeat, "It's not for sale."

"Do you play this violin before audiences?"

"No way," Jack said. "I guess you'd say I just fiddle around. Jack-of-all-trades, you might say." He laughed lightly. Georgio acknowledged the comment with a nod, yet his gaze held curiosity.

Seeing Al's smile and Eva's stiff expression, Jack figured he might as well admit openly what he'd learned about his own limitations. "I don't have the concert violin touch, if that's what you mean. I could play it, yes. But not with the feeling you put into it with the first movement of the bow across the string. I'm sure that was recognized at an early age."

Georgio accepted that. It wasn't a compliment, just a fact. He gazed longingly at the Alono. "I've heard everything has its price. Think about it."

Jack didn't have to think about it. He was aware that the sale of that Alono could set him up for life without his having to start at the bottom and work his way up. It was best not to think about it. He picked up the Alono and moved it to its case. "I'll leave it here, and you're welcome to play it if I or Al or Eva are here."

Eva turned not only her head, but her entire body away from Jack at that remark.

"Thank you." Baldovino gazed a moment longer at the Alono, then the case of his Strad. Jack knew he didn't want to leave either. Then his gaze moved to Eva. "I would feel better with some kind of security. If I can't have the violin, I would like to take the girl."

Eva looked over at him, then flashed a gorgeous smile when he added as if he were modest, "That is, with her permission." While their gazes locked, Baldovino walked closer to her. "If you are willing to go with me, I would love to see some of those places we talked about last evening."

Eva nodded, without a trace of uncertainty. Her confidence had grown along with her maturity, as well it should. She had every reason for confidence. She was beautiful, intelligent, successful—what more could a man want in a woman?

"I would like that," she said.

Walking toward Jack, who stood at the end of the partition, she darted him a resentful glance and her silence spoke louder than words. It reminded him of a mild version of the way she'd looked at him four years ago when she'd stormed, "That violin should be mine, not yours!"

He wondered what she was thinking now. She no longer cared for the jack-of-all-trades with the Alono. She had shifted her affections to a master concert violinist with a Strad.

As she walked around him and toward Baldovino, Jack realized the violinist had watched every move, every nuance. Baldovino's parting glance held Jack's for a lengthy moment with something akin to challenge in his gaze. He opened the door, allowing Eva to pass in front of him. With a nod, as if he had finished a performance, Baldovino walked away from the shop with Eva.

Jack knew, without a doubt, this was a man thing.

As plain as the sunshine streaming through the glass panes, Jack knew what Baldovino's gaze had meant. He might as well have said, "It's your call, Jack. You want the girl. I want the violin. How about a trade? If you won't let me have the violin, then I'll take the girl."

The idea that Eva would have something to say about that did nothing to assuage the uneasiness Jack felt. He had asked Eva to accompany him to his prospective shop. Her response had been to walk out and get into a black European convertible with Baldovino.

Chapter 4

Eva assumed Georgio was unattached since no female was with him, nor had one been mentioned. She didn't protest when Georgio said he would like to drive, if she didn't mind. Driving was both a challenge and a pleasure for him since he was accustomed to being chauffeured so much of the time.

She felt cocooned in a world of luxury after she and Georgio were ensconced in the luxury car's deep maroon interior. Likely she would soon awaken to find this was all a dream—like an admiring fan suddenly riding around with a famous movie star. She had found Georgio easy to talk to last evening, but suddenly felt—

"Eva?"

She quickly turned her head to face him, noting that he was turned toward her with one arm draped over the steering wheel. A faint scent of musky male cologne mingled with the car's aroma of leather warmed by the midmorning sun. "Oh, I'm sorry."

"You are deep in thought," Georgio said.

She might as well be honest. "I was thinking that I feel very much the amateur in your presence."

His glance and smile were reassuring. "That is very good for my self-esteem. It gives me the opportunity to try to impress you."

"Your playing does that. I have a recording of your playing with the Vienna Philharmonic."

"Were my feet not so big, that might never have happened."

Eva looked down. "Your feet?"

Georgio laughed lightly. "You know the saying about an artist's difficulty of getting his foot in the door. It helps to have accomplished parents and relatives who have a musical history. The doors were open before I was born."

"There's something to be said about your talent."

"The genes, I think that's called." Georgio shook his head. "I doubt that any of my relatives have genes that aren't musical."

Eva laughed as he smiled. "I shudder to think what practice would have been like without the genes. Being a Baldovino, I had to become a success."

"You sound American," Eva said.

He shrugged slightly and looked over at her with a smile. "My mother is American, my father, Italian. I speak with an Italian accent when there. You know the saying, 'When in Rome, do as the Romans do.' "

"That sounds biblical, like something the apostle Paul said. Are you. . .a Christian?"

"I didn't realize that was a biblical quote." He straightened in his seat and turned the key in the ignition. "I have visited some of the finest churches in the world, but generally I have time for nothing but the violin. That is why this time of relaxation before the upcoming concert is so important to me. That

286

is why I am enjoying your company so much. You are a breath of fresh air."

Eva loved the compliment, but she felt that was a charming way of his avoiding the subject of religion. He backed the car out of the parking space and headed down the long driveway.

"Have you been to Miami before?" she asked.

"Yes, but not to sight-see. I'm staying at our family's beach house, which is used by various relatives. My visit to Miami has been primarily as a beachcomber. Of course, I do know a little about the city, the main roads, et cetera." He stopped at the end of the driveway. "Now, what sights would you like to show me?"

Eva mentioned several places including Vizcaya, hoping to get into the conversation about the quartet's invitation to play there. However, as he pulled out onto the road, he broached the subject she'd rather leave behind.

"If I'm not being too personal, what is this between you and Jack? What does that fellow do? Is he a relative? A friend?"

Eva hardly knew how to respond. "He's been a friend of the family for years. His parents are part of a professional touring choral group. Jack has a wonderful voice and has sung at the restaurant in the past. As a teenager, he stayed behind in school while his parents traveled much of the time. He and Grandpa hit it off from the first time Jack performed at Alono's. After that, Jack came often to Grandpa's shop. Jack has perfect pitch and was a great help with tone. In return, Grandpa taught Jack a lot about violin making."

Georgio nodded, with a sympathetic look, as if he were familiar with that lifestyle.

"He began to hang out at the restaurant, even worked there in the summers, and also became attached to Grandpa. Grandpa was a mentor and like a father or grandfather to Jack."

"I hope I'm not being too personal and of course you don't have to answer. But, were you in love with Jack?"

She wished he hadn't asked. "Well," she hedged, "as much as a silly teenager, and later a college girl, could be."

"You're not now?"

"Oh, please. I was a young girl. I always looked up to him because he was a few years older and all my friends swooned over him, thinking he was so magnificent. You see, when he wasn't at the shop or the restaurant, he was a knight with a Renaissance group. He wore armor and rode a white horse. I suppose, for awhile, I saw him as a real knight and I as some sort of princess to be rescued from the humdrum of life. That was. . .fantasy. I'm. . .not a teenager anymore."

She really didn't want to reveal how she'd felt rejected by Jack. However, the words spilled forth despite her preferring to change the subject. "After Grandpa gave him the Alono, he left to make his mark in the world. And stayed away for four years."

Georgio seemed to be concentrating on the traffic for a long moment. Then he spoke in a low tone. "You don't like Jack's having that Alono violin."

Eva's heavy sigh preceded her honesty. "No."

"Neither do I," Georgio said. "You and I have that in common."

❧

Eva was eager to return to her tour-guide role and switched the conversation to Vizcaya. She explained what a wonderful opportunity it was for the quartet to play at the famous museum, that it was a long-awaited goal of the group and now seemed only her goal.

Georgio raised his hand from the wheel, lifting it into the air. "Then why not give Vizcaya an affirmative answer? You would be taking nothing from the quartet. Surely they would be as receptive to a trio, duet, or even solo."

Now why hadn't she thought of that? She might even mention it to Vizcaya.

She gave Georgio a brief description as the house and grounds came into view. "Miami's famous Vizcaya Museum and Gardens is a Renaissance masterpiece," she said, "on Biscayne Bay."

He took on an appreciative look as he gestured toward the scene before him. "Ah, this resembles a lavish Italianate villa."

"It's one of South Florida's leading attractions. It portrays the history of Miami and four hundred years of European history. The architecture represents the Italian Renaissance."

"Impressive," Georgio said as he turned the wheel and the sports car crept along through the immaculate grounds.

"Around two hundred thousand people visit the museum each year," Eva said. "There have been such dignitaries as presidents, queens, kings. Also the Summit of the Americas was held here with the president and thirty-four leaders of the Western Hemisphere. Oh," she added, facing him and smiling, "and perhaps will be visited by a renown violinist."

Georgio's dark gaze and smile held warmth. "I would love to have you lead me on a tour if my schedule permits. Today, however, I would like to get my bearings here in Miami and go by the concert hall and look at the stage, if you don't mind."

"You're driving," Eva said.

He nodded and his foot pressed the accelerator.

After driving past the concert hall, Georgio said he would

like to take her to his beach house for lunch. After Eva agreed, he used a cell phone to make a call.

"Elena," he said. "I'm bringing a guest for lunch. Great. See you soon."

He didn't explain who Elena was. Obviously, he had a wife or someone staying with him. When the house came into view, Eva was mildly surprised it was an older style, then recalled Georgio said it had been in the family for a long time.

"The spectacular part of the house," Georgio said of the structure situated on an incline, "is the glass walls and windows that reveal an incredible view of the ocean."

Georgio parked alongside a rental car and a late-model economy car.

They walked up onto the open porch. At the side was a glass-enclosed piazza.

The beach house looked as comfortable and cozy inside as the middle-aged man and woman that Georgio introduced as an invaluable married couple, Elena and Victor. "They take care of the house when it's unoccupied and take care of us when we vacation here."

Eva shook their hands and got a strong impression by the pleasant way they responded to Georgio's remarks that they were not just hired hands, but they liked each other. They both excused themselves from the room.

Her eyes were drawn to a doorway across which a man, talking on a phone, paced back and forth.

"That's Hastings," Georgio said. "He is agent and public relations executive for the upcoming concert and anything that might come up as a result of the promotion." He lowered his voice and leaned near when Hastings again appeared and glanced their way. "I think all this could be done from New York via the phone and computer, but Hastings insists upon the personal touch. Frankly," he said, "I think he just likes the beach and a few days away from his wife and kids."

Eva laughed with him. "This is a beautiful place."

Hastings appeared at the doorway, covered the mouthpiece, and lowered the phone. "Sir, are you available to speak with the concert manager?"

He nodded. "Eva, would you mind waiting for me on the piazza? We can eat out there."

Soon, Elena joined her with salad, delicate sandwiches, a platter of fresh fruit, and a plate of pastries.

"Mr. Baldovino's favorite drink is coffee. But we have—"

Eva lifted her hand. "Coffee's fine with me." The two of them engaged in conversation about the lovely weather and the wonderful view.

Georgio soon joined Eva at the small white wrought iron table. He apologized for the phone call and explained a few appointments he had coming up. She wondered how he found time to relax.

Eva spread her napkin on her lap and Georgio did the same. She wondered if she should just say an open-eyed silent blessing. Her glance across the table, however, revealed him smiling.

"Do you always play an invocation," he asked, "or do you use words?"

Eva laughed. "Since I didn't bring my violin, I think words would be appropriate."

He gestured with his hand toward her and a slight nod. Eva bowed her head and said a few words of thanks for the food.

Eva really wanted to know Georgio's personal status—wife,

former wife, fiancée—but didn't want to chance giving the impression she expected something personal to develop between the two of them.

She needn't have worried. Georgio asked about her studies at the university, where she had majored in music and had started the quartet during her senior year in college. "Grandpa said he taught me to play the violin as soon as I could hold a bow."

Georgio nodded understanding. "I doubt I've ever had a day without some form of music. I consider myself fortunate for that. Speaking of music," he said as they munched on pastry and drank coffee, "why does Jack want to hold on to his violin when he claims no particular interest in playing it? Yet, he had it out this morning and offered to allow me to play it with supervision. Was he trying to impress me?"

Eva shook her head on that one. "No. Jack doesn't think like that. He would want you to appreciate it."

Georgio looked at his coffee cup for a long moment. Then his gaze met Eva's. "Do you think," he asked, "that your grandpa could make me an Alono like Jack's?"

"If he really wanted to," Eva said, "I think he could. He studied tone scientifically to discover why the violin does what it does. But—"

"Uh-oh," Georgio said. "Now comes the negative side of this."

Eva nodded. "Grandpa considers that Alono his crowning accomplishment. He's not trying to compete with other violin makers or the Strad."

She looked at Georgio's thoughtful expression as he gazed out over the ocean. She remembered that Grandpa had said he could teach her to make a violin like the Alono. After Jack left with the Alono, she wanted to show them both that she could make her own. She tried for awhile, then gave it up. Grandpa had said one must put love into the making of a violin for it to be great. She realized that if Grandpa was right, and she continued, her masterpiece would emulate a heartbreak.

That dormant ambition of hers began to stir. "Perhaps," she said and waited as the word brought Georgio's attention back to her. She lifted her chin slightly. "Perhaps I will make you an Alono."

Chapter 5

Jack sat on the front row in the sanctuary of the church, waiting to make his announcement. He wondered what he would see when he stood before the congregation on Sunday morning. Would he have to look out at Eva and Baldovino?

A part of him would be glad if Baldovino was a Christian and going to be serious about Eva and she about him. However, another part of him wanted to let Eva know how the four years away from home had changed him and had made him realize there was no other woman who touched his heart like she did. He had returned with the intention of finding out if there might be a future for them together.

Perhaps he already had his answer.

Then the pastor was introducing him, saying that most of the congregation would remember when Jack played the piano and sang solos as well as sang in the choir. "He's been in France for several years studying bow making and has returned," the pastor said, then mentioned that Jack had talked over an idea with him and the choir director. They were delighted to endorse the plans Jack had for his life and for the church.

"Jack Darren," the pastor said.

Jack walked up onto the dais. "First," he said, holding on to each side of the wooden structure in front of him, "let me say how good it is to be back. I feel like I've come home. Not only to the city, but to the Lord. I've had my training and opportunities. Now I want to give something back to this area and this church."

He glanced toward the pastor and Jim, the choir director, and mentioned that they had endorsed his idea. "We would like to form an orchestra for the church." He knew there were several in the congregation who played instruments.

"If you're interested, meet with me and Jim in the choir room after the service. The players need to have a certain level of experience. Also, in our talking about a music ministry, some of us want to teach those who would like to learn to play an instrument or learn more about singing. Just like you have your children's choirs, you can also develop a children's orchestra. This does what we are supposed to do. Train up our children in church and encourage them to use their talents and abilities for the Lord."

Jack had tried not to look directly at Eva, or anyone for that matter, but he'd felt drawn to her gaze before he returned to his seat on the front pew.

Would Eva join the orchestra? Her participation would almost ensure success. He could play the piano, she and Al the violin. Her quartet might join them. He knew a couple others in the church who played instruments, and there were surely high school band students who could learn to play church music as easily as they learned marches and tunes for their school concerts.

But, would Eva join? Four years ago she had asked him to

help her start a string band, but he had left to go to New York, then Paris. . .with the Alono to which she felt entitled.

Jack could barely keep his mind on the congregational singing, the choir's special anthem, and the pastor's message. As soon as it all ended, he hurried to the choir room. When Al came in without Eva, Jack's heart sank. When Eva walked in, his heart sang.

He felt as if the music of his heart were audible and as if a visible warm glow had spread over him. She must surely detect his pleasure at her appearance. "Eva. You'll be—"

He didn't finish saying what an asset she would be to the orchestra. She was shaking her head. "I'll hurry and get out of your way. I just wanted to ask if it will be okay if I take the Alono to Georgio's beach house for him to practice this evening."

Jack felt a rebuke form in his throat and tried not to verbalize it. After all, he had been magnanimous enough to tell Baldovino he could play it in the presence of Al or Eva. He hadn't expected it to be at the man's beach house. "This evening, you say?" managed to escape from his fractured voice box.

Eva nodded. "All afternoon he will be at the home of the concert hall's administrator, meeting Miami's important people."

"No need to explain." Jack didn't want to hear that after Baldovino associated with those "important people," he and Eva would be alone at night, at a secluded beach house by the ocean.

"Do you want the Alono to stay at Grandpa's?"

"No, no. That. . .that's fine. Of course you may take it. I made the offer, remember?"

"Thanks." She turned and walked out of the choir room, leaving him feeling like a song that wouldn't be sung.

He remembered the Eva of four years ago. The light in her

eyes each time she had looked at him indicated a young girl who wanted to be the special person in his life. He'd pretended not to notice.

Now she looked at him with mere tolerance, when she looked at all.

What were her dreams now?

To be a concert violinist?

To be the special person in the life of one?

Eva parked near the cars that had been there the day before. Georgio came off the porch when she opened the trunk to take out the violins.

"The Alono," she said, handing it to him. "And Grandpa said the Strad is dry. He doesn't like to do business on Sunday, so you can pay him at your convenience if it's repaired to your satisfaction."

He thanked her for bringing the violins. Inside, she again saw Hastings pacing past a doorway. Georgio laughed. "I think he cannot live without a telephone at his ear."

He led her into a small music room in which a baby grand piano was most dominant. They set down the violins. "You did come prepared to join me for dinner, as I asked?"

"Even if I hadn't," Eva said loudly enough for the ears of Elena, who she could see in the nearby kitchen and walked toward it, "that aroma of food would be too enticing to refuse."

A smiling Elena served them a wonderful dinner at a long, narrow table in a dining area adjacent to the kitchen, separated only by an island.

After dinner Georgio asked if she'd like to walk on the

beach. "Elena and Victor often leave after dinner," he said, "but they will stay until after we return from our walk. Although it's secluded here, I will not leave the Alono unattended." Eva appreciated that kind of thoughtfulness.

Eva enjoyed the cool breeze, the quietness of the scene except for the sound of the ocean's rhythm beneath a tranquil sky.

How different from a couple of days ago when she fretted about not having a mate. Now she walked along the beach with an extraordinarily talented man. She decided to let him lead if there were to be a conversation. After all, he had come here to relax.

"Eva," he said, after they'd walked for awhile. "Do you have a special boyfriend?"

"I haven't had time for that." Eva laughed, thinking of her full schedules for years. "After high school, there was Grandma's long illness. I moved in with Grandpa and tried to help, but Grandpa wanted to do as much as he could for Grandma and wouldn't leave her side for long. Jack and I helped keep the shop going. After she died, I had college, the quartet, and the restaurant. In the past couple of years, the quartet has had several local performances and even a cruise."

"Sounds like you have a full life," Georgio said.

Eva sighed. "Now, it looks like the quartet may break up. They're all getting married."

She felt like this might be a time to ask a pertinent question. "Are you married or anything?"

"I haven't had time for that," he said, mimicking what she had said. "I've been on a world tour for the past three years. That is how one becomes world famous. Once I have achieved a certain amount of fame, then I can refuse bookings. However—"

He spread his hands. "Am I not then obligated to the public? All is not as perfect as it might seem. Once you have reached the top, you're expected to be perfect. I must practice every day."

Eva was well aware that if she missed a day's practice, she could tell a difference in the ease of playing. And yet her requirements were nothing like Georgio's. "Is that a burden?"

He smiled. "No. I love it. It's a vital part of me. I care for my violin like a father would care for his baby. Perhaps better. But lately, I have had visions of grandeur, like finding a wife and raising a family. It would be such a change. But I am ready to think about those things."

"You have found someone you want to settle down with?"

"There should be love, no?" He spread his hands in what she was becoming accustomed to his doing often. "Oh, I know about finding women attractive and spending time with them. But, how do you know if you're in love?"

Eva thought it was love when someone was always present in your mind. When your heart leapt at the sight of him. But, even children claimed to be in love with young boys. Married people divorced who had claimed to be in love. "I'm. . .not sure," Eva said.

"Neither am I," Georgio said. "That is one reason I decided on a vacation here. To get away from the disturbance and to clear my mind."

"Is it working?" Eva asked.

He stopped and turned to face her. "I think it's beginning to. And a big part of that can be credited to you. Thank you."

Eva looked up at him and met his thoughtful, questioning gaze. Was Georgio trying to forget someone?

Could Georgio make her forget what she had felt for

Jack—both the love of the past and the resentment of the present? She didn't protest when Georgio lifted his hand, placed a finger beneath her chin, and bent to gently press his lips against hers.

The sweetness of the kiss was like a thank-you.

He straightened and said, "You are so kind to spend time with me. I am grateful. You are teaching me many things."

"I? Teach you? What would that be?"

"About your city, you, those around you, your everyday life, confiding in me about some of your hopes and dreams and disappointments. I was never allowed to express any doubts or fears or apprehensions about myself or life. You do not. . .um. . .take relationships lightly. What I mean is, you are a Christian. You do not just. . .enjoy life and have fun."

Eva wasn't exactly sure what he was asking. "I do enjoy life and have fun, but I don't consider fun being anything that can harm my body or emotional well-being. You're right, I don't take relationships lightly."

He was nodding, saying, "Umhmm. You have that morality faith as was expressed at your parents' restaurant."

"I'm a Christian," she said. "And morality is part of it. Are you?"

"No. I believe in God, but I think there are many roads that lead to Him. Why do you not believe that?"

Eva wondered if she were adequate for this debate. "Anything I might say doesn't really matter. It only matters what God says. And the Bible, which I believe is His book to us, says that Jesus is the only way to God. I'm not saying it. God said it."

"Really?" He looked rather surprised.

Eva felt so inadequate. "Well, I don't know how else to say it."

"You did fine," he said. "Just fine."

Eva watched him as he looked out at the ocean with a rather amused look on his face and that mysterious twist of his lips resembling a smile. He did not look disturbed or intrigued. Apparently he wasn't and didn't take her words to heart as he gazed out toward a horizon that had disappeared into the sky.

Suddenly he stopped. "Shall we return to the beach house? I suspect you and I could make beautiful music together."

If she'd been chewing any, she would have swallowed her gum. Since she wasn't, she swallowed a gulp of air and had to struggle not to cough.

Did he mean they might make music together. . .personally?

She looked over at him, and he gave her a sideways glance. A small light sparked his dark eyes, and he smiled as they walked back toward the beach house.

He led her into the music room. "Would you like to play the Alono?" he asked.

She stared at it. She would not be able to play it with ease, not with those old feelings rising up inside her. "No, I really wouldn't."

He played briefly on the Strad. "The tone sounds as good as ever to me," he said. "Would you like to play this one?"

She gladly took it.

From the instant she placed the violin on her shoulder and lay the side of her chin against it, Eva felt what Georgio had said about this being one's baby. Her own violin was a huge part of who she was and what she did. Hers was a fine violin; however, Georgio's was the world's best. She was afraid her hand would tremble and she'd be the world's first to screech a bow across the strings of a Stradivarius.

Willing herself to relax, she drew the bow across the G, D, A, and E as a warm-up. The tone was so easy, smooth, and clear. They played together some classical fun tunes she knew by memory that the quartet often played.

Georgio placed Johann Sebastian Bach's *Concerto for Two Violins in D Minor* on the stand. She played, looking at the music, while Georgio played from memory on the Alono.

Yes, they made beautiful music together.

Afterward, Georgio played solo while she became the captivated audience.

When he finished, he bowed to her applause. He returned the Alono to its case and handed it to her.

"The Strad is my baby," he said. "But I wouldn't mind having a second child. I would need to play more on the Alono to make sure it is all I believe it to be."

Eva understood. "And I wouldn't mind playing more on the Strad."

"Deal," he said. "I don't want to take you from your daily activities, and I have appointments tomorrow. All right if I call you?"

"Sure. If I'm not in, leave word with Grandpa or on the answering machine."

He smiled as he walked her to her car. "We did indeed make beautiful music together, no?"

She returned his smile. "Yes."

❧

After returning home, Eva took the Alono to her room and opened the case. She looked at it a long time. Then she reached out to touch it. She hadn't wanted to play it.

She had loved Jack with all the love a young girl could have. Now, she could understand his going away to music school, then Paris to learn bow making. She couldn't blame him for taking the violin since Grandpa had wanted him to have it.

Why couldn't she put the past behind her? Why, as she looked at the Alono, couldn't she see the face of Georgio Baldovino instead of the smiling, handsome face of that blond, green-eyed man that she'd be better off to forget?

Needing to get things settled in her mind once and for all, Eva went into the kitchen, where Grandpa was having a snack, like he always did before going to bed.

She sat across from him at the table and told him about her evening at the beach and how much Georgio admired the Alono.

Grandpa nodded and smiled. "I knew the moment he heard it, he was impressed with the tone."

"He really wants it," Eva said.

"If Jack were going to sell it, that would have been done while he was trying to find out where he fit in with the music field. I don't believe he will ever sell it now."

Eva decided to ask what she wanted to know for four years. "Grandpa. Why did you give the Alono to Jack?"

He looked over at her for a long time. She thought he wasn't going to answer. Finally, he took a deep breath, then exhaled. "I know you didn't understand that, Eva. And I felt bad about it. But I have to do what I think is right. You remember what I told you, when I said I was going to give it to Jack?"

Eva nodded. "You said I should make my own."

He nodded. "You didn't take that the way I meant it. You

wanted to be a violin maker. Then your goal should not be to have the Alono, but to make a comparable one."

"I. . .tried for awhile," she said.

"Yes, I know. But a violin that plays beautiful music must be made with love, not resentment. That's why I couldn't make Alonos every day of the week. I reached my goal. I had nothing more to prove. Afterward, I just wanted to make wonderful instruments for musicians to play, not those only for the rich and famous. You understand?"

"Yes, and I could understand if you wanted to keep it or have it put in some museum or music center or rented it out to classical violinists. But. . .give it to Jack?"

Grandpa nodded. "I did that for two reasons."

She waited.

That incredible look, full of love, crossed his face. . .the look of love and of teacher, older, wiser, and she felt she was in for a lecture.

"Because he needed it, Child. The same principle as when Jesus was asked why He ate with sinners. He said that the well don't need a physician but the sick do. Jack was at a turning point in his life. A young man with dreams, uncertainties, opportunities, beginning to get off the straight and narrow. You had me and your family. Jack had a piece of wood."

Finally, he said, "If you had that Alono, you wouldn't need to make your own. But if you wanted to be a great violin maker, you don't need my Alono. You make the best violin you can, using the mathematical equations with all the ingredients. Then you listen for the tone and with your heart. When it stirs your emotions, you have made a great violin."

She waited. He didn't speak further.

"Grandpa, you said you gave it to Jack for two reasons. What's the other one?"

"That," he said, in a kind but firm tone, "is not for me to say. Both the Alono and the explanation now belong to Jack."

Chapter 6

On Monday, Eva and Tristan went to Vizcaya to finalize plans for their playing instead of chancing their response being lost in the mail. That done, they set up a practice session for the next morning.

When she returned home, Grandpa said Georgio had come and paid his bill. He also said the sound of the Strad was perfect and thanked him profusely. He asked Grandpa to give her the message that he was expecting a call from California and would not be able to practice on the Alono that evening, but he hoped they could get together soon. He wanted to test the sound of the Alono further.

Eva wondered if Georgio would call for her to bring the Alono to his beach house again on Tuesday.

Ironic, she thought, that it was the Alono that played a part in her facing facts that Jack hadn't cared for her in a special way. Now the Alono was one of the reasons she and Georgio spent time together and had enjoyed a wonderful evening the night before.

That night, before falling asleep, she prayed that she might stop thinking of Jack and how she used to feel about him and resenting him for not returning her affection.

As she thought of Jack and Georgio, she admitted to herself that one could not force oneself to think of another in a romantic way. She drifted off to sleep with the memory of the music that she and Georgio had elicited from the Strad and the Alono the night before.

On Tuesday morning, Eva went downstairs shortly before nine o'clock. Tristan was talking with Grandpa, who was replacing a broken string on a child's violin.

Tristan greeted Eva, and the two of them headed for the music room, where Rissa's voice became audible. Eva stopped short at the doorway for an instant when her gaze met Jack's. For an instant when their eyes met, she seemed transported back to four years ago when that green gaze had melted her heart.

Immediately she shook that thought away and hoped the others would simply take her moment's hesitation as surprise at seeing Jack there, holding the cello.

"Tyrone can't come this morning," Tristan said. "I asked Jack, since we need to get things finalized about what we'll play at Vizcaya."

Jack hadn't been concerned four years ago, so she preferred he not be involved now. She quickly reprimanded herself for that attitude.

"Before we get into that," Rissa said. "Eva, Jack and I were just talking about his orchestra. I'm planning to participate when I can. How about you?"

Eva didn't want to do anything to infer that she still had feelings for Jack. She preferred to keep her distance. Opening up her violin case, she said, "All I have on my mind right now is Vizcaya."

"One good thing," Tristan said. "If any one of us can't make it, Jack could fill in."

Not wanting Jack to think she still cared about him, Eva said flippantly, "Oh, that's good to hear. Who knows where I might be? Perhaps touring the world with none other than the great Georgio Baldovino."

"Yeah, yeah," Tristan said. "Rissa's been telling wild tales about things like that. When you dream, you dream big."

"Really. I told him we practice mornings whenever we can. He said he would like to come some morning when he's free."

"Sure," Tristan said and laughed.

"It's true," Rissa said. "She's been to his beach house and everything."

"Everything?" Tristan said ominously.

"Not. . .everything!" Eva said. "You guys are embarrassing me." She had a sudden urge to make sure Jack knew she didn't care if he had that Alono. "But. . .who could resist a man with a Stradivarius?"

The others were grinning like crazy while she did a little shimmy with her shoulder and lifted her chin in a mock "better-than-you" playfulness.

They didn't laugh. Jack lifted his eyebrows and looked beyond her with a bland gaze. Tristan looked as if he'd choke on a laugh. Rissa drew her eyebrows together and was making funny motions with her eyes.

Eva was trying to figure out what was wrong with them when she heard a familiar voice say, "My lucky day or what? I just happen to know a man who has a Stradivarius."

Eva gritted her teeth, squeezed her eyes shut, and grimaced.

Georgio laughed and the others joined in.

Eva turned to face him. "I. . .was just being. . .silly."

"Good," he said immediately. "I could use a little silliness in my life. I'm beginning to realize I've been much too stodgy for too long."

"Well, you've come to the right place to loosen up," Tristan said.

Georgio walked over to Jack. "You're part of this group now?"

"Only as a friend," Jack said. "And a fill-in when needed. The cellist couldn't come this morning. "I'm number one jack-of-all-trades. I play many instruments but none too well. I'd better warm up before we get into the practice."

"Maybe you can give us some ideas," Tristan said to Georgio.

"I'm sure you know what you're doing. Let me hear what you have in mind."

He listened as they played.

"Very good," Georgio said when they finished. "You have played this before, right?"

"Oh, yes, many times," Eva said.

"Locally?"

"Yes," Eva said, "but we want this to be absolutely perfect for Vizcaya."

Georgio nodded. "I suggest you vary the program some-what. Likely, the music lovers of the area have already heard you. They would like the old favorites and to be introduced to something new."

"Or something old," Jack said.

They all looked at him. He shrugged a shoulder. "It's not my call, but you're playing during the Renaissance Festival. Shouldn't you go with that theme?"

"I wasn't aware of the festival," Georgio said. He looked at Jack. "I think you're exactly right about keeping with the theme. Consider the Baroque composers."

Jack and Georgio entered into an animated conversation about early music as they mentioned Corelli and Bach.

Jack made an offer. "I hadn't ordered any early music for my shop, but I'm sure we can find some around."

Georgio lifted a shoulder and an eyebrow. "Anything can be faxed, can it not?"

Jack laughed. "Perfect answer."

Rissa was skeptical. "Will we have time to learn the new music?"

"We don't have to memorize it. Even the best—" Jack stopped speaking suddenly and glanced at Georgio. "Well, maybe not the best." He laughed lightly. "But even symphony orchestras have their music in front of them."

The rest of the practice session was a fun excursion of their playing classical music. Georgio played the Alono. At Jack's suggestion, they turned to contemporary Christian music.

Eva couldn't help smiling. If Georgio Baldovino wasn't too good to use sheet music, then certainly the quartet could use it at Vizcaya.

❧

For the rest of the week, Eva settled into the routine of practice in the mornings, working in the shop in the afternoons, and spending evenings at Georgio's beach house. They'd have dinner, walk on the beach briefly, then play music.

Georgio had the Baroque music that had been faxed to him. With his instruction, Eva found the Renaissance music much easier than if she'd had to tackle the violin part alone.

"You'll do fine," Georgio complimented after a particularly good session on Friday evening.

"Thanks," Eva said. "But it won't sound nearly as good on my violin as on the Strad."

He held out the Alono. "Play this one."

Eva's breath caught in her throat for a moment. She felt her face grow warm under the scrutiny of Georgio's questioning gaze.

"I'd. . .rather not. I've gotten over my resentment of Grandpa's giving it to Jack, but I wouldn't feel right asking to play it. I don't want Jack to think I care about it."

"I see." Georgio took on that mysterious playful look she'd noticed several times. She hoped he didn't detect the uneasiness she felt when he talked about Jack or when she was around Jack.

"You're not playing in Jack's church orchestra?"

"I. . .have my other practices and recently I took up playing the Strad."

He laughed. "Ah," he said. "Priorities." He smiled so sweetly at her. "You were able to do a fine rendition of Bach and the early composers with little practice. I daresay you could whip out a hymn or two with no problem."

Eva felt torn. She could justify not being in the orchestra by what she just said. Those were excuses though, not reasons. She would love to play in the church orchestra and was rather envious that she hadn't started it herself. But as long as being around Jack made her so. . .uncomfortable, she couldn't possibly be a part of it.

Georgio put the Alono in its case and zipped it up. "Have you asked Jack to sell the Alono to you?"

Eva laughed at that. "I could never afford it."

He grinned. "A reduced price, perhaps. Or finance it." He shrugged. "Even I could buy it and you could make payments to me. If Jack would sell it."

She shook her head. "Jack won't sell it. But even if he would, I don't want it. I mean, if Grandpa had given it to me as an heirloom, then I'd treasure it. It's the principle that disturbs me."

"The principle," Georgio repeated. "You don't want the Alono. Jack doesn't want to play it. Your grandpa gave it away." A short laugh escaped his throat. "Then why ever can't I have it?"

Eva laughed, too. It wasn't funny, but ironic. "I honestly don't know."

"Tomorrow," he said. "Let us go to his shop and face your Jack once again."

"He's not my Jack," Eva said more sharply than she intended.

Georgio nodded. "I should have said, 'the Alono's Jack.'"

Eva turned from him to put the Strad in its case.

"I have used the Alono long enough to know its quality," he said. "I would like to return it to Jack and thank him. Will you accompany me to his shop in the morning? I don't know where it is."

Eva faced him and nodded. "I need to take some of my violins over there anyway."

Georgio walked her out to her car as usual. He closed the door, then leaned down at the open window. "Thank you, Eva. I sincerely enjoy the time we spend together."

"So do I," Eva said.

She returned his smile. Driving away from the house, she turned on the Bach concerto. While it played in the background, she thought of how she never would have thought she'd be comfortable spending time with a famous concert violinist like Georgio Baldovino.

And yet, she felt so uncomfortable just hearing the name of Jack.

Jack wasn't surprised to see Baldovino and Eva together. He'd learned from Al that the two of them spent each evening together at the beach house and that Eva had begun work on her own Alono.

He was surprised, however, that Eva came into his shop. She seemed to go out of her way to avoid him. Maybe she wanted to impress upon him that she no longer cared for him the way she had years ago.

Jack helped them bring in some of Eva's violins. Then Baldovino set the Alono on the glass cabinet top.

"This entire wall," Jack said, motioning behind himself as he stood behind the glass partition, "is for the display violins. I will keep beginner ones in a back room since those will be most of the sells."

Eva nodded. "This is quite impressive, Jack."

"Thank you," he said, realizing that was the closest she'd come to being more than tolerant of him since he'd returned. She quickly walked away and looked around at the walls on which hung some guitars, fiddles, and banjos. She touched some of the same kind of instruments leaned against the walls and on stands.

Baldovino drew his attention again as he began to talk about his gratitude to Jack for allowing him to play the Alono. "I suspect you knew I would find the Alono irresistible and you'd raise the price. If so, you were right. I will pay what you ask."

"Sorry," Jack said. "It's still not for sale."

"Then why did you have me play it?"

Jack's glance met Eva's after Baldovino asked the question, as if she, too, wanted to know the answer to that question. She quickly turned toward the racks that contained music books of many levels of expertise and CDs of country, bluegrass, contemporary, and classical music.

Jack glanced back at Baldovino. "I offered it because your Strad was being repaired. And also because I wanted someone of your stature to play it."

With a lift of an eyebrow, Baldovino seemed to accept that. "My offer will stand," he said. He glanced around. "Nice shop. Could I see some of your bows?"

Jack slid aside the glass door and handed him one. He knew it was strong, evenly balanced and weighted, stiff but light.

Baldovino checked it out. "Appears to be excellent. Where do you get your hair?"

"Usually from horses," Jack said.

Even Eva could not help laughing at that. Bows were strung with horsehair.

Jack unzipped the case, and Baldovino took the Alono and tried the bow on the strings. "Yes, this is symphony quality. Very smooth tone. And I see you have not bleached the horsehair. Although some violinists disagree with me, I think the darker hair grabs better; it produces more volume. And of course the stick is made from Pernambuco wood from Brazil."

"Of course," Jack agreed. "Fiberglass is adequate for beginners, also for their parents' pocketbooks."

Baldovino returned the Alono to the case and zipped it.

"You mentioned once that you were a jack-of-all trades. I rather think you are a master of many."

Jack wasn't sure what he meant by "many." "I studied with the best in France. And most of my horsehair comes from the Moroccan horses of China."

"The more I see of you, the more I feel you and I have a lot in common."

As far as Jack could see, they had nothing in common. "What's that?"

"A knowledge of music, a love for it. We both have. . ." He looked up toward the banjos hanging on the wall. "How shall I say it? Ah—an appreciation for the finer things in life."

Baldovino's fingers grazed over the Alono case as he glanced toward Eva, who was examining some shakers in the form of fruit and vegetables. His head dipped slightly, but he looked up at Jack beneath raised eyebrows.

Like before, Jack got the clear impression Baldovino wasn't referring to the Alono just then. However, he spoke of it again. "Will you keep the Alono in your shop?"

"No," Jack said. "It's not for sale, and I don't want to chance its being stolen. I will keep it at my house."

Baldovino nodded. "On display there, like a valuable piece of art."

Jack shook his head. "It's more valuable to me than that."

The violinist looked thoughtful for a moment. "I sense there's a story here."

Jack nodded. "Oh, yes. Perhaps there will be opportunity to share it with you."

Baldovino didn't invite Jack to do that. He obviously wasn't intrigued enough to carry the conversation further. He walked around the shop. Every once in awhile, Baldovino touched Eva's shoulder or leaned near her and gestured toward an instrument or a CD or a music book. They both said a casual good-bye to Jack and walked out together.

Jack looked after them long after they'd vanished from sight.

A sense of loneliness invaded him. The words of a song ran through his mind. *Tic Toc. Tic Toc. The clock stopped when the old man died.*

His glance swept over his shop. So many musical instruments and items of music. Yet not a note of music sounded in the shop.

He looked at his valuable, expensive stringed instrument.

He had a violin he said he wouldn't sell.

He had an Alono he rarely played.

He even had a story nobody cared to hear.

Chapter 7

Jack generally didn't consider himself a bow tie sort of person, but this occasion called for it. Any other time he would have welcomed the opportunity to sit in seats reserved for special guests of performers. Tonight, however, he found the idea miserable. He, Al, and Eva were Baldovino's guests for the evening.

If Baldovino's Strad had not needed to be repaired, then perhaps Jack would be escorting Eva to the concert instead of being her and Al's chauffeur for the evening, only to leave her to be Georgio's dinner guest after it ended.

And tonight, when Eva would be Baldovino's guest at dinner, all the "important" people in music would know her and that would increase her opportunities considerably. Yes, Baldovino could give Eva the kind of life that Jack couldn't imagine anyone not wanting. He had wanted it once. Then he discovered that was not so important. He hadn't been willing to concentrate on one area of music and become an expert. He didn't have the desire to be top in any particular musical field.

After his studies in music, he'd worked in various clubs as a pianist, a soloist, and later a backup fiddle player for a well-known country music singer. Then he remembered that Al had taught him how to make bows and had said the finest bow makers came from France. He checked it out and decided he needed something more substantial as a career than clubs and backup for a fading star.

He'd let the years go by without letting the people he loved know that he loved them. He'd been too young and foolish for his mind to listen to his heart. Years passed. Then he discovered what he was looking for deep inside was not center stage at all. It was a filling of the empty spot in his heart that only the Creator could fill upon his complete commitment to the Lord.

Now, Jack felt like he was coming apart at the seams and there was no glue to put him together again.

He knew why Baldovino invited Al. He was grateful for Al's having repaired his Strad. Jack figured he invited him, perhaps to soften him up, hoping he'd change his mind about selling the Alono.

There was a certain playfulness about Baldovino, like some kind of smug knowing in his expression and thin smile. Or was it a twist of sardonic humor knowing Jack cared about Eva and yet she was spending time with the great violinist?

Jack leaned over closer to Eva. "Is Baldovino a Christian?"

"No," she said, and her voice sounded sad. "He believes in God and right living, but doesn't believe Jesus is the only way to God." She paused, glanced away, then back again. "But our mission as Christians is to enlighten unbelievers, isn't it?"

"Exactly," Jack said, but he wondered if Eva was thinking about the Bible's warning against relationships with unbelievers.

He straightened in his seat for two reasons. One, this wasn't the time or place to discuss the matter of faith since the orchestra was coming onto the stage and the audience began to applaud. Two, the fragrance of Eva's delicate perfume had an unsettling effect upon his senses. Or, maybe it was just the nearness of Eva herself.

She looked particularly beautiful in a form-fitting black dress with rhinestones along the vee-cut neckline and her hair back in a chic French chignon.

But he must control his thoughts, dispense with his hopes about Eva. Perhaps she and Baldovino were meant for each other. Saying "God's will be done" was one thing. Feeling good about it was another.

Jack joined the applause. The first violinist played his tuning note. The conductor strode out on the stage and shook hands with the first violinist. He bowed to the audience, stepped up on his box, lifted his baton, and the orchestra began transporting listeners into a sublime world of music, playing Franz Liszt's *Les Prelude, Symphonic Poem no. 3.*

When the soprano came onstage, Eva leaned near Jack and with a delighted smile and eyes dancing with pleasure, she pointed to the program that listed the musical poems in French with the English translation beside them. "You understand all this," she said.

"So can you, if you can read English," he said.

She looked at him with dancing eyes and a warm, uninhibited smile. For awhile Jack thought she liked him, but when Georgio Baldovino appeared, striding out like he owned the world, Eva looked at the violinist as if he really did. The expression on her face glowed with awe and anticipation as she turned her attention away from Jack and joined the thunderous applause for Baldovino, who took center stage and bowed magnificently.

The concert was to be a special treat, combining themes of great composers. Usually an orchestra chose one theme for a concert. Tonight, they combined Liszt and Bach.

To make matters worse, Jack liked Baldovino. He liked the fact that such a gifted, famous man saw the worth in Eva.

From the moment Baldovino's bow touched the Strad, he drew out the most heavenly music Jack had ever heard as he played Johann Sebastian Bach's *Violin Concerto no. 1 in A Minor*. Jack found himself smiling broadly after the initial exposition, then Baldovino entered into what seemed to be a musical dialogue with the orchestra as if the two clashed, reminding Jack of dueling banjos. In the final gigue of two extended solos, Baldovino used a bowing technique that resulted in a curious croaking effect, delighting the audience.

In Bach's *Violin Concerto no. 2 in E Major*, Baldovino opened with an impassioned melody, followed by serenity, and ending with a dancelike finale.

The audience rose in another standing ovation.

The concert concluded with Tchaikovsky's *Symphony no. 4 in F Minor*.

Not being able to come up with a more apt example, Jack felt himself much like a Cinderella at the stroke of midnight, who turned away from the magical evening and faced the reality of returning to his place among the cinders.

For an instant he jealously told himself that perhaps he should have excelled in something more glamorous than bow making.

Jack gazed at Eva going against the flow of the crowd as she made her way backstage after the concert. Jack felt bereft, as if he had lost her without ever having really found her. Her being in love with him had been an ego trip for him years ago. When he settled down to seriousness, he began to realize what a wonderful person Eva was.

He'd returned with the determination that if she were not already taken, he wanted to pursue a serious relationship with her. Perhaps that would have worked except for the appearance of Georgio Baldovino.

Eva was beautiful and would easily make Baldovino shine even brighter by being his dinner guest with the orchestra.

Baldovino had. . ."everything."

Even Al recognized that. On the way home, he said, "Looks like our Eva hit the jackpot."

"Not a 'Jack pot,' " he replied. "Looks more like a 'Baldovino pot. . .of gold!' "

He glanced at Al, who stared at him with that "what are you gonna do about it?" look. Jack never had been able to hide anything from Al. It had been Al who had cautioned him about Eva's fragile feelings when they were younger. Jack had flippantly replied that Eva was but one in a long line of admiring females.

"Sometimes I'm tempted to give her the Alono," Jack said.

Al harrumphed. "If she doesn't like you now, would she like you if you gave her a violin?"

"No," Jack said. "She would just like the violin. She's angry with me."

A light laugh escaped Al's throat. "Reminds me of how I got mad at Ruth for dying and leaving me."

"At least she's not indifferent to me."

"That's something," Al said. "What you do with your violin is up to you. But you remember what I told you about it."

"That's what changed my life." Jack took a deep breath and let out a long sigh. He admitted to himself what had been nagging at the back of his mind for quite some time. Almost as if an audible voice had spoken, he knew there were two things he had to do.

One, despite any rejection he would likely receive, he had to let Eva know he loved her.

Chapter 8

J ack became more nervous by the moment about what he
intended to. All day he vacillated between telling himself
how foolish such an action would be and telling himself he
must follow through.

What would he do if Baldovino were there? Was today the
time to do it? Was it too late? Was Vizcaya the place? Was he
just setting himself up for humiliation for the rest of his life?

Determined, he decided on dressy/casual attire and not to
wear a suit as Baldovino likely would. The quartet had talked
of wearing their matching outfits of navy and white since they
were not out-front performers, but would provide background
music to the guests touring the museum.

He arrived after noon, knowing the quartet was to play for a
couple of hours inside the museum in the morning, afternoon,
and evening between the outdoor Medieval activities. Deciding
afternoon was not the time to carry out his mission, he watched
a little of the Medieval jousting and remembered when he was a
knight and when many young women, including Eva, admired
him much the way Eva was now admiring the famous violinist.

One big difference. She'd been a young college girl then.

She was a woman now.

If Baldovino were there at Vizcaya, then Jack saw no way he could get Eva alone and talk with her. He didn't see him.

He listened to the quartet playing their Renaissance music in the evening. Most guests took the music for granted. A few took time to lightly applaud. The sound was good enough to merit enthusiastic ovation.

"Eva, could I talk with you privately?" he asked when the quartet was putting their instruments into their cases.

She laid her violin in its case, then straightened and looked at him curiously.

He must have looked as ill as he felt. This was the turning point of his entire life. He had to know if there was a chance for him, although he felt he already knew. He was bold in most areas and never self-conscious. This weak-kneed, butterfly stomach sort of thing was entirely new to him.

He kept telling himself that he and Eva had known each other for years. They were like family in many ways. He could say anything to her. She was not an unkind person. However, his ego and pride played a part in this, too. But, he mustn't let pride stand in the way of at least facing what he felt for her and letting her know, regardless of the consequence. He felt like a coward, but not telling her would be even worse cowardice.

If the truth were out, and he received her rejection, then he wouldn't have to wonder and could move on, as difficult as that might be. But he didn't want to live out his life having been a coward.

"Is Baldovino here?" he asked.

"I haven't seen him," she replied. "His tour manager was to fly in this morning. Georgio said he'd come tonight if he could.

"Is something wrong?" she asked quickly, likely seeing some horrible expression on his face. "Have you seen him?"

"No. Nothing like that. I was just asking."

"Is Grandpa all right?"

"He's all right. It's. . .me."

"You? Jack?" Her stare filled with concern. "Are. . .are you ill?"

"Ill?" He expelled a deep breath. "Not in the way you're implying. I feel rather like I've got the flu, but—"

"Oh, Jack. Well, go home and take something and get in bed."

Tristan, Tyrone, and Rissa were looking at him now. "Do you need to leave with them?"

"No. I drove," she said.

"Could we. . .talk in private?"

"Sure," she said.

The others said their good-byes, and Eva left her violin with an attendant.

Jack led her out into the fan-shaped garden of Italian-clipped topiary, water displays, and French parterres. A beautiful setting for having one's heart broken. Perhaps he could stick his head in a water fountain and drown.

"Orange juice and aspirin and rest won't help what ails me," Jack said. "I don't have the flu. I just. . .feel like it. . .sort of. I have a problem."

"A problem?"

He followed her lead now as she passed through a double grotto and entered the high-walled secret garden.

"Eva," he said, lest she continue toward the maze garden in which he'd likely end up at a dead end, which was the way he felt already. A scent of jasmine wafted on the light evening breeze as the sky deepened to a deep blue hue.

She stopped and looked up at him with concern in her expression.

He couldn't stand it any longer. *Say it. . .get it over with.* This was not some romantic interlude in which he should get on his knees. This was a confession to a woman who resented him. Was he crazy? Probably. But he'd decided to do it and do it he would.

He'd even rehearsed but couldn't remember how to say it. He supposed there was no way but to blurt it out.

He grasped her upper arms, lest she slap him and run away before he finished.

"I love you," he said.

She stared. She seemed like one of the statues in the garden. She didn't blink. She didn't open her mouth. Had she ceased to breathe? Had he shocked the life out of her?

He'd said it. Maybe he should explain it.

"I always cared for you. But I saw you as one of many girls who seemed to think I was that knight in shining armor on a white horse. I reveled in it, but in those days I took no girl seriously. I knew you cared for me, but so did others. After I went away, I realized what you really meant to me. More than any other woman. I've related to others, but my heart always returned to you. I found myself, so to speak. I found the Lord in a more committed way. I needed a career and had an opportunity to learn a trade. I realized my heart was here in my own hometown. I longed to see the Alonos again. And you. I wondered if your presence in my heart was only because I missed each of you so much. I had to return and find out. The moment

I saw you that first night at Alono's, I knew. I love you."

He wondered if he'd spoken in French or English. She didn't seem to comprehend.

But she hadn't moved away.

When you've come this far. . .why not. . .

He drew her to himself, enfolded her in his arms, lowered his face to her uplifted one, and his lips met hers. No sweeter music ever played than the tune so eloquently stirring in his heart, mind, and body.

Reluctantly, he moved away. She stood staring at him with her lips parted, her face stark, and her eyes wide with astonishment. Her shoulder seemed to move slightly upward as if there were a shrug in it, and her head seemed to shake slightly. He could not read that body language. Did her shoulder shrug mean that his declaration meant nothing? Did the shake of her head mean she could not accept his love? She looked like he had said the most asinine thing one could say.

He felt heat begin to rise into his face, and he felt a weakness throughout his body. "I'm sorry if I offended you. I just thought you should know. Forgive me if I was out of line."

Maybe her heart already belonged to Baldovino.

Did she let him kiss her?

She seemed to have melted into his arms. Her lips seemed welcoming. Or had she just been too shocked to resist?

He was so caught up in the emotion of it, he couldn't even be sure if she had responded or simply tolerated his embrace and his kiss.

She continued to stare.

"I had to let you know how I feel. You don't have to say anything."

She didn't.

He turned and walked away, hardly knowing what direction he was taking, but hoping he wouldn't end up in the maze garden, where he'd never find his way out.

∽

Eva didn't know how long she stood there, oblivious to anything around her. Not until she heard Georgio's voice did she return to some semblance of normalcy and realized her fingers lay gently on her lips that Jack had so thoroughly kissed.

She lowered her hand and faced Georgio.

"I tried to get here sooner," he said. "But that was impossible. Fortunately, I have already heard you perform your Renaissance music."

Eva could only nod. Making a sudden switch from the happenings with Jack to the presence of Georgio proved to be a difficult transition.

"I'm dry," Georgio said. "Could I get you something to drink?"

Eva nodded and felt she'd just begun to learn to talk. "Wa–water, please."

She still stood in the same spot when Georgio returned with two glasses of water with a slice of lemon on the edges. He looked around and spoke of the lovely evening.

After a few sips in silence, Georgio spoke. "Could we stroll through the gardens? I've never seen them."

When they came to a secluded spot, he turned to her. "To my regret, my agent tells me my vacation must end soon and I must return to my obligations elsewhere. I have so enjoyed our times together."

"Oh, I have, too," Eva said with exuberance. "I will never forget it."

"Neither will I," he said. "Could you join me tomorrow night at the beach house? There is something very important I'd like to discuss with you."

"Yes," Eva said.

He looked at her for a long moment, but she could find no words to say. He smiled then, reached out his hand, and touched her arm. "Are you ready to leave?"

"Not just yet," she said. "I. . .I will see you tomorrow."

"Very good," he said and smiled. "Good night."

Eva found a bench beneath a tree and lowered herself to a sitting position.

Why wasn't her pulse racing because Georgio said he had something "very important" to discuss with her? She would be ecstatically anticipatory if things had remained as they had been with Jack.

But. . .Jack kissed her. He said he loved her.

A few weeks ago she had no one special.

And now. . .would she have to decide between two men. . . one who had come into her life so recently. . .and the other one whom she had loved so ardently for years?

With her hands clasped on her lap, Eva took several deep, needed breaths, as if she were Miss Muffet on a tuffet, expecting a spider to come and sit down beside her.

Chapter 9

Now that Jack had done one of the two things he'd intended to do, the time had come for the second task, which might prove to be as unacceptable as when he told Eva he loved her.

He got the phone number that Al had while repairing the Strad and called Baldovino. Soon he was on his way to the beach house.

A man led Jack into a front room that had a spectacular view of the ocean. Baldovino laid aside a magazine and stood when Jack came into the room. He offered Jack refreshments, which Jack refused, and the man who'd led him in left the room. Jack accepted the offer to sit in a chair across from Baldovino.

Jack laid his violin case across his knees. Baldovino simply glanced at it, then gazed blandly at Jack.

Jack plunged in. "This is the Alono." He laid his hand on the case. "It can be yours."

Baldovino lifted an eyebrow and looked as if he'd expected that all along. "How much?"

"It's a gift," Jack said. "On one condition."

Baldovino leaned farther back against his chair. "Ah, this

sounds like a business transaction. I get the Alono and I return the girl to you."

"No," Jack said. "I love Eva. I would not attempt to do something like this underhandedly. I can't buy her. You can't give her to me." He paused a moment. "Frankly, I'm more inclined to give you the violin because you have the girl. She deserves the best, and a man trying to live without the Lord is not the best."

Baldovino looked amused. "I seem to be doing all right." He lifted both eyebrows and gave Jack a quick once-over as if he might be the one who needed help.

Jack nodded. "You seem to be. But if it hasn't happened already, the time will come when you feel there's an empty spot in your heart and life that even fame and money can't fill. I've been there. Only God's spirit can bring that kind of filling."

Baldovino gestured with his hand as if that subject didn't matter. "Getting back to the Alono. You say I can't give you Eva. You don't want money." He shrugged. "What's your condition?"

"My condition is that you listen to the reason I'm giving it."

"Proceed." Baldovino crossed his arms over his chest.

Jack took a shaky breath. "This violin should be played by a master. I'm not that. I'll say to you what Al said to me that I couldn't escape. I hope you won't be able to escape it, either. It's a free gift demonstrating the gift of eternal life with God. You can't buy it. You can't accomplish enough to earn or deserve it. It's a free gift. You only have to believe Jesus is the Son of God. He died as forgiveness for our sins and He rose from the dead. You accept that in your heart and turn to a life of serving Him, and that's called salvation from eternal separation from God."

They sat in silence for a long moment.

Georgio didn't speak or move, reminding him of Eva's reaction the night before.

Jack knew his condition had been met. Georgio had listened. There was only one thing to do.

Jack stood. He picked up the violin case by the handle and held it out to Georgio.

Georgio's dark eyes searched Jack's. "You're taking a chance on losing the Alono and Eva, too."

Jack nodded. "I know. And that is even more reason to want you to find salvation, to be the kind of man she deserves. You can't be that without the Holy Spirit in your life. You can't have the Holy Spirit without believing and following Jesus Christ." Jack blinked as if the bright midmorning sunlight against the windows were accosting his eyes.

"You know what this violin is worth?"

"Yes, of course," Jack replied. "But not as much as my eternal soul. Jesus paid with His life. He gave Himself up to die for me. Anything I have to give is small in comparison."

"And if I don't believe or accept what you've said, I must return the violin?"

"No. I will be pleased if one of your ability plays this violin and brings pleasure to others. But I would hope this gesture will do what Al hoped it would do for me. I couldn't forget that, and you won't, either. Al said the violin was mine to keep, to hide, to throw away, to give away, to play. When a gift is given, you shouldn't tell the recipient what to do with it. But never forget why it was given. I hope it will have the same effect on you."

Jack took a small tract out of his shirt pocket. "This briefly tells of the plan of salvation much better than I did."

Georgio stared at it, while awkwardly his hands lay on top

of the violin case lying on his knees.

It occurred to Jack that Georgio might not believe the Alono was in the case. He took it, laid the case on the couch, and unzipped the lid. He took it out and showed Georgio Al's mark on the back.

"I'm willing to pay you for it," Baldovino said.

"No," Jack said. "This is not about money. It's about your eternal soul. Your salvation."

Baldovino spoke thoughtfully. "I impress women with my violin playing. You could win Eva's favor, if not her love, by giving her the Alono." He shrugged. "Yet, you will not."

"No. Al said someday I would know what to do with this violin. I know. . .this is what I want to do."

Baldovino still looked skeptical. He spoke slowly. "So. You will give up your prized possession because of your faith."

"Yes."

Baldovino shook his head and a scoff escaped his throat. "Amazing."

❧

"I want to talk to you about love," Georgio said.

Eva stopped short on the sandy beach where the two of them had been strolling after a lovely dinner prepared by Elena. She put her hand to her chest. "Oh. . ." She thought the world of Georgio. But she couldn't consider making any kind of commitment at this time. Not since—

Georgio raised both hands. He laughed lightly. "No. No. Don't worry. I know you are in love with Jack."

"What?"

"Whether you want to admit it or not, you're in love with Jack."

Eva scoffed. "How can you say that?"

"For one thing," he said. "Last night I arrived at Vizcaya earlier than I let on. One of your friends said you had gone into the garden. I walked out there, then saw you and Jack. I made a hasty retreat back into the building."

"Oh, I'm sorry. I didn't expect that to happen."

"No. No. I'm not asking for an explanation. That is your business. I suspected you loved Jack that first night I met you two at the Alono Restaurant."

"I didn't give Jack the time of day that night."

Georgio lifted a finger and looked mischievous. "That was the first clue. But that night, you did not miss a note in your violin playing although you were obviously impressed with my being a successful violinist." He smiled. "You spilled the water at the sound of the voice of the one who touches your heart. I have kept that in mind."

Eva relaxed somewhat, now that Georgio wasn't asking her for a commitment nor expressing undying love for her.

She said coyly, "Then why did you kiss me that night, right here on the beach?"

He spread his hands and looked askance. "That was a kiss? Ah." He scoffed then. "That was more like the tuning note before the violinist plays. I can do much better."

He leaned forward and Eva jumped back. They both laughed.

"Actually, though," he said, "let me count the reasons. You are a beautiful woman and I am a man. I like you. Beyond my own selfish reasons, I wanted to confirm to myself and to you that you are in love with someone else, whether or not you choose to admit it."

"I. . .tried not to."

"Now, a kiss is more like what you and Jack did in that garden."

"He kissed me. I. . .I don't think I kissed him."

"Oh, ho!" Georgio exclaimed. "If that was not a kiss, then God didn't make little green apples."

Eva ducked her head and looked down at the sand. "I really don't know what happened. I was surprised. Then shocked."

Georgio lifted her chin with his fingers. "Let me shock you further."

❧

Shocked she was, when Georgio told her what Jack had done in giving him the Alono.

As he continued the story, Eva realized, however, that she should not be shocked. It sounded so much like Grandpa, and now she realized how Jack demonstrated his commitment to the Lord in his settling down to a business, being faithful to the church, and using his musical ability for the Lord.

But this was a much bigger issue than what she thought of either Georgio or Jack as men. "Did his gift have an impact on you?"

Georgio sighed. "I suppose I'm reluctant to be too serious about all this. But Jack was right. I left that Alono on the couch all day. I wouldn't touch it. I'd pass through the room or in the hallway and look in its direction. I no longer see it as just a wonderful violin. I see it as possibly the only way to a relationship with God." He looked up toward the darkening sky. "Jack was right. I cannot face the Alono without knowing there is a decision for me to make."

Before she could even ask if he wanted to talk about such a

decision, he stopped walking and faced her again. "How does this make you feel that Jack gave away the Alono?"

The seagull that spread its wings, lifted off from the beach, and soared out over the ocean simulated the burden that left her heart.

Tears welled up in her eyes. "I realize I was never really so much upset about Grandpa giving the Alono to Jack. My resentment of Jack was because I felt rejected by him. I loved him."

"You love him now."

Eva nodded.

"I will give you the Alono. It belongs to you and Jack."

"No." Eva was adamant about that. "I understand Grandpa now. The Alono is a witness to his faith in Jesus Christ. Now it has been that to Jack. Whatever it might become to you, it is something that should be played by a person of your ability. And. . .Jack's having given it to you makes me love him even more."

Georgio sighed. "You could not love him if he gave you the violin you wanted. And yet you love him for giving away the violin you wanted. Women! Who can understand them?"

He laughed and put his arm around her shoulders. "I do love you in a special way, Eva."

She looked up at him and nodded. "And I love you, Georgio. For the person you are. Not just because you're a great violinist."

He smiled. "Let us seal this mutual admiration society with a temporary farewell dinner Friday night at the Alono Restaurant. Okay?"

Chapter 10

J ack didn't know what it was about. Baldovino had called his shop and invited him to dinner at the Alono Restaurant on Friday night. He was led to the table where the violinist and Eva sat.

She looked particularly beautiful in a colorful Spanish-style dress and her hair back in a French chignon. The glow of the candle danced with light and shadow on her face, which wore a soft expression, and her eyes seemed to glow with warmth. Was that the look of love—for Baldovino?

Was this a thank-you dinner for the Alono and for Eva? Maybe Baldovino wanted to gloat that he had won the girl.

Baldovino had a silly grin on his face. Eva spoke to Jack but avoided looking into his eyes. She and Baldovino seemed to be speaking an indecipherable eye language. Jack felt like knocking his water glass over and making a dash for the back door.

As if there were no issues, and perhaps there were none, Baldovino began to talk about bows. "Before I leave Miami," he said, "I would like to buy one of your bows."

Jack met his gaze. "Are you trying to repay me for the Alono?"

Baldovino laughed. "I daresay a bow wouldn't come close to what the Alono is worth."

Jack acknowledged that with a nod. "True. But the best ones are expensive."

"I'm aware of that," Georgio said. "My bows are made by French masters—likely your teachers."

Jack was aware that the sale of one of his best bows meant he would have no business worries for quite awhile. It meant his business could grow slowly without his worrying about it. Any other time Jack would be overjoyed at what this man just said.

At the moment, however, another thought burdened his mind. Baldovino would buy his bow. Baldovino would be Eva's beau.

He didn't know if he could get through this dinner gracefully.

"My cue," Eva said. She pushed away from the table and walked up onto the stage. She reached for the violin lying atop the piano, then began to play, "There's a Sweet, Sweet Spirit in This Place."

Jack stared at Eva. She was not playing her violin. The tone had to be either the Alono. . .or the Strad. Feeling as she had about his having the Alono, he felt this had to be Baldovino's Strad.

His spirit was anything but sweet at the moment. He took a deep breath and told himself to accept the inevitable and prepare for the worst.

Baldovino kept glancing at him with what appeared to be a twinkle in his eyes. Maybe it was just the candlelight. Maybe it was a gloat that the best man won. Perhaps Baldovino was the best man. . .for Eva.

When Eva returned to the table, Jack didn't ask if she'd

played the Strad. Over salad, Baldovino asked how Jack's business was going. After some idle chitchat, Al came over. After greeting them, he spoke primarily to Baldovino. "I heard you'll be leaving soon. Just wanted to say how much I've enjoyed meeting you. Your concert was fabulous. And I appreciate how happy you've made my granddaughter these past weeks."

Georgio stood and shook hands with Al, expressing his gratitude for all he'd done, including having such an adorable granddaughter. Al returned to the Alono family table. Eva seemed to concentrate on her salad, making only a few remarks here and there. Jack suspected her being unusually quiet meant she was embarrassed for his having declared his undying love for her.

Roberto Alono then took the microphone and after a few words, he and Bev began their flamenco dance while waiters removed salad plates.

During the main course, Baldovino took the subject where Jack hadn't expected, but had hoped and prayed about.

"I want to thank you both for the time and attention you've given me. And you, Jack, for the Alono. If you would take money for it, I would gladly pay it."

Jack shook his head.

Baldovino nodded and smiled. "I do want you both to know that I'm not some infidel. I have attended church. I have read much of the Bible. I am familiar with the great hymns and spiritual music."

He gestured with his hands, including his fork.

"Almost everyone knows of Handel's *Messiah*. I have played those great religious songs. Have heard them sung. I know the words. I think they're wonderful. How can anyone listen to beautiful music and say there is no God? It is beyond man. My playing is a result of many factors, and yet it is still beyond me. I am as amazed as my fans at the beauty of music and the ability of a person to be a part of it."

Jack didn't take another bite while Baldovino was expressing his belief in God. This had turned out to be much bigger than his own personal wants. An eternal soul lay in the balance. When Baldovino paused to take another bite, Jack said, "Almost everyone believes there is a God. That's not the main point."

Baldovino lifted a finger while chewing, then swallowed. Then he nodded. "I understand that now. I never doubted that Jesus maybe was the Son of God. Who else does so much for humanity than those who believe that? I thought that was one way to God—not the only way." He sighed and shook his head. "I didn't know one needed to take a stand on it."

He tackled his food again, so Jack decided to do the same. If Baldovino understood it, then what more was there to say? The matter now lay between him and God.

Eva excused herself from the table without having eaten much of her food.

As soon as she was a few steps away, Baldovino leaned toward Jack. "I know you love her."

How quickly a subject could change from the spiritual to the personal. What could he say? He wasn't sorry. He didn't have to explain his actions to Baldovino. Or did he? He could try. "If I had known—"

"No. No." Baldovino lifted his hand. "That was just an observation. I wonder. . .do you think you and I could be friends?"

Was this guy rubbing it in? "I don't know," Jack said. "How involved were you with the woman I love?"

"Ah!" Baldovino said. "I do not kiss and tell."

Jack felt like punching the guy in the face. However, maybe Baldovino felt like doing the same to him.

"I will say," Baldovino began, "Eva is a masterpiece. What does one do with a masterpiece? Perhaps you were inclined not to play a fine musical instrument. But I. . .hey, am a master of performance."

He raised his right hand with his index finger like one making a very fine point. "Wait! Wait!"

Jack wasn't sure what to make of the egotistical, triumphant attitude of Baldovino that turned playful. The violinist shook his head and gave Jack a look of one reprimanding another.

Baldovino laughed then, and Jack knew it likely was at his own reddening face. "You have nothing to worry about. I happened upon the garden at Vizcaya and witnessed you and Eva making emotional music together. That kind of melody has not existed between her and me. Besides, one of the reasons I took these few weeks away from people and activity in which I am normally involved was to ponder the relationship with a woman who has been special to me for some time. A serious commitment would involve changes in careers of one or the other of us. She is an acclaimed soprano with a touring philharmonic. I have studied the relationship of you and your Eva."

"Studied?"

Baldovino nodded. "You see, I came here to get away from Maria and her morality faith. I prayed to God that if there was something to the Jesus thing, then let me know. Then He smacked me in the face with it at every turn, beginning with the first night when Eva played an invocation, then her parents expressed their faith, and on it went. Then your giving me the Alono and a sermon."

The two of them laughed lightly. Jack loved the way God could work in lives when humans felt so helpless. "I think you've played a few games there."

"Well," Baldovino said with a lift of his aristocratic chin. "The relationship between you two fascinated me. It reminded me of my own with Maria. But I will say I enjoyed spending time with Eva. She helped me understand Maria. I believe Eva and I have become friends."

Jack was having trouble processing what was taking place. Then his attention turned to the stage, where Eva had again taken the microphone.

She announced to the quieting patrons that there was a special surprise tonight. She introduced Baldovino, who rose to the rousing applause and made his way to the stage. He reached for the violin and bow that lay on top of the piano while Eva returned to the table. Jack watched her expression as she gazed at Baldovino with unabashed appreciation. Or was it. . .something else?

Baldovino said he and Eva hadn't fallen in love. But. . . could he speak for Eva?

Baldovino began to speak over the microphone. "I will be playing on an Alono violin, one of the finest in the world. Also, I would like to play in tribute to the maker of the violin, the one who gave me this priceless instrument, and the one who gave me weeks of pleasure when I was a stranger in your city. Most of all, this is an answer to the Maker of my soul."

Jack knew by the second note that Baldovino was playing

"Amazing Grace." Eva faced him then and looked straight into his eyes. He couldn't read the expression, however. The tears, from her eyes, or his own, perhaps both, obscured visibility.

He closed his eyes and thanked God that a soul had been saved from eternal separation from his Maker. One in a position to tell a wide audience of their need for Jesus Christ. The amazing sound of music that enveloped the room from a master violinist expressed with indescribable beauty the grace of God.

❧

Eva looked up at Georgio as he stood at the table, violin case in hand. "I will not stay for dessert," he said. "I will say good-bye, but I hope we keep in touch."

Eva stood, and so did Jack, who shook Georgio's hand. Eva hugged him, and he kissed her cheek.

"Thank you both," he said. "If you will excuse me now, I have an important call to make to someone else who has been concerned about my soul. If things go as I hope, then perhaps we can be friends as couples."

Eva looked after Georgio until he was out of sight. He had filled her life in so many ways. She could see now that God had a purpose in it, too. That was a lesson she must remember—that people who come into our lives may not be for our sake only, but for their eternal souls. She was grateful for that special man who had touched her life in such a beautiful way.

"Eva," Jack said. "You're ignoring me."

With a sideways glance, she shrugged. "How long did you ignore me?"

"Oh, no." He groaned. "You're going to make me wait four years before you tell me if there's a chance for us?"

"Four years?" She huffed. "You ignored me even before that.

So. . .just give me time. I'm. . .thinking."

"Okay," he said. "I can sit here for four, six, eight years. However long it takes."

Eva picked at the dessert that was set before her, knowing that Jack had begun to eat his. She had wondered how to tell Jack that she loved him, too. Somehow she couldn't just blurt it out. That simply wasn't romantic enough.

She'd returned to trying to make a great Alono. After all, that was her name as well as Grandpa's. She'd looked at the plaque Grandpa kept over one of his workbenches. She'd read the verse hundreds of times—

> *Now finish the work, so that your eager willingness to do it may be matched by your completion of it, according to your means.*
>
> *For if the willingness is there, the gift is acceptable according to what one has, not according to what he does not have.*
>
> 2 CORINTHIANS 8:11–12

Maybe she could make the best violin she could and give it to Jack to replace the Alono and to show him she no longer resented his having had it but was grateful to Grandpa's wisdom in making it an object of one's witness to one's faith.

Suddenly, Jack rose from his seat, tossed his napkin on his plate, and strode away from the table. Eva drew in a quick breath. Had he given up? So soon? Had she behaved like a silly schoolgirl, when he would expect a woman to return his love? Should she run after him?

The next thing she knew, he'd hopped up onto the stage

and grabbed the microphone. "This is unconventional and not part of the program," he said. "So feel free to leave if you wish. I can't perform like the great Georgio Baldovino, but I want to express my love with my music to the one who can turn my life's song into one of beauty or one of despair. The last time I heard this song, I was not ready to accept true love nor was I capable of giving it. This is for the love of my life. I want this to be. . .our song."

Eva stared as he sat down on the piano stool, stretched out his arms, placed his hands on the keys, and began not only to play but to sing "So in Love."

Eva laid her fork down and put her hands on her lap. When Marco came near, she gave him her car keys and instruction. He nodded and grinned.

When Jack finished, he came to the table. With his hands on the edge, he said, "I can't wait four years. I can't even wait four minutes. Do I stand a chance that you could love me?"

Eva tried to look demure. "Could you meet me on the back veranda? I will then give you my answer in about four seconds."

"I hope it will be accompanied by three words," he said.

She smiled demurely. "Follow me."

Outside, she picked up the violin she'd had Marco put on a table and walked over to a shadowed spot, lighted only by the moonlight and twinkling stars.

She began to play "So in Love," and Jack joined in with the lyrics of being "close to you beneath the stars." He came nearer, singing, "So in love with you am I."

He took the violin from her and laid it aside and then took her in his arms.

"I love you, Jack," she said. "Since the first time I saw you.

Oh, I think it was a crush at first, but it grew. Even when I tried not to love you, I did."

He held her. "I've always loved you, too, Eva. As a young girl, as a friend. And now I love you as a woman. I want us to build a life together. To marry, have children, love each other." He took a deep breath and took on a troubled look. "I couldn't give you the Alono. I can only offer my heart, my lifetime commitment, my love."

"That's all I want," Eva said.

This time, she knew she responded to his kiss, perhaps even initiated it.

Georgio could play the Alono. Jack played the strings of her heart.

And she could name that tune. It was love.

YVONNE LEHMAN

As an award-winning novelist from Black Mountain in the heart of North Carolina's Smoky Mountains, Yvonne has written several novels for Barbour Publishing and its Heartsong Presents line. Her titles include *Mountain Man*—which won a National Reader's Choice Award sponsored by a chapter of Romance Writers of America, *After the Storm, Call of the Mountain, The Stranger's Kiss*—Booksellers Best Award winner, *On A Clear Day*, and a hard-cover novella, *His Hands*. Yvonne has published more than two dozen novels, including books in the Bethany House "White Dove" series for young adults. In addition to being an inspirational romance writer, she is also the founder of the Blue Ridge Christian Writers' Conference. She and her husband are the parents of four grown children and grandparents to several dear children.

A Letter to Our Readers

Dear Readers:

In order that we might better contribute to your reading enjoyment, we would appreciate your taking a few minutes to respond to the following questions. When completed, please return to the following: Fiction Editor, Barbour Publishing, Inc., P.O. Box 719, Uhrichsville, OH 44683.

1. Did you enjoy reading *Strings of the Heart?*
   - ❏ Very much—I would like to see more books like this.
   - ❏ Moderately—I would have enjoyed it more if _____
   _____
   _____

2. What influenced your decision to purchase this book?
   (Check those that apply.)
   | ❏ Cover | ❏ Back cover copy | ❏ Title | ❏ Price |
   | ❏ Friends | ❏ Publicity | ❏ Other | |

3. Which story was your favorite?
   - ❏ *The Great Expectation*
   - ❏ *Harmonized Hearts*
   - ❏ *Syncopation*
   - ❏ *Name That Tune*

4. Please check your age range:
   | ❏ Under 18 | ❏ 18–24 | ❏ 25–34 |
   | ❏ 35–45 | ❏ 46–55 | ❏ Over 55 |

5. How many hours per week do you read? _____

Name _____

Occupation _____

Address _____

City _____ State _____ Zip _____

E-mail _____

_H_EARTSONG ❤ PRESENTS

Love Stories
Are Rated G!

That's for godly, gratifying, and of course, great! If you love a thrilling love story but don't appreciate the sordidness of some popular paperback romances, **Heartsong Presents** is for you. In fact, **Heartsong Presents** is the premiere inspirational romance book club featuring love stories where Christian faith is the primary ingredient in a marriage relationship.

Sign up today to receive your first set of four, never-before-published Christian romances. Send no money now; you will receive a bill with the first shipment. You may cancel at any time without obligation, and if you aren't completely satisfied with any selection, you may return the books for an immediate refund!

Imagine. . .four new romances every four weeks—two historical, two contemporary—with men and women like you who long to meet the one God has chosen as the love of their lives. . .all for the low price of $10.99 postpaid.

To join, simply complete the coupon below and mail to the address provided. **Heartsong Presents** romances are rated G for another reason: They'll arrive Godspeed!

YES! Sign me up for Hearts❤ng!

NEW MEMBERSHIPS WILL BE SHIPPED IMMEDIATELY!
Send no money now. We'll bill you only $10.99 postpaid with your first shipment of four books. Or for faster action, call toll free 1-800-847-8270.

NAME _____

ADDRESS_____

CITY _____ STATE_____ ZIP_____

MAIL TO: HEARTSONG PRESENTS, P.O. Box 721, Uhrichsville, Ohio 44683
or visit www.heartsongpresents.com